Amuse Bouche

A Russell Quant Mystery

Amuse Bouche

A Russell Quant Mystery

Anthony Bidulka

INSOMNIAC PRESS

Edited by Catherine Lake
Copy edited by Adrienne Weiss
Designed by Marijke Friesen

Library and Archives Canada Cataloguing in Publication

Bidulka, Anthony, 1962-
  Amuse Bouche / Anthony Bidulka.

ISBN 1-894663-91-8

I. Title.

PS8553.I319A8 2005   C813'.6   C2005-900278-6

The publisher gratefully acknowledges the support of the Canada Council, the
Ontario Arts Council and the Department of Canadian Heritage through the Book
Publishing Industry Development Program. We acknowledge the support of the
Government of Ontario through the Ontario Media Development Corporation's
Ontario Book Initiative.

Printed and bound in Canada

Insomniac Press
192 Spadina Avenue, Suite 403
Toronto, Ontario, Canada, M5T 2C2
www.insomniacpress.com

An idea, a dream, brought to life through words. You fed and encouraged it and made it grow. And then like a flash we spent a day in the sun and a night by the fire and realized giddily that it was real. You inspire me. You teach me. You bolster me. You accept me. You amaze me with your generosity, perspicacity, consistency and enduring love and championship. Without you these pages—and perhaps I—would be blank.

For Herb.

Chapter 1

I HAVE TO BELIEVE THAT HERCULE POIROT and Jessica Fletcher along with the current slate of mystery novel and television detectives had to start somewhere. Somewhere unworthy of a book or possible syndication rights. They didn't all begin with "The Case of the Smoking Gun" or by tracking down an ingenious serial killer. Or did they? I'm assuming they didn't, but I don't know that for a fact. Yet, that assumption gives me some comfort when I look back on the last twelve months since I began my life as a private detective. If someone were creating a TV show about some of the cases I've had in the past year, they'd have to resort to episode titles like "The Case of the Hiding Pussy Cat" or "Midnight Surveillance Sucks."

To celebrate my one-year anniversary, I drank passable champagne from a bottle I'd chilled in the small fridge that holds up one end of my office desk, and then finished the paperwork on my most recent case. My client had been a local woman who vacations in Arizona from late fall to early spring every year. She had hired me to track down a couple whose motor home had sat next to hers in the trailer park the previous winter. Apparently the next door neighbours had forgotten to return a favourite piece of Corning Ware and my client wanted it back. I mailed a bill for fifty-three dollars and fifty cents, for time *and* expenses, and closed the file on "The Case of the Missing Casserole Dish."

My name is Russell Quant. I'm thirty-one and a former police constable for the city of Saskatoon in the province of Saskatchewan. At about 215,000 people and smack in the middle of the Canadian prairie, Saskatoon is not action central, but neither is it the end of the world. It's safe and clean. It has four distinct seasons, some of the friendliest people on the globe, and it's home.

My office is on Spadina Crescent, just out of downtown, in an old character house that used to be called the Professional Womyn's Centre. Back in the early eighties when it was cool to delete the reference to "man," a group of professional women bought the building and rented space to female tenants who ran female-oriented businesses. For several years the Professional Womyn's Centre was a success. But as the nineties matured and women overall became less hung up about the "man" thing, what was once politically correct became a bit of an embarrassment and serious-minded tenants moved out. They headed for buildings with less controversial names like The Templeton Complex or better yet, no name at all. A couple of beadmakers and crystal readers later, the owners were near bankruptcy and the house fell into dis-repair. In 1998 a young lawyer, Errall Strane, purchased the property, did some remodelling and in deference to a piece of history, renamed it the PWC Building. I believe, if I was to ask the average "myn" on the street what PWC stands for, they wouldn't know.

After renovations, PWC was left with four office spaces. Errall runs her one-lawyer practice out of the largest suite on the main floor, the balance of which is rented to Beverly Chaney, a psychiatrist. Two smaller offices on the second floor belonged to Martha Plume, a book editor, and Alberta Lougheed, a psychic. Unfortunate for her but fortunate for me, Martha passed away about the same time I was looking to hang my shingle. My good friend Kelly Doell knew I was searching for four walls and convinced her partner,

Errall, to invite me to join the household. I am the first male tenant in twenty years. It was a difficult decision for Errall, one that at times I know she regrets, but…too bad, I've got a lease. Mine is the smallest office, but it's the only one with a balcony and the view more than makes up for the size—from the small deck I can look across Spadina Crescent into beautiful Kiwanis Park and the swiftly flowing South Saskatchewan River. And, oh yeah, the price is right.

I was standing on my balcony, drinking coffee on a chilled late September morning, when the first case of my second year as a private investigator began with a phone call. From the beginning I knew it was going to be big.

Trying not to spill a drop, I raced to my desk to answer the call before my message manager picked it up. "Russell Quant." Nice, short, succinct, what more do you need to say?

The person on the other end of the line hesitated for the count of five but decided to continue. "Mr. Quant, I understand you're a private detective."

"Yes," I told the deep voice. So far so good.

"My name is Harold Chavell."

The name told me a lot. Harold Chavell was a local entrepreneur who owned several successful businesses in the province. Off the top of my head I knew about a trucking company and a paint manufacturing company both with subsidiaries across North America. Simply put, he was one of Saskatoon's who's who. I was surprised to hear his name. I was surprised he was calling me.

"Yes Mr. Chavell, how can I help you?" Mr. Professional at your service.

"I may be in need of your expertise and was wondering if we could arrange a meeting. I don't wish to discuss it over the phone and not at work. It's a personal matter." His tone was direct and businesslike.

"Of course. What would be convenient for you?"

"Not tonight, but this can't wait much longer." I heard the sound of a turning page and an impatient sigh as if he was having difficulty finding a time slot to fit me into. "How about tomorrow afternoon, one o'clock?"

I glanced at my Daytimer and took a second to note that Tuesday was blank. So were the other days of the week but he didn't need to know that. I flipped a few pages rather loudly but held off on the impatient sigh. "That should work out fine," I said, with a hint in my voice that I'd pushed a few other things around to accommodate him.

Harold Chavell gave me directions to his home and the conversation ended. As I finished my coffee I tried to recall what I knew about the man from the *StarPhoenix*, Saskatoon's daily paper. He was apparently rich, obviously successful, heavily involved in the community, and friends with the mayor and every bank manager in town. Not the type of guy you'd expect to hire a detective who'd just billed a client fifty-three dollars and fifty cents. What did this man want with me?

I spent the rest of the morning going through mail, reading the paper and tidying up a few administrative details on old cases. I was expected at the vet with my dog, Barbra at 2:00 p.m. Time for her annual check-up.

Cathedral Bluffs is one of a plethora of acreage communities that sprung up around Saskatoon in the late 1990's and early 2000's. It's about a dozen kilometres northeast of the city and features five-to-ten-acre parcels of land off either side of a gravel road that lazily snakes its way through the development. At the end of a lengthy, sapling-lined driveway I found Harold Chavell's ostentatious house. Its considerable bulk was crammed at one end of the lot to take full viewing advantage of the South Saskatchewan River valley over which it was dramatically perched. No expense had been spared. Money sprouted from the ground, spurted out of sprinklers, covered the roof, filled the garages and floated in the pool. He was either trying to prove something or had nothing better to do with his cash. Or both.

I pulled up to a twenty-foot-high portico. I hoped my 1988 Mazda RX7 convertible wouldn't leak fluid on the faux rock, burgundy-dyed driveway. Oh well. Isn't that what driveways are for? I rang a doorbell that was actually a small, square pad of light and waited for its symphony to bring someone to the door. I was surprised when Chavell himself appeared. Had he given the servants the afternoon off so we could talk in private?

"Mr. Chavell, I'm Russell Quant."

He shook my hand and studied my face with something more than casual interest. "Thank you for coming, Mr. Quant. Please, come in."

Stepping inside I was transported into the foyer of a five-star luxury hotel. It was gorgeous. Slate floor, high ceiling and ancient looking pedestals displaying sculptures of things I couldn't readily identify. Two of the walls were designed to resemble the shear face of a mountainside, replete with rivulets of water dribbling from summit to base. His own natural mountain spring? I guess it would save on Evian bills. At the centre of the room was a marble-topped table that seemed barely large enough to support an impossibly huge arrangement of fresh cut flowers. I looked around for the check-in counter but saw none.

"I have refreshments in here," he said.

I followed him from the main entrance into a big room that looked like an office doubling as a sitting room. From this vantage point I was able to assess Harold Chavell without being caught. He was a man of sharp profiles, each handsome and interesting in a way that came only with certain age and experience. I guessed him to be in his mid- to late-forties—a worn around the edges soap opera star who'd appeared in a few too many episodes. His build was not dissimilar from my own. He was just over six feet tall, wide-shouldered and slim-hipped. Although it was difficult to be certain with the suit he was wearing, he appeared fit. His outfit was elegant but bland, and expensive. When we shook hands earlier I noticed he wore no jewelry except for a pinkie ring, platinum I think, on his right hand.

While he fixed our drinks, coffee for me, Pellegrino with a twist for him, I sat on an eggplant-coloured, leather couch. I was mesmerized by an oval piece of glass in front of me that seemed to be floating on the backs of two frolicking, solid bronze dolphins. After serving the drinks he sat in one of the two armchairs on the other side of the fish. I'm not even sure how to describe the colour of the armchairs, kind of peachy-orange maybe? It actually worked well together, the eggplant, the orange, the sea life. A nice package.

"I called you, Mr. Quant, based on the recommendation of an acquaintance of mine. He assured me that you could be counted on to recognize the special sensitivity of this matter. Even so, I will need your personal assurance today that everything we discuss will remain confidential."

I wanted to ask who'd referred me, but thought better of it. I'd find out later. "You have that assurance," I told him. "Assuming you are not about to tell me anything of an illegal nature."

The man gave me a restrained smile, one he probably reserved for unpleasant business matters. "No. Not illegal, but definitely personal in nature. What I'm about to share with you is not common knowledge and I do not wish it to be so."

"I understand."

"Three days ago, on Saturday night, I was to be married."

His tone told me congratulations were not in order. I already knew his ring finger was naked. I remained silent.

"I was to be married to another man."

Now this I didn't expect. Juicy. His hesitation after this revelation, led me to believe he wanted a response. I decided against "juicy."

"I'm sorry it didn't work out for you."

"Not as sorry as I am. Obviously my relationship with Tom was…is not well known in the community. We're not completely in the closet, but neither is the door wide open, you understand? Our ceremony was to be a private affair. We had sixty guests here in my home. Most were friends, family and some close business associates who are included in our personal lives." Chavell paused here and sipped his sparkling water. His presentation was cool, almost impassive, and I wondered about what I was seeing in his face. Hurt? Anger? Embarrassment? Maybe all of it. Maybe something altogether different. He carefully placed the crystal tumbler back on the coffee table and continued, "Tom and I are deeply in love. We've been together for almost three years. We are dedicated to one another. For him not to show up, to leave me standing there alone, like a fool, at the altar, never mind to not even call, is just…well it's something I can't accept."

"I hate to be blunt." A lie. "But it did happen. Don't you *have* to accept it?"

"No. I can accept that the ceremony did not occur, but I cannot accept that he stood me up on purpose. I think something is terribly wrong."

"So he hasn't been home since the evening of the ceremony?"

"I live here alone," Chavell said formally. "Tom has an apartment in the city."

I gave a little shrug. "Okay. So you haven't heard from Tom since Saturday?"

"I haven't seen or heard from Tom since the rehearsal party the night before the ceremony."

"Oh."

"Yes! Oh! That's just not like Tom. He would never do that."

"What about his friends? Family? Have they heard from him?"

"No," he answered. "I've contacted a couple of his friends but they tell me he hasn't called and they have no idea what's going on with him."

"What do the police have to say about this?"

"Nothing."

"You haven't reported him as a missing person? He disappeared Friday night; this is Tuesday afternoon. What about his family? Haven't they gone to the police?"

"Tom isn't missing, Mr. Quant."

Now I was confused. I'm sure the look on my face conveyed that message all too clearly.

"I know where Tom is."

"So you want me to find out why he stood you up?"

"First you have to find him. And then, yes, I want you to find out what happened."

More confusion. "But I thought you just said you know where he is."

"I know roughly where he is, not exactly where he is. He's in France."

"How do you know that?"

"The day after our ceremony, Sunday morning, we were to leave for Paris on our honeymoon."

"So you think he went on the honeymoon without you? I don't know if…"

"I thought it was crazy too. But his luggage is gone and then I found his plane ticket was also missing. Both our tickets and copies of the itinerary were right over there on the desk."

I glanced over at the expansive mahogany desk as if doing so would help. "When did you notice the ticket was missing?"

"Not until Monday morning, right before I called you. I was too distraught and busy doing whatever I could to track Tom down. Until then I never imagined he'd left the country."

"What about you? After the embarrassment of being jilted, you never thought of escaping it all by going to France anyway?" Okay, it might seem like a stupid and insensitive question, but sometimes those are the best kind.

"Of course not! Up until Monday I was seriously considering Tom might be dead or have been in an accident. It was the only thing that made sense…"

"Until you found his ticket wasn't where it should be."

"Yes."

I may have been shaking my head when I said, "He could be anywhere."

"You see, I don't think so. There's more. I studied at IMEDE in Switzerland and have travelled extensively in France. I am quite familiar with that part of Europe, but Tom…well he barely knows how to speak a few words in French. He'd have significant trouble getting by on his own, unless everything was already planned for him."

I was catching on. "So you suspect he will follow the plans you made for your honeymoon?"

"Yes. My travel agent and I pre-arranged almost every step of the trip, what routes we'd take, hotels, dinner reservations, everything. It's all spelled out in a very detailed itinerary. And more than that," Chavell said as if scoring the winning point, "I now have proof that he is following that itinerary. Our first stop was to be in Paris where we were to visit an old friend of mine, Solonge Fontaine. I called her this morning to tell her what's happened. Tom showed up as planned."

"Tom visited your friend in Paris?"

"Yesterday. Monday evening. Or rather, what was Monday evening in Paris. It would have been around noon here in Saskatoon. He had nowhere else to go, he knew she was expecting us and she speaks English. Imagine the state of mind he must have been in at that point. And tired and jet-lagged. Even though she was a virtual stranger to him, he'd be in need of a friendly face."

"Did he tell her what was going on?"

"It doesn't sound like he told her much of anything, but that's where I need your help. Solonge is a marvellous woman and tremendous friend, but she is also somewhat eccentric and can, at times, be a little vague. She may know something important without knowing she knows it."

"You want me to give her a call?"

"No, Mr. Quant. I want you to go to France. Meet with Solonge. See what you can find out. And then I want you to find Tom. The easiest thing for him to do is follow our itinerary. You should be able to catch up with him in no time."

"Not if he doesn't want to be found. It's the last thing he would do."

"If he didn't want to be found he wouldn't have gone to France and he wouldn't have visited Solonge."

He had a point. "So you think he wants to be found, maybe even expects you to come running after him?"

Chavell had an odd look on his face. "In a way, yes, that's possible."

"Then…why don't you?"

Chavell sat up straight in his seat and gave me a steely look used to strike fear into the hearts of his competitors. I, however, took it much better than that. "Are you not interested in taking this case, Mr. Quant?"

"In a case like this, Mr. Chavell, you have to be prepared to answer some difficult personal questions. If I feel I can't ask them, or that you will not answer them honestly, then the answer is no, I am not interested in this case."

He nodded as if thinking over my words. "I'm sorry. You're right."

"That's fine." I could see he was upset, but I couldn't afford to let him get me off topic. "So, why are you not jumping on a plane to France? Why don't you save yourself a bunch of money and go find him yourself?"

A lesser man might have gotten up, walked a few feet away, and spoke the following words with his back to me. I had to give Harold Chavell credit for staying in his seat and facing me with his emotions. "I've been through many tortured hours believing Tom might be hurt, or worse, dead. Grieving for him. Although it was the most gruesome of possibilities, it was the only one I could accept as the reason why he didn't show up for our wedding. When I found he had taken his ticket, flown to Paris without me and turned up on Solonge's doorstep, I…I just…"

I began to understand. "You became angry."

He was quiet for a moment. Now he did turn away and stared into the grate of an unlit fireplace.

I helped him along. "Even if Tom wants to be chased, you're not in the mood to do the chasing."

"It's petty, I know," he said, turning back to me. "But as much as I can't face him right now, I still have to know why he did this."

"I'm sure you've given this a lot of thought. Do you have any guesses as to his reasons?" If I was going to go ahead with this, I wanted as few surprises as possible. "Had you been fighting? Was there something else that was going on in Tom's life that might have impacted his decision about the marriage? Family? Friends? Ex-lovers causing problems? A current lover outside the relationship?"

Chavell gave me a nasty look that told me I was treading on thin ice as far as asking difficult, personal questions. "No," he said. "Nothing. This was not some fling, Mr. Quant. We had a serious relationship. This ceremony wasn't just another excuse to throw a party. We wanted to stand up in front of a room full of people who cared about us and proclaim our love for one another. We had no doubts. Neither of us." Then he shook his head and grimaced. "But I guess I was wrong about that, wasn't I?"

I shouldn't have, but I nodded. I looked in his face and wondered if this man was telling me everything. I felt there was something missing from the story.

"Can you give me Tom's address? I'd like to check out his apartment. And I'll need the names of friends, co-workers and family who were close to him and a list of the wedding guests. I'd like to talk with them myself. Also…"

"I can have the lists sent to your office. But right now there's no time for that," Chavell told me. "I've booked you on a flight tomorrow morning. I hope your passport is in order. I want you there immediately. Although I'm certain he'll stick to the itinerary as planned, I can't guarantee for how long."

I'm not much of a dawdler when it comes to business, so I could appreciate Harold Chavell's sense of haste. Sort of. Even though my Daytimer was empty, leaving the country with less than twenty-four hour's notice was not my idea of filling it. I was also a little uncomfortable taking the trip without the opportunity to do a little background work first. But Chavell informed me my Air Canada ticket to Paris was paid for and waiting for me at the airport. I told him I charge ninety-five dollars per hour plus out-of-pocket expenses and applicable taxes. Without wincing even once, he signed the contract I'd taken the liberty of preparing that morning. He gave me a healthy retainer, a copy of the itinerary, and a picture of Tom Osborn. Business concluded.

I was going to Paris.

Chapter 2

IT WAS CLOSE TO THREE O'CLOCK when I pulled into the gravel lot behind PWC. I hustled up the metal staircase that hugs the rear of the building and takes me directly to the second floor. I think at one time it was meant to be a fire escape, but now the ancient railings are so unstable I'm the only one who dares use them. They're handy when I want to slip into my office without being detected. As I unlocked the second floor door I couldn't decide whether I was excited or apprehensive. The tightness in my stomach could have been a sign of either. I love to travel but usually I'm thinking about whether I can get away with a Speedo rather than bulky trunks, not how to find a missing person in a foreign country. I tiptoed across the hallway and let myself into my office, soundlessly shutting the door behind me. I didn't want Alberta, our resident psychic, to know I was in. How impossible is that? Alberta is as wonderful as she is weird, and she loves to talk. Generally I enjoy our chats, but I didn't have the time right then for the latest gossip from the spiritual world.

I sat at my desk and pulled a cola from the fridge beneath it. Desk drawers are overrated and usually end up full of stuff you never look at again. I have a garbage can for that. I booted up my computer to begin making notes on my meeting with Chavell. I noticed the message light on my phone blinking red. Why did it have to be red? It reminded me of an ambulance light or stop light, things that needed immediate attention. Blue would be a nice change or even purple. I tried to ignore it. That damn machine had to learn that sometimes it was not the number one priority. But the red light flashed in the corner of my eye with the insistence of a lighthouse. In the battle of wills between man and machine, I was a failure.

I activated the speakerphone and listened to the recorded message. "Quant, it's Darren Kirsch. I have the information you wanted on Queasy. 975-8241." Click.

I had to shake my head. Detective Darren Kirsch. The formality of his phone message was hilarious. As if we hardly knew one another. And he had to know I had memorized his phone number ages ago. I had used it often enough in the last year. Maybe it was his way of saying, "Please understand that we are not friends or even acquaintances. Here is my phone number to be used to call me back. Just this once; don't use it again." I often wondered why Darren Kirsch *did* return my calls. Was he simply too polite not to? Did he think it was his professional duty? Did he know he was the only cop in the entire Saskatoon Police Service who ever bothered? The rest of them just ignored me.

Most cops, and I know this because I used to be one, think private investigators are unprofessional money-grabbers that will suck information out of you and give nothing back in return. And sometimes this is true. But I knew if I wanted to make a go of being a private detective, I'd need some friends in the police department. And a smart cop would know that being friendly with a detective who wasn't employed by the city and out there on the streets was not altogether a bad idea either. The jury was still out on whether Darren was a smart cop or just a naïve one who didn't know he could blow me off. Darren was now a detective in the Criminal Investigations Division so I guess he couldn't be that naïve. He and I had trained together at the Saskatchewan Police College in Regina and we both ended up in the SPS, Saskatoon Police Service. Every so often we had worked together but we never hung out or really talked to one another. A few years later when I decided life in uniform was not part of my long-term goals and left the force, I don't think he missed me.

Queasy, by self-description, is a sixty-two-year-old bum who has crossed my path more than a few times over the past years, first in the course of my duties as a police officer and then as a private detective. He is a PI's worst nightmare: a client who is always in trouble but can never pay to get out of it. Everyone has to do a little pro-bono work, and Queasy is mine. I'd heard the old fella was back in trouble and called Darren to find out the scoop. I wasn't ignoring the fact that Darren has more serious things to do, but I just happened to know he too has a soft spot for Queasy and tends to keep an eye out for him.

I dialled Darren's number and he answered on the first ring.

"Kirsch? Quant here." Two could play at his game. I didn't have to like him any more than he liked me.

"Hold on, I have his sheet right here." Such a friendly guy.

"Doing pretty good, thanks. You?"

He ignored that and updated me on Queasy who was being released that morning.

"He's just bored," I said. "And too smart. He gets to sing and dance in the bus mall while we're working our butts off."

I thought I could almost hear the detective smile. "Queasy thinks you work your butt off?"

Oh, clever man. Nice shot. Now I was sure he was smiling. "You know how it is, Kirsch. Actually I'm getting on a plane for France tomorrow. Compliments of a client. You know France, it's in Europe, the place with all the wine, fine food, the Riviera."

"Drafty hotels, snooty waiters, thirteen dollar cups of coffee."

"You're jealous."

"You're dreaming. Local client? Anything I should know about?" Darren keeps his ear to the wall.

"Missing person…sort of."

"Oh? Local?"

Although I was not in the habit of revealing details of my cases to the police, over the past several months Darren and I had begun to develop an understanding. We helped each other when we could. We were still working on figuring out where the line was that we shouldn't cross. When that happened, generally we'd hang up on each other. But this time I had a reason to continue with this conversation. Chavell wasn't giving me a lot of prep time. I had to do some fast digging. Chavell had told me Tom hadn't been reported as a missing person, but at the beginning of any case the last person I trust is my client. If the police knew something about this case or anything at all about Tom, I wanted to know about it. "Fellow by the name of Tom Osborn."

I could hear Darren mulling over the name before he responded. "Don't ring no bells."

"I didn't think so," I quickly told him. If Tom wasn't on the police radar screen I didn't want to put him there. "Anything else about Queasy? He going to be okay?"

"Your guess is as good as mine. It'll be the same ol' story as always."

"Okay. Thanks for the call."

I replaced the receiver and took the last swallow of my drink before lifting the phone again and dialling a familiar number.

"On Broadway," sung a friendly voice after a couple of rings.

"Kelly, it's Russell."

"Hey bud, how ya doing?"

"Good. Hey, I know it's short notice but would you and Errall be able to take Barbra for a few days?" I knew the chances were good the answer would be yes. Not only is Kelly one of my oldest friends, but she and Errall own Barbra's brother, Brutus, and the two dogs get along famously.

"Oh sure. No problem. When?"

I winced even though I knew Kelly couldn't see it. "I'm on a plane tomorrow morning."

"No problem. I can pick her up before work. Your alarm code the same?"

Good ol' Kelly. "Thank you, thank you, thank you. Yes, the code is the same. You sure you don't mind? I shouldn't keep you, you probably have customers." Kelly owned a small pottery and craft studio on Broadway Avenue.

"Yeah, I should go, but no problem. You tell Barbra that Brutus will pull out all his toys tonight." It's a running joke between us that I've never bothered to provide enough doggie toys for Barbra to play with. And it's true. I don't think to buy pull ropes or rubber chickens with bells in their bellies. But Barbra never complains. Only Kelly and Errall. "Where you off to?"

"France. But I'll tell you all about it later. You get back to your customers. And thanks a bunch, hon. I owe you."

"Nah you don't. Have a good trip. Bye."

"Bye."

I stepped out onto my deck realizing I could just as easily have walked downstairs and talked to Errall directly about taking care of Barbra. But somehow it felt more natural and comfortable to call Kelly. I studied the photo of Tom Osborn. It was a five by seven of professional quality, taken perhaps for business purposes. He was wearing a suit and I estimated his age to be thirty or thirty-five. His face had more curves than angles and I had a difficult time deciding whether he was handsome or merely cute. He had sandy brown hair, straight and clipped short, a smallish nose and plump lips. By far his most attractive feature was his friendly, smiling, green eyes. Even reproduced, they sparkled. His was a face you might not pick out of a crowd but one you'd easily grow fond of and miss when it was gone. I stared at Tom Osborn and wondered what made him run. I felt sad for Harold Chavell.

For a while I sat. I watched the sluggish traffic on Spadina. I studied the trees in the park. Their leaves would soon lose their verdant green in favour of autumn's bright hues. I love this time of year. So fresh and invigorating. But that didn't relieve the growing sense of discomfort I'd begun to feel after I left Cathedral Bluffs hours earlier. I was uneasy about boarding that plane tomorrow with no background information on Tom Osborn.

But I knew there was something I could do about that. I jumped out of my chair.

There are times in my career when I find myself doing things that are "less than completely legal." I prefer "less than completely legal" to "illegal" which has a decidedly negative sound to it. Semantics. Breaking and entering is one of those things. I do not commit myself lightly to such an act. Rather, I must believe it to be the most efficient and expedient means to an end without causing undue harm to person, place or police investigation. I believed this to be such a case. Tom Osborn was in another country so he certainly couldn't complain about what I was about to do. I'm a pretty fine lock-picker and tidy snooper, so I could guarantee I'd leave his apartment just as I'd found it. And, completing my rationalization, I'd just been told by Darren Kirsch that Tom Osborn was not under police investigation so I knew I wouldn't be treading on some cop's toes. As I parked my car a half block away from Tom's place I had myself entirely convinced this was the right thing to do.

My client's boyfriend was living in an area called Grosvenor Park near the university. His building was the newest construction in a complex of five sitting semi-circle around a green area and the only one that had gone condo. Once I was inside the main foyer I glanced about and was grateful to see no evidence of a surveillance camera. I approached the security intercom system. Often with these systems, there's a listing on the wall displaying the names of tenants along with their intercom number. No such luck here. Apparently if you lived in this building you'd have to furnish visitors with your address *and* intercom number. Shit. I was not in the mood for scaling walls tonight. I should have tried to get a key from Chavell. Oh well, no time for that now. This would make things harder but not impossible. I began with two digit codes. One-one. One-two. One-three. I worked my way up to two-five before deciding to try three digits. One-zero-one. One-zero-two. I kept this up for a few minutes. Nothing. I'd found that intercom codes are rarely four digits. Too hard to remember. I returned to two digits with a zero in front. Zero-one-zero. Bingo. Zero-One-Zero yielded me a cautious "Hello."

"Yes, hello," I said as charmingly as I could. I hate the sound of my voice when I'm trying to be charming. "This is Danny Bonaduce from the third floor." I hoped this person didn't know *Partridge Family* trivia. "I just moved in last week and I've got my apartment key but I forgot the one for the front door." I had to talk fast to get in my whole sob story before I got a yes or no. "My last place didn't have such a fancy security system. But it's great we've got this one. I was just wondering…"

She must have been bored with my story or wanting to get back to the television. I heard the buzzing sound that would unlock the door that led into the main lobby. Swell. I love it when things work out like this. It makes me believe I've learned a thing or two in the past year.

The building was eerily quiet and smelled clean. I knew Tom lived in apartment 303. I wondered if his intercom number was zero-three-zero. But then what would the intercom number be for apartment 304? I dislike confusing number systems. There was an elevator but I chose to take the stairs. Less chance of running into anyone. Especially the woman from zero-one-zero. Conceivably she could have been a *Partridge Family* fan rushing down to the lobby with her autograph book.

I reached the third floor and Tom's door without incident. I knocked twice, making up an excuse should the unexpected happen and Tom answer. He didn't. I waited a moment to listen for sounds of impending departure from other third floor tenants. Not much seemed to be happening. I pulled my prized set of lock picks from my jacket pocket. They are small, concise instruments made of something strong, don't ask me what. Any failure I had experienced with them was due to human error and not their capability. It took me two or three minutes. When I heard the click of success I had to restrain myself from cheering. Every time I do this I get a little better at it.

Once inside I took a moment to wipe the sweat from my brow and settle my racing heart. The apartment was dark. I couldn't think of a reason not to switch on the lights so I felt around the wall next to the door and flipped up the first protuberance I touched. I was in a short hallway. To my left a closet door. To my right was an alcove shelf covered with a collection of stuff: paper chits, a bowl full of change, a pair of weightlifting gloves and a portable CD player. Further down was the entryway to the rest of the apartment. Throwing on lights as if I lived there, I walked first into a smallish dining room, which gave way to an odd, triangular-shaped kitchen. Over a marble-topped island I could see the living room and another hallway which I guessed would take me to the bathroom and one or two bedrooms.

As was my habit on such expeditions, if I had the luxury of time, I spent the first few minutes getting a feel for the place and the person who lived there. My first impression was one of sparseness. Tom Osborn was neat and organized. His taste in furniture, art and do-dads was good. Quality over quantity. I guessed he probably was a fairly new tenant. It had that just moved in look. This surprised me. I would have thought if Tom and Chavell were about to get hitched, they'd also be planning to move in together. So then why would Tom move into a new place? I also suspected this was not a place where Harold Chavell would have spent much time. There was nary a luxury item in sight. No wine cellar, no humidor, no Persian rugs or pantry full of foie gras. How could he possibly survive?

The apartment did not appear to have been abandoned or left in a hurry. It did not look like a place from where someone had been abducted. Chavell was probably right. The last time Tom Osborn left his apartment, it had been under his own terms. I checked the closets. No suitcases. Very few clothes. And what there was looked like work clothes: suits, shirts, ties, shiny dress shoes.

It was time for a closer look. The first thing to catch my eye was a cardboard package on an armoire pushed up against the wall near the dining table. I picked up the small box and spied remnants of tape on its underbelly sticking to snatches of torn gift-wrap. This had been a present. Perhaps a pre-wedding gift? There were no markings on the box and there was no card. I opened it and pulled out a burgundy case, also unmarked, and swung up its lid. Inside, nestled in cream-coloured silk was a silver chain and attached to it a gleaming pendant. I lifted the chain out of its box for a closer look. The pendant was also silver and looked to be the left half of what was once a heart shape. Unique. I wondered who owned the right half. I found it interesting that Tom had decided to leave without it and that he had left it out in plain view. He obviously planned to do something with it. Did he not want it? Was it a gift he planned to return? Had it been sent to him or was it personally delivered? The heart shape said romance to me. My best guess was that it was a gift from Chavell. A gift Tom decided to leave behind when he took his luggage and left town.

I pulled a pen and blank cheque from my jacket pocket. On the backside of the cheque I did a quick sketch of the jewellery. When I was done I carefully replaced the gift where and how I'd found it and continued my search. Drawers and nooks and crannies that are often home to secrets, revealed none. I felt under furniture, checked behind pictures and in the refrigerator, rifled through books, sock drawers and stacks of papers, but came up empty.

I had learned from Chavell that Tom was a partner in QW Technologies, a high technology firm he co-founded with a college buddy. Except for a few technical manuals with chapters full of gobbledygook it appeared he kept his work at work. Not even a computer. Odd. Most computer geeks like to keep a computer nearby at all times. Actually, almost everyone has a home computer nowadays. But maybe he owned a portable laptop and took it with him. As I continued to snoop around I was beginning to get the feeling Tom not only kept his work away from home, but he kept his home away from home too. There were a few framed photos of Tom, Chavell and others who I assumed were either family or friends, but nothing seriously hinted at his relationship to Chavell or the upcoming wedding. There were no signs of a hobby or forms of entertainment other than a small TV. There was little of a personal nature to find. About as much as I'd expect to see in a cabin or weekend retreat. I knew Tom had packed enough clothes and personal supplies for two weeks in Europe, and maybe that would explain the absence of T-shirts and jeans and funky sweaters, but why was there no hamburger meat in the freezer, no dirty sneakers, no shelf full of novels and magazines?

I picked up the phone and heard the telling beeps indicating Tom had messages, but without his SaskTel password I wouldn't be able to access them. I hit the "redial" button to check the last phone call made from Tom's phone and reached the answering machine for someplace called TechWorld. I made a mental note. I punched *69 which gave me the last number that had called Tom's phone. It was Chavell's home number. No surprise there.

I pretty much concluded Tom didn't really live here. At least not often. This apartment was likely a ruse to make it appear that Tom and Chavell did not live together as a couple. But I was certain they did live together and I'd bet it was at Chavell's castle rather than in this modest apartment. An expensive ruse, but one that I'm sure worked well. Perhaps it was family or co-workers who had made creating and maintaining this falsehood a necessity in their lives. And if this was a fake home, I had to question how much authentic information I was bound to collect here. Even so, I could not leave without performing the worst job. I always saved it for last. The kitchen garbage.

Unappetizing as it sounds, it's a must-do in any thorough search. Often I ended up with nothing but smelly hands, but now and again, amongst the apple peels and eggshells, was a gem of knowledge. And knowledge is power. The key to this part of an investigation is to have some idea of what you hope to find or what could be important. Otherwise garbage and clues can look surprisingly alike. In this case, the best I could hope for, would be anything that might tell me how Tom spent his time between the Friday night rehearsal party and his Sunday morning flight to Paris. There were two slightly soiled dishes in the kitchen sink so I expected I might have to rifle through leftovers. I also hoped to find a card that might have accompanied the silver chain. Lady Luck wasn't on my side. I didn't find either. Tom must have recently taken out the trash. The refuse barrel was empty except for a scrunched-up, brown paper bag. I retrieved it and flattened it out on the kitchen counter. Embossed on the front was the name of a vegetarian restaurant near Broadway Avenue called The Blue Carrot Café. I got the carrot part, but why blue? Inexplicable use of colour bothers me—first the answering machine light and now this. I tossed the bag back into the garbage.

Before leaving premises I have not been formally invited into, I generally find it a wise practice to sneak a peak out the windows. Just to see what I can see. Not that I expect a squadron of police cars with lights flashing and cops with guns drawn awaiting my exit, but you never know. I pushed my fingers through two slats of venetian blind and peered through the space I'd created. The window I'd chosen looked over the parking lot behind the building. In the light of a street-lamp I could see a densely populated bicycle rack and roughly twenty vehicles. Over half were of the ubiquitous sports utility vehicle variety—Blazers, Jimmys, Jeep Cherokees. Didn't anyone drive a car anymore? I wondered if one of them belonged to Tom. Chavell hadn't mentioned whether Tom owned a vehicle or whether or not it too was missing. Did he use it to get to the airport? Did he call a taxi? Or did someone pick him up? More for the list of things I did not know.

As I was about to switch off the hallway light on my way out, my eyes fell on the glass bowl filled with change sitting on the alcove shelf. I had almost missed it, but among the metallic money was a small gold key. I picked it up and examined it closely. It was on a thin silver ring with a tiny fob in the shape of an elephant's head. Based on its shape and size I immediately ruled out it being for a vehicle or a standard door. Just to be sure I slipped it into the lock on the apartment's front door, but, as I'd guessed, it was much too small. In my mind I mentally retraced my steps throughout the apartment to see if I could recall coming across anything locked I couldn't get into. There was nothing, no safety box or diary or even a stray padlock. What was this key for? Tom had kept it in an easily accessible spot telling me he probably used it on a regular basis or at least wanted to ensure quick access to it.

Leaving the apartment, I ran down the stairs to the lobby doors. Again the key was obviously too small. I glanced around for other opportunities for a tenant to use a key. I spied a wall of mailboxes next to the elevator. That had to be it! As luck would have it, the mailboxes yielded yet another nonsensical numbering system that did not appear to have any apparent relationship to the intercom or apartment numbers. This was probably a good security measure, but a pain in the ass for someone in my profession. I had no choice but to try them all. Again I was thankful for the lack of security cameras.

Minutes later I remained stymied. The key was about the right size for the mailboxes, but it had failed to unlock one. I returned to the apartment and took another quick tour looking for someplace to stick the mysterious key. Nothing. Drat. I knew if I didn't find out what this key was used for, I'd wake up in the middle of the night thinking about it.

I glanced at my watch. Almost seven. I was hungry, I knew Barbra would be too and I still had to pack. I pocketed the key and ran around the apartment switching off the lights. For the second time that night I was about to extinguish the hallway light and pull open the door to leave when suddenly I froze in my tracks. This time it wasn't a key that stopped me. It was a knock at the door.

Shit!

I could taste my heart in my throat and it didn't taste good. I had been way too close to opening that door and stepping into the arms of someone who'd be expecting to see Tom Osborn. Not good. No, worse than that. Stupid and careless came to mind. And it got better. Could they see the hallway light under the door?

Suppose whoever it was out in the hallway had seen me flicking lights on and off like a disco strobe? I glanced down but couldn't tell how wide the space was. How far was I from being the subject of a 9-1-1 call?

Another rap on the door.

I stood there trying not to breathe as if the sound of it might pass through the door.

Again. This time the knock was accompanied by a man's plaintive voice, "Tom? Tom? Are you in there? We should talk about this!"

As if walking on hot coals I approached the door. I leaned in close until my right eye met the peephole. He was young and blonde with dark brows gathered together in a frown.

I heard another voice. A woman. Goddamnit, how many of them are there out there, I wondered. I saw the man's head turn to his left.

"Excuse me?" he said.

"I sez yer wasting yer time," the woman's voice said. Or sez. "He's not home. So stop all that knockin' and wailin.' Are yeh hungry? I've got some cutlets over here."

The man looked confused. Can't imagine why. Cutlets? He stepped out of the peephole's visual range but I could still hear his voice. "Are you talking about Tom Osborn? Do you know him?"

"Of course I know 'im. We're's neighbours, aren't we?"

"I guess. Not home, huh?"

"Nah. But he's never around much."

"Oh. So you haven't seen him around in the last couple of days?"

"Nah. Hasn't been home for days. I'da seen or heard 'im if he had. Yer not hungry? Yer a skinny boy."

I hoped the young man at least smiled or shook his head. If not, his sudden departure was rather rude. Eventually I heard a door close which I hoped meant cutlet-lady had gone back into her apartment. Even so, I waited another full five minutes before concluding it was safe to move on. I switched off the remaining light and left Tom Osborn's apartment, making sure the door was locked behind me.

My home is my castle, a place where I re-energize and take refuge from the world. The house is on a large lot at the dead end of a quiet, little-travelled street. A grove of towering aspen and thick spruce neatly hide it from view of the casual passer-by. Even some of my neighbours don't know the house is there. When I first saw the lot it felt to me like one of those enchanted fairy tale forests, the kind with elves and fairies and mischievous gnomes. I knew I'd fit right in. Inside the house is a unique mix of open, airy rooms and tiny, cozy spaces, each that appeal to me, depending on my mood. The backyard had been a labour of love of the previous owner from which I now reap the benefits. A six-foot-high fence encircles it and its population of fountains, birdbaths and trellises. It is a wonderful never-never land of lovingly planted flora, well-placed clay pots and metalwork benches, and stone-laid pathways that lead into leafy enclaves hidden throughout the expanse. Although I knew little about gardening when I moved in, I am now an avid student and it has quickly become a much-loved summertime hobby. At the rear of the lot, accessible by way of a back alley, is a two-car garage with a handy second storey I use for storage.

When I first came to the big city from small town Saskatchewan to attend university, my mother's brother, Lawrence, took me under his mighty wing. It was not, however, through any sense of duty or responsibility for his sister's kid, for in actuality I hardly knew him before then. He and my mother did not get along. Lawrence helped me out because, as I later learned, he saw in me a younger version of himself. I don't know how accurate he was, but I'm glad he thought so. Lawrence hosted extravagant dinners and parties populated with bizarre and interesting people and I was always invited. He was larger than life. He was attractive, well-mannered, well-educated and well-heeled. I wanted to be him. When he travelled, which was often, I was given the keys to the house, the cars, and the impossibly bountiful lifestyle that went with them. It was almost too much for a nineteen-year-old farm-boy. I'll never know why, but he trusted me implicitly with all of it. Tragically, Lawrence did not return from his last trip. He was killed in a skiing accident. He was fifty-one at the time.

In his will, Uncle Lawrence left me a sum of money with one simple instruction: Buy a Dream. I was a Saskatoon police officer when Lawrence died. I wasn't unhappy with my job, but I wasn't thrilled with it either. I liked the work but I just wasn't cut out to wear a uniform and drive a car with a bubble. I knew becoming a detective in a small Canadian city was a risk, career-wise and financially, but in all other ways it promised a much superior lifestyle. No bosses. No shift work. No doughnut jokes. And, I still got to solve criminal riddles, help good guys and get rid of bad guys. Perfect. In theory. The Saskatoon Yellow Pages reveal only a handful of investigators for hire. Is it a matter of less population equals less crime, or is Canada simply a less PI-oriented country? All I knew was that this was one career that guaranteed a rocky start. So, it was the money from Lawrence that allowed me to quit my steady police job, pay off the mortgage on my house, and survive the first months of my new life. As instructed, I had bought a dream.

It was after 11:00 p.m. when I finished packing. I was about to pour a glass of wine and relax but Barbra had other ideas. Barbra is a robust, four-year-old Standard Schnauzer with a wiry pepper and salt coat, strong, rectangular head and cropped ears and tail. Barbra is affectionate but not effusive, lively but not restless, fairly independent, occasionally playful but usually laid back and serious. She prefers communication by way of eye contact rather than barking. If I am the king of my castle, she is the queen. We are wholly compatible housemates. Usually.

She was standing as still as a wax figurine at the front door. It was time for a walk. The nice thing about Barbra is that she won't whine or bark incessantly until I agree to take her out. She simply stands at the door and stares at me whenever I happen to pass by.

If I continue to ignore her, she'll eventually begin following me around the house with a look of utter disappointment in her eyes. It wasn't worth it. I dutifully retrieved a harness for her and a coat for myself. She didn't reveal any particular excitement. I had simply met her expectations for regular exercise and she was glad, but there was certainly no reason to jump about and act silly. A self-disciplined animal.

I had planned to leave a message for my neighbour the next morning asking if she would keep an eye on the house while I was away, but as we passed her home I saw Sereena on her front porch. She was leaning against the railing studying the stars, a wineglass in her hand. Sereena Orion Smith is best described by that song from the early eighties, "I've Never Been To Me" by Charlene. She is probably forty-something—I don't know, I don't ask. Once a raving beauty, Sereena's past life of drugs, alcohol and all-night partying shows in her roughened face. I have no doubt that indeed she has been "undressed by kings...and seen some things that a woman ain't s'posed to see." And now, she is simply relieved to have survived, maybe a little disappointed things turned out the way they did, but content to live a quieter life. She never boasts of her travels or experiences or the famous people she once knew and is never impressed by anything or anyone—like someone who has seen and done it all and knows it ain't so great. Many people consider her abrasive and gruff. And maybe she is. But the thing I like about Sereena is that what you see is what you get. There's no bullshit when it comes to her. My other neighbours are friendly enough, but Sereena really listens, really cares, she's someone who still gives a damn.

Barbra and I made our way down the short pathway to Sereena's porch. "See anything up there?"

She didn't look down at first, as though our approach was not of particular interest to her. "More than you think."

"I just wanted to tell you I'm going to be out of town for a few days. Barbra is going to visit Brutus but I was wondering if you'd keep an eye on the place."

She gave me the look. Even with her excess-ravaged face, in the softening moonlight Sereena Smith is a stunning woman. "That depends on where you're going. Perhaps I'll join you."

With anyone else this would have been an idle joke. With Sereena that wasn't necessarily true. "Paris to start. After that, I'm not sure."

"I love to travel that way. Plan the first day and wing it after that. Are you in need of company, sweetheart? I could get away."

"Maybe next time. It's work."

"Really?" She patted the railing next to where she stood. An invitation to join her. "Wine?"

I shook my head. "Thanks. I have an early flight."

She glanced at her watch and scoffed. "Can't be that early. Of course I'll watch the house. How long? I assume my key will still work."

"Yes it is. Don't know. And yes it will."

"Don't know? I can't promise to be here indeterminately. Life is full of unexpected opportunities."

"It won't be that long. Maybe a week?"

"Fine. Do you speak French?"

I grinned. "Just enough to piss them off."

"Good boy. Au revoir, Monsieur Quant." Her accent was perfect.

"Au revoir, Madame Smith." Mine wasn't.

Chapter 3

I LOVE SASKATOON. Living in a small, Canadian, prairie city is one of the best-kept secrets in the world. Not too small, not too big, relatively safe, relatively inexpensive, clean and only the unimaginative cannot find enough to do. Even so, Saskatchewanians do have wanderlust. From the oldest wheat farmer to the poorest university student, it seems they've all travelled, oftentimes far beyond the province's rectangular border. With temperatures that can dip below minus forty degrees Celsius, fitting in a short getaway during the winter months is often a popular choice. Let a tropical sun colour your cheeks. Get jostled about on one of the great retail streets of the world. Experience the culture of another country. Hear foreign languages, smell the unfamiliar, taste the exquisite. What a rush. The only problem is physically getting out of town. It's a sad fact that the Saskatchewan traveller cannot get anywhere flying direct from Saskatoon. Connect, connect, connect and then maybe you've made it out of the province. I'm exaggerating—slightly.

I left Saskatoon at 11:00 a.m. Wednesday morning and landed in Toronto at 4:00 p.m. It was only a three-hour flight but at this time of year, there's a two-hour time change between Saskatchewan and Ontario. My flight to Paris left Toronto at 7:30 that evening and I arrived at Charles de Gaulle Airport seven hours later at 8:30 a.m. The total time change from Saskatchewan was now eight hours and I felt every one of them weighing down on my eyelids as I made my way to the plane's exit. I should have been nestled in my bed entering REM sleep rather than greeting a bright new day. What made it worse is that everyone seemed a co-conspirator in the perverse charade. The steward wished me a cheery good morning as I stepped past him. Hadn't he been on the same flight as I was? It wasn't morning. It was the middle of the night and no amount of scrambled eggs and orange juice served in plastic containers was going to convince me otherwise. I grumbled at him. I can be a grouch in the morning.

Even though I'd been to Paris once before, I still needed my wits about me to navigate the international airport terminal. I found the baggage carousel without trouble and was pleasantly surprised when my bag was the first one to appear. The airline gods were looking out for me. I pulled the suitcase off the turnstile feeling somewhat superior to my fellow travellers. They looked at me with various degrees of dislike, some half-dazed from lack of sleep, and some half-crazed from lack of nicotine. I walked away without an ounce of guilt, pretending to be a VIP who rightly deserved his luggage first. Opportunities like that don't present themselves often. It's important to take full advantage when they do. Sereena taught me that.

I entered a flood of swiftly moving humanity. By now Chavell would have contacted Solonge Fontaine and told her to expect my call. I was to arrange a meeting time with her as soon as I landed. Good idea but it would have to wait until I found coffee. It didn't take me long. I paid the exorbitant price, found a table to lean against and took the first exquisite sip of the dark, full-bodied, French café. No matter what a label tells you or waiter promises, there is nothing like it in Canada. As I savoured the caffeine, I watched the constant stream of travellers—a people-watcher's delight. Not only for the eyes but for the ears as well. There seemed to be as many languages spoken as manners of dress and colours of skin. It was a United Nations fashion show.

After I finished my drink I found a telephone booth where I waited in line behind a tall, elegant woman made even taller by her mile-high, multi-coloured turban. I didn't mind. When I had to, I could nap on my feet. When it was my turn at the phone I spoke with someone I understood to be Solonge Fontaine's assistant. I might have gotten that wrong as my French was a little rusty. (At Uncle Lawrence's suggestion, I had taken French immersion classes several years before. He said it was the language of good taste and sophistication and that I'd be unprepared to enjoy the world without it.) The assistant told me "Madame" was expecting me and could receive me mid-afternoon at her apartment. I wrote down directions and hung up. I had a few hours to kill.

A lovely young woman behind the Sixt car rental counter presented me with the keys to the C180 Mercedes Chavell had arranged for me. She warned me against taking the vehicle into Italy. Apparently expensive French rental cars were common targets for Italian thieves. I assured her I had no intention of driving into Italy and got the feeling that if I had, I'd be looking elsewhere for a vehicle. I found my car in the Sixt parking lot and acquainted myself with its features. Except for the language used on the dashboard instruments, everything looked familiar save for one button that seemed to indicate I could eject a fellow passenger through the sunroof. That could come in handy. Suddenly I felt like James Bond. I opened my map of Paris and laid it over the steering wheel to plot my course.

Later, as I headed into the bowels of Paris, I was grateful for the proliferation of signs telling me in no uncertain terms where to go. Signage was not the problem—it was the millions of cars and trucks and vans and motorized scooters whizzing by me like a

Anthony Bidulka

movie on fast forward. I've always thought there should be a tourist's lane. But no one pays attention to my ideas. The last time I was in Paris I drove around the Arc de Triomphe traffic circle several times, each time helplessly watching my exit sign speed by before I found the reckless courage to go for it. Now, on a multi-laned highway leading me into the core of the great city, I kept my speed as slow as I dared. I knew from past experience that most of the honking going on around me wasn't road rage but rather drivers saying, "Hey, I'm here and I want to get in front of you." I always let them. Europeans tend to use horns as a means of communication, not an expression of anger.

My hotel, Residence Concorde, proved difficult to find. There wasn't a noticeable exterior sign or expansive driveway like most North American hotels. There were no tell-tale valets or bellhops standing curbside anxiously waiting to serve me. Exasperated, I found a parking spot near where my map suggested the hotel should be and continued my search on foot. I didn't have far to go. Only two doors down from where I'd parked, and voila! There it was. Residence Concorde. I knew this from a tiny, brass plaque next to a green door on a nondescript five-storey building that butted right up against the sidewalk. Under the plaque was a black-nosed buzzer. This was the extent of the hotel's exterior presence. How could I have missed it? This was definitely not the Sheraton.

I rang the buzzer. After a moment an elderly porter opened the door. Without conversation he grabbed my bag with a gnarled hand and led me up a narrow flight of stairs. Normally I would have felt badly about having an old man lug my heavy suitcase all that way, but I was too busy worrying about where the hell he was taking me. From what I could see on our way up it appeared we were in a run down apartment building. Where was the hotel? Where was the foyer with marble floors? Where was the concierge desk? And where, for goodness sake, was the lobby bar? On the third floor landing the porter deposited my bag and stood back expectantly. I smiled and shrugged my shoulders. He looked me square in the eye and said something completely unintelligible. I began to panic. Was that French? If it was, I had taken the wrong class. I glanced about and noticed a small, square-shaped opening the size of a hardcover book at chest height in the scuffed up wall in front of me. I stepped forward, crouched down and peeked through it. I saw a severe-looking woman watching us without any particular interest. I smiled. No noticeable response.

"Is this Residence Concorde?" I asked in what I hoped was passable French.

She replied something that sounded a bit like French at supersonic speed.

"I'm sorry," I said, speaking slowly, hoping it would encourage her to do the same. "S'il vous plaît, parlez moins vite? Can you speak slower? I didn't understand what you said. Could you repeat it?"

"You're looking for Residence Concorde?" she answered slowly and intelligibly.

"Yes!" I suppose I didn't have to sound so excited, but I was glad to have understood her.

"Then you are there," she stated.

For a moment we kind of stared at one another, not sure who should make the next move.

"Name?"

"Russell Quant." Finally, something I could say in English.

"Would you like to see the room?" she said after mercifully finding my name in the register book and placing a big checkmark next to it.

Was there only one? "Yes. Thank you."

I heard a buzzing sound and the woman's slanting eyes directed me to a door on my right. The porter had disappeared. I guess the rest was up to me. Maybe he was mad I hadn't tipped him? I opened the door, grabbed the handle of my bag and pulled it behind me into the depths of Residence Concorde. Beyond the door was a high-ceilinged, dim passageway that smelled of yeast. Perhaps someone was about to bake bread? Madame-Behind-the-Window greeted me with a tight nod. She briskly led me down the hallway pointing out the amenities of the hotel as if she were a tour guide. I caught less than half of what she said. We passed a small alcove crowded with four small round tables. My translation suggested a continental breakfast would be served in this room from 7:30 a.m. to 9:00 a.m. and not one second earlier or later. (I inferred the last part from her tone.) The further we went the darker it seemed to get. I was glad her shoes made a click-clacking noise on the swarthy, wooden floors. Soon I would need the auditory clue to keep me from getting lost. Sure enough we almost collided a moment later when she made an abrupt stop. She unlocked a door and threw it open, announcing, "Une chambre pour une personne!" as if she had unveiled a magnificent piece of art. I nodded, she handed me the key and away she went.

Although I admit to sometimes (well, maybe always) packing more than I could possibly need, I had reason to believe my suit-case was of normal proportions. But once I'd deposited it in my suite, there was no remaining floor space on which to walk. The bed was cot-size but still too big for the room. It was wedged against the door of what was probably a closet. I'd never know. The only other piece of furniture in the room was a dresser that at home would be considered an antique. Here, I wasn't so sure. I could pull the drawers open only partway before they were blocked by the bed's headboard. Apparently if you wished to deposit items in the drawers they had to fit through a three-inch space. I could imagine getting everything in there, but how would I get it out? Another door opened into a Barbie-sized bathroom. I've been in small hotel rooms before but this was the winner. I pushed my luggage into the bathroom so I could sit on the bed with my feet on the floor. I took a moment to console myself with the thought that at most I'd be here only one night.

I crawled over the bed and pulled aside the drapes. A street view was too much to hope for. Instead, I could see the wall of the neighbouring building across the alley. Unlike those in most modern hotels, this window had a latch that allowed me to open it. No temperature-controlled environment here. As the casement swung out I felt a rush of cool air wash over my jet-lagged face. It was glorious. I leaned out and looked down. Three floors below, halfway down the alley, a single table and two rickety chairs were perched on the cobblestones. A colourful tablecloth fluttered in the breeze. A young man cockily sat half-sprawled on one of the chairs. He wore a dark blue peacoat and a white scarf hung from his neck. His large, square hands looked odd as he raised a minuscule cup from its saucer to his lips. The door in the building behind him opened. A beautiful young woman in a flimsy blouse came through it. He barely turned to look at her. She stood for a moment behind him and said something. He cocked his head but still did not look at her. I thought they might be having an argument. Instead, she threw back her head in what I decided was a lusty laugh and leaped into his lap. They kissed, bringing beauty and life to a grey, deserted alley. I fell back onto my bed and stared at the ceiling with a smile on my face. Suddenly the size of the room no longer mattered. I was a prairie boy in Paris! Yahoo!

I must stay awake. I must stay awake. This was my mantra as I strolled down the Champs Élysées. A chilly temperature and occasional dollop of rain helped. I had to stay awake as long as I could. I wanted nothing more than to take a nap, but if I had a sleep in what was now the middle of the day, I knew I'd spend the rest of the trip awakening at 2:00 a.m. and reading until dawn. The Eiffel Tower beckoned from a distance, but I was certain my aching legs wouldn't take me that far. Shopping wasn't an option unless I was prepared to spend Chavell's retainer on a belt. Instead I chose one of numerous cafés, ordered an expresso and paid the extra fee, which allowed me to sit at a table rather than stand at a counter. I could wait here until it was time to visit Solonge Fontaine. She lived nearby and that, I guessed, was why Harold Chavell chose Residence Concorde for me. I was certain *he* had never stayed there.

At 2:00 p.m. I presented myself at the door of Madame Fontaine. She lived near the top of a high-rise apartment building. It looked run down from the outside but was neat and clean inside. I was let in by her assistant and shown into a room that she called the parlour. The apartment was moderate in size. Oddly enough, most of the furniture appeared larger than life as if meant for a giant's castle. Still, everything was so cleverly arranged it wasn't nearly as crowded as it might have been. I didn't wait long before my hostess presented herself. Solonge Fontaine was a striking woman in her sixties. Her steel-grey hair was pulled back from her face into a tidy bun. She was in excellent shape, wearing one of those tight pants and floopy sweater outfits Mary Tyler Moore used to wear on the *Dick Van Dyke Show*. Sixty-year-old women in Canada rarely dressed like this. But on her, it worked.

"You'll have coffee? A small drink, perhaps?" Finally some French I could understand. Her voice was deep and smoky. I'm not quite sure what that means, but I know it applied. "My, you are a lovely-looking man."

I blushed. "Thank you. Coffee would be wonderful." More caffeine was good. Not surprisingly, I was beginning to feel quite awake and confident in my ability to speak and understand French.

After instructing her assistant to fetch drinks, Solonge Fontaine settled down on a thinly padded armchair, tucking her slender legs underneath herself. She gave me a quizzical look. "I'm not quite certain, Mr. Quant, why you are here? Please, sit with me."

I hoisted myself into the chair opposite hers. I was horrified to see my feet barely touching the ground. Should I also tuck them under me? Should I let them swing? "Didn't Harold Chavell call and explain the purpose for my visit?"

"Of course, of course, but I didn't really pay attention. Once I'd heard he was sending you I thought I'd wait until you arrived and understand from you in person." Interesting thought process.

"You were aware Harold and his friend, Tom Osborn, were to be vacationing in France?" As I struggled with sentence structure I remembered Chavell had told me Solonge knew how to speak English. It was too late to switch now. Besides, I needed the practice.

"Yes of course. Harold is one of my oldest and dearest friends. He and his lover were most welcome in my home." The way she said lover, *amant*, made it sound both mysterious and naughty at the same time. "I looked forward to entertaining them."

"But only Tom arrived," I pushed her along. She had the irritating habit of saying each sentence as if it were the conclusion of the story.

"Yes. Strange that."

"Harold thought so too. That is why I'm here. To find Tom."

"Oh my, my, my. Then you've made a long voyage for nothing I'm afraid."

I hoped the translation in my head wasn't accurate.

"Tom Osborn is no longer here," she told me. "He stayed only an hour or so."

Instant relief. I was worried she was about to tell me Tom had booked passage on a freighter sailing for Tunisia. "Yes, I know that. You see Harold had hoped you could give us some information about Tom. Anything you might have learned during your visit with him would be helpful. Any idea where he might be heading next." I had the itinerary but no guarantee Tom would follow it.

"Well as you know, it was my first time meeting Mr. Osborn. We had much to discuss."

I crossed my legs but quickly uncrossed them when I realized how silly it must look with me in the impossibly huge armchair. "Did he explain to you why he arrived without Harold?"

"Yes. Of course he did."

Prod. Prod. Prod. "What did he say?"

"I'm uncertain whether I should divulge such information to you, a total stranger."

"But your friend, Harold Chavell, has sent me here especially for that reason," I said, probably sounding a little exasperated.

She chuckled at that as if glad to have been reminded of the fact. "Yes, yes, of course, you're right, he did."

"What did Mr. Osborn tell you, Madame?"

"He told me his heart was troubled and that he and Harold needed time apart."

I doubted this was an exact quote from a Canadian computer geek. And perhaps my translation of Solonge's French wasn't one hundred per cent accurate.

She continued. "I was, of course, very surprised to receive him alone. But it was obvious he was a young man in pain. Poor Mr. Osborn seemed nervous and distracted and very sad. He asked me not to contact Harold, but of course I did. After all, Harold is one of my oldest and dearest friends. Well, actually Harold telephoned me, but I was certainly considering it."

"Did he seem afraid?" It was a guess. "Tom I mean."

She considered this for a moment. "No. No, I did not feel he was afraid."

"Did he explain why he decided to leave Harold at the altar? Why was he troubled? Did he and Harold have a fight or did something else happen to make him run away?"

"No, no, nothing like that. It wasn't something that happened between the two of them. It came from within."

Huh? I gave her a blank look.

"I can only guess at this, but based on my experience in matters of the heart, which is not inconsequential, I'd say it was more a case of Mr. Osborn looking within himself and being unsure of what his heart was telling him."

"Meaning he had doubts about marrying Harold?"

"Yes and no. He had doubts about getting married. But no doubts about Harold. He needed to run away. To think. Sometimes that is the only intelligent thing left to do. There were moments when he spoke of darling Harold when I sensed they had almost become complete strangers. Shame, that."

"Okay." Chavell was right about Solonge. She was vague. It seemed he had also been telling the truth about his relationship with Tom. He told me there had been nothing amiss between the two of them. No big fight. Nothing readily apparent to suggest the relationship was doomed. If what I thought Solonge was saying was correct, this could simply be a major case of cold feet. "Did he tell you where he was going?"

"He asked about renting a vehicle and about maps. I don't know much about such things. I wasn't much help to him I'm afraid."

I was about to conclude Solonge Fontaine wouldn't be much help to me either. I didn't get the sense she was hiding anything. She just didn't know anything more and I was starting to suspect the whole subject was beginning to bore her.

I thanked her and hopped off my chair. I landed safely. She followed me to the front door where her assistant materialized to open it for me. Solonge and I shook hands and as I was about to leave she stopped me with a soft touch on my shoulder. "One thing. One thing I heard."

I turned to face her. "Yes?"

"He asked me one more thing. He asked me if I knew if the weather was better in the south this time of year. Which it is. There was a strong rain in the city the day he arrived. It was very cold. He may be going south? No?"

I smiled at her. It wasn't much, but it did jive with the itinerary Chavell had given me. They had planned to head south after their stop in Paris. "Thank you, Madame. That is very helpful."

She smiled back, convinced her bit of information had conclusively solved the mystery of Tom Osborn's whereabouts.

If only it were that easy.

Back in my cubicle at Residence Concorde, chomping on a ham and cheese sandwich I'd picked up from a corner *supermarché*, I studied the itinerary for the aborted honeymoon. Would Tom really follow the route exactly as Chavell had planned it? The answer might be yes only if he truly wanted to be found. I tried to put myself in Tom's shoes and reconstruct his actions in my head. First he'd have to conclude he did not want to marry Harold Chavell. Maybe he still wanted the relationship but not the wedding? So when did he make that decision? The week before? The night before, at the rehearsal party? The morning of the wedding? I didn't know the answer. But certainly if he'd come to his decision before the Saturday morning of the ceremony he would have told Chavell, wouldn't he? If for no other reason but to save the man he supposedly loved from the humiliation of standing alone at the altar in front of sixty friends and family members. Or was that exactly what he wanted to happen? And, if Tom didn't decide to run until Saturday morning, when did he have the opportunity to snatch his plane ticket from Chavell's desk? I couldn't figure that one out either. I'd have to remember to ask Chavell when he'd last seen Tom's plane ticket before he'd found it missing on Monday morning. Was this a spur of the moment decision or something Tom had planned for some time? I was beginning to really look forward to finding Tom Osborn and getting answers to my questions.

Since the night before the wedding, Tom had successfully avoided speaking to or seeing anyone (according to Chavell) until Sunday morning when he boarded the plane for Paris. By the time he arrived in Europe on Monday, he would have had several hours to think about what he'd done. Was he remorseful? Regretful? Shame-faced? Or was he still in a running mood? At that point he could have simply disappeared. Instead he chose to stick to the itinerary and visit Chavell's best friend, Solonge Fontaine. Chavell thought Tom sought out Solonge because she could speak English and he'd be in need of a friendly face. But there were plenty of English- speaking people at the airport. And, Tom had never met Solonge before. How could he be certain she wouldn't be furious with him for leaving her "oldest and dearest friend" standing at the altar? He took a risk. But maybe it was all part of his plan. He'd show up at her doorstep, the picture of a tortured soul, begging her not to contact Chavell but knowing full well she'd do exactly that. Chavell, hearing his groom was in France, would hop the next flight and come after him. And as the musical score rises to a dramatic crescendo the two lovers are reunited in the middle of a vineyard toasting each other with glasses of Premier Cru. The End. Yuck!

I screwed up my face with the thought that I'd been tossed into the middle of a pissy little lover's quarrel. Maybe Chavell enjoyed the feeling of spending money, buying me to chase his boyfriend, to increase the dramatic quotient of the experience. How was I to know? Without the chance to do any background work I had no idea what type of people my new client and his partner were. The sooner this was over with, the better, I decided. And, I realized with little gusto, if this scenario were true, Tom Osborn would not be thrilled to see me instead of his almost groom. Oh well, sometimes life sucks.

I refocused on the itinerary searching for a way to get ahead of my quarry. I'd feel much better if I were in front of Tom Osborn rather than behind. Based on the original plan, Chavell and Tom were to stay in Paris one night, after which they were to travel down the Loire Valley for a couple of days. On Friday, which was tomorrow, they had a reservation in a hotel called Domaine des Hauts de Loire, near the town of Onzine. I looked at my watch. Not yet four o'clock. Still early. I unfolded my map on the bed. It never failed to amaze me how close together everything is in Europe. Travelling by car, it is possible to have a baguette for breakfast in France, fondue for lunch in Switzerland and spaghetti for dinner in Italy. I found Onzine situated between the larger centres of Blois and Tours. Judging the distance and seeing I could take the autoroute almost the entire way, I decided to try for Onzine that afternoon. When Tom arrived tomorrow, I'd be waiting for him.

Madame-Behind-the-Window was nonplussed as I checked out only a few hours after checking in, but I just smiled and happily paid not to spend a night in that trés petite room.

There are over four hundred Relais & Chateaux properties situated in about forty countries. My next destination was one of this elite chain of mostly privately-owned and operated hotels. Each property is unique but promises the outstanding quality necessary to be included on the peerless list of Relais & Chateaux establishments. Guests are guaranteed a certain standard of accommodation and cuisine, oftentimes the finest the host country has to offer. They also pay dearly for this perfection.

I reached the north end of Onzine without incident and followed short, squat, wooden signposts planted at irregular intervals that directed me through town and into its southern outskirts wherein somewhere lay Domaine des Hauts. The white and gold Relais & Chateaux guidebook I'd obtained before leaving Paris described the property as a former hunting lodge. The main house was supposedly hidden amongst the rolling hills of a heavily wooded piece of farmland. I was beginning to think it was too hidden when I finally came upon a tall iron gate with a sign welcoming me to the estate. I made a sharp turn off the main road onto a narrow, winding drive. The foliage of amazingly tall and thick-trunked trees met somewhere above me to form a solid canopy that effectively shielded the roadway from light and precipitation. I imagined men on horseback who wore tights and maidens in distress and thought Robin Hood would have felt right at home in this dim and mysterious place. Even though it was getting dark and the weather was cool, I rolled down my window to breathe in the scent of damp plant life and moss. I could hear my tires squishing through a deep cushion of fallen leaves.

Lost in the aura of the forest, I was caught by surprise when I rounded a bend and suddenly found myself confronted by the grandeur of Domaine des Hauts. At first it looked to me like an impressively large house rather than a hotel, and of German architecture rather than French. There were several smaller buildings gathered beside the main house, which sat before a large cement patio, and, not far off, a heavily populated duck pond. There were a dozen cars in a parking lot meant for three times that many. I found a spot and unloaded my bag from the trunk. The sky was darkening with night, or an impending storm, and I was exhausted from this day that had begun on one continent and did not seem to want to end on another. As stinging spits of rain dotted my hot head I knew I'd soon need an attitude adjustment.

I staggered into the tiny hotel foyer feeling chilled and more than a little damp. I had my good friend from Residence Concorde, Madame-Behind-the-Window, call ahead to reserve a room, so at least I was assured a roof over my head. The reception desk was no larger than a podium. This did not bode well for the size of my accommodations. The young woman behind the desk was friendly, professional and quick. I was moving into a better mood until she informed me there were no elevators in the building and my room was on the third floor. Still no bellboys. And I couldn't very well ask her to carry my bag, although she offered with amazing sincerity. I accepted the room key attached to a ridiculously oversized fob and manipulated my big Canadian suitcase up the tiny French staircase.

My room made up for everything. Not only was it larger than a standard North American hotel room, but it also displayed a style that I believe is meant by the phrase "very well-appointed." Two sets of floor to ceiling windows draped with billowy sheers looked out onto the front courtyard now bathed in the romantic glow of dusk. A large four-poster bed, swathed in similar material and piled high with thick coverlets, sat in the centre of the room amidst a heavy wardrobe, two armchairs and several small, ornate tables. The bathroom was thankfully utilitarian with both a bathtub and shower.

Longingly eyeing the tub, I realized I was starving and needed food sooner than a relaxing soak. I'd had little to eat all day. I glanced at my watch. Almost seven-thirty. I searched near the phone for a room service menu. Finding none I dialled the front desk.

"Bonsoir," answered the voice in lilting French. I was certain it was the same woman who'd checked me in.

"This is Mr. Quant in Room 33." I realized I was imitating the singsong quality of the receptionist's voice and urged myself to stop it.

"Yes, Monsieur Quant? Is everything satisfactory?"

"Oh yes. I was just wondering if the hotel had room service?"

"I'm sorry?"

"Room service. Sending food up to the room." I wasn't sure whether it was my French or the concept she didn't understand.

"If you can make it down to the salon before eight o'clock you can absolutely make the last seating in the dining room." I guess that meant no room service.

"I see."

"Will that give you enough time to prepare for dinner? Jacket and tie is appropriate. We'll be very happy to have you."

Hmmm. Was she telling me to get cleaned up, you bum, or else no grub for you? "Eight o'clock in the salon. Where is the salon?"

"Main floor, east door off the foyer. We'll see you at eight o'clock, Mr. Quant." She clicked off.

I was anxious for a leisurely bath but made do with a hurried shower. Wrapped in a complimentary bathrobe that was too thin to keep me warm but looked rather dashing, I opened my suitcase and surveyed the treasures therein. I generally maintain a modest wardrobe consisting of wrinkle-free cotton pants, T-shirts and wrinkle-free cotton shirts. My two extravagances are coats and footwear. Living in Saskatoon where it is cold, or cold and snowing two-thirds of the year, it makes sense to have several coats of many styles, colour and quality. Coats are the piece of clothing you wear most often. They're what everyone sees. The same goes for shoes. Everything else is simply there to keep you from walking around naked. I do however maintain a few articles of what my menswear-boutique-owning friend, Anthony Gatt, calls finery. I admit, finery sometimes comes in handy on the job, or when trying to impress someone or, like at that moment, if I was hoping to enjoy an expensive meal in an upscale restaurant without looking like a schmo. Out of the suitcase I pulled my "wonderpants." They are black, never wrinkle, and I've owned them forever yet they're always in style and, most importantly, I've been told that they make my ass look great. Simple white shirt, black silk tie, checkered, black-and-grey sports coat, shiny loafers, hair slicked back and I was ready to go.

I stood in front of the mirror. Not too shabby. I'm six feet tall plus a bit, with green eyes, finger-combed sandy hair and a toothy smile. Based on how often I have to go to the gym, my body is certainly not a gift of nature, but rather something I have to sweat over to keep it looking okay. It's nicely shaped, I guess, but one weekend eating Doritos and ice cream in front of the TV and my mid-section starts pooching out. It never did that when I was in my twenties.

It was a few minutes after eight when I finally made my way down the stairs and back into the foyer. It was unrecognizable. In less than an hour it had become *the* place to be. The space now seemed twice the size with two sets of French doors thrown open, one to the east end salon and the other to the west end restaurant. The lighting was dim and mystical music floated on air heavy with the smell of bougainvillea, fresh rain and simmering sauces. Another woman and three young men, all in matching black-and-white uniforms, now joined the young woman who'd checked me in. They greeted and directed and made nice with exquisitely outfitted guests drifting in from the courtyard and parking lot. I guessed that many of the patrons were not hotel guests at all but locals making a special trip to visit the restaurant. Always a good sign.

The salon was a long and narrow room with a dozen, knee-high tables of varying shapes and from various historical periods. I found a two-seater near the unlit fireplace and tried to get comfortable in the unforgiving, wooden chair. Immediately a gigantic man approached my table. Bouncer?

"Mr. Quant, welcome. My name is Jacques," he said in a delicate voice that belied his size. "Perhaps a cocktail to begin the evening?"

I smiled at him, impressed he knew my name. "Do you have a wine list?"

He handed me a leather-bound folder and said, "Perhaps monsieur would care to begin with champagne?" I studied his tone for any sign of haughtiness but heard none. Even though I'd only had champagne as a celebratory drink, usually late at night, I accepted his professional recommendation and off he went. I opened what I assumed was the wine list. Wrong. Food menu. I flipped through the thick pages but saw no mention of liquid refreshments. Well, at least I could decide on my dinner. A quick perusal of my choices told me I was in for a culinary treat. I glanced at the price of the first entrée listed and did the conversion math. Did it again. Decided to ignore the prices. Jacques returned promptly with a flute of champagne and asked if I needed help with the menu. Oh yeah. We began on page one under a heading that read *Amuse Bouche*. I was sure my translation couldn't be accurate because I thought it meant "Party in Your Mouth." (I'd have to remember to serve that back home!) Eventually I figured out that *Amuse Bouche* is a much less salacious term referring to appetizers.

Once Jacques left to order what I was sure would be the most extraordinary meal I'd had in years, I happily sipped away at my champagne until the sommelier paid me a visit. He was a tall, rangy man with an oversized, hooked nose and way too much energy for the room. He gesticulated wildly and described each wine in a hushed tone that was louder than my normal speaking voice, and in terms a man usually reserves for a lover. I quickly accepted his suggestions and was rather relieved when he gallumphed away in his size twelve shoes. I looked around the room but no one seemed to notice or mind his performance. About then a waiter, not Jacques, came into the salon and escorted a couple that were seated nearby across the foyer into the restaurant. I began to understand how the system works. Apparently the tradition is to begin one's evening in the salon with champagne and witty repartee. It is there that you order your meal and wine. But not until the precise moment that they are ready for you in the restaurant, are you invited in to be seated just as your first course, the *Amuse Bouche,* is being delivered.

Forty minutes later sated with champagne but a little short on repartee, it was my turn.

The meal was out of this world fantastic. Little mounds of tomato mousse, a fish velouté, cold mackerel topped with raspberry purée, coq au vin, unbelievably huge pimentos stuffed with lobster, and a lime soufflé that looked as if it might float off the plate. The wines, a half-litre red and a half-litre white, were incomparable. (From the sommelier, I'd learned it was not only acceptable but recommended to switch wine selection and colour during a meal.) I could only manage a small hunk of goat cheese when the cheese trolley came by. My wonderpants were beginning to wonder whether they'd be able to contain me much longer.

After a quick walk on the patio I returned to my room and gave in to sleep. It had been a full first day.

I woke at 2:00 a.m. and read.

Sun streaming through those damn large windows jolted me awake at the crack of dawn. The room was so bright I considered reaching for my sunglasses. I sat up and swore at the no longer beloved gauzy curtains. Would I have to start wearing sunblock to bed? It wasn't until I shifted my feet to the floor that I noticed the wooden shutters on either side of the window. Oh well. Early bird gets the worm. And my worm was arriving today. I cleaned up and headed downstairs. Since I had to pass by her desk anyway, I decided to check with the receptionist before heading into the salon for breakfast.

"Bonjour," I said to her. Same woman as last night. They must work killer split shifts.

"Bonjour, Monsieur Quant. Did you have a wonderful rest?"

"Yes, absolutely."

"And the restaurant. Did you enjoy your meal?"

"It was fantastic." Aside from the early morning tanning session, I was a pretty happy guy. "I wonder if you could help me?"

"I will try, Mr. Quant." She still had that pleasant singsong quality to her voice. It probably irritated her husband all to hell.

"A good friend of mine is arriving today and I was wondering if perhaps you knew what time he was expected."

She looked a little uncertain but didn't shut me down. "What is your friend's name, Mr. Quant?"

I guessed Tom Osborn would have checked in under Chavell's name. "Harold Chavell," I told her.

"Ah, yes, Mr. Quant." This sounded hopeful. "Mr. Chavell left very early this morning."

Pardon? I didn't say anything at first, going over the translation in my head to make sure I'd gotten it right. "He left?"

"Oui."

"This morning?"

"Oui."

"Mr. Harold Chavell?"

"Oui."

I was grateful the woman showed no outward signs of being impatient with me. "Is there anything else I can help you with this morning?"

"I'm a little confused," I told her. I'm sure she'd already figured that one out. "My information says Mr. Chavell was not to arrive at Domaine Des Hauts until today."

"Yes, that is correct."

Okay. Something was not working between this woman and I. "But he left already? Even though he wasn't supposed to arrive until today?" This was not easy to put into French.

She laughed. "I see the problem now. You're wondering why he has already checked out?"

Bingo! "Oui!"

"Mr. Chavell called to change his reservation to yesterday, rather than today. He was fortunate, as you were Mr. Quant, that we were able to accommodate him on such short notice. The tourist season is nearly over, you see. We can do such things easier this time of year."

Fortunate? I did not feel fortunate. Tom Osborn had been right under my nose and I'd missed him.

What was worse, he was no longer following the itinerary.

Chapter 4

OVER BREAKFAST OF RAVEN DARK COFFEE and soft breads oozing butter
and slathered with chunky jam, I studied the itinerary yet again. I
was irked to have missed Tom Osborn and by such a narrow margin.
I was also more than a little worried about his deviation from the
itinerary. He had come to Domains des Hauts a full day earlier
than planned. What did that mean? Was he playing some kind of
game? Was he trying to make Chavell work for his prize? Would
he abandon the itinerary altogether? I hoped not. It was my only
chance of finding him. All I could do now was choose a spot and
try to get there before he did. From the itinerary I knew Chavell
and Tom had planned to eventually drive east from the Loire
Valley into the Rhône Valley and head south after that. I studied
the map and chose a place called Cliousclat. They had a reservation
in the small town's hotel for the day after tomorrow. If I drove
hard, I could make it before nightfall. My only worry was, would
that be a sufficient leap-frog to catch up to my prey?

After breakfast, to hedge my bet, I sweet-talked the concierge
into calling the hotel in Cliousclat to confirm a booking for
Chavell. She proved to be helpful. By the time I returned to the

foyer with my luggage, she had not only confirmed that Chavell's reservation remained unchanged but booked a room for me as well.

Never underestimate the power of sweet-talk, straight white teeth and full lips. I can be a shameless flirt when I want to.

I noticed a marked difference as I crossed France from the Loire Valley into the Rhône. While the Loire appeared dry and lifeless and the river sluggish, the Rhône was rich and green and the river flowed with vigour. Not that I saw much of either, travelling almost exclusively on the autoroute, which allowed me speed in excess of one-hundred-and-forty kilometres an hour. And still cars passed me. I stopped only once, around noon, for a quick sandwich. The weather had greatly improved and most of the day was warm and cloudless. Road signs were plentiful and helpful. As long as I knew approximately what direction I was heading and the names of towns near my destination I could almost navigate without a map.

Almost.

My car was pointed up and chugging into the hills outside of Loriol, a modern town on the verge of becoming a city. I was on a steep, winding road that became narrower with each passing kilometre. I'm sure the view of the valley I was leaving far below would have been picturesque in daylight but it was now darker than pitch and my headlights, the only illumination, were having a hard time slicing through the black of night. I had been on the near-vertical road for such a long time I was certain I'd passed through a layer of clouds. The whole scene was beginning to feel too spooky for my liking. Here I was, in the middle of a foreign country, in the middle of the night (well pretty late anyway), driving a rental car and chasing after a stranger to some little hamlet, both of which didn't seem to want to be found.

I considered going back. I could get a room in Loriol and try again in the morning. But the road had gotten so narrow there was barely enough surface to keep my car on, never mind turn around. There wasn't even a decent ditch. Cliff to the right of me, mountain to the left. I began to contemplate what I would do if I met another car on the road. There was no way two vehicles could pass. I decelerated until it seemed the car was barely moving forward. My sweaty palms tightened around the steering wheel and I could feel a knot develop between my shoulder blades. I continued in that state of discomfort until, thank you stars above, I saw a cheery sign welcoming me to Cliousclat.

Entering the village was like entering someone's farmyard. After a minute or two you've seen it all. Yet, difficult as it had been to get there, I sensed I had stumbled upon a special place. A place where you could easily believe time had stopped centuries ago. Not unlike the drive up, there was only enough clearance in the street for one vehicle. Unfortunately, the vehicle the street builders had in mind was something more like a horse and buggy or a big bicycle, not an oversized, fat-ass Mercedes that stuck out like a Tonka truck on a street made for Hot Wheels. Finding my hotel, La Treille Muscate, was not difficult and I was grateful to see a parking lot sign. I had to get my monstrosity off the street. Even foot traffic could not get by me—people had to duck into doorways and side alleys to make room as I chugged by at the speed of cold molasses. I made the right turn and immediately felt the entire chassis lurch forward and down. The postage-stamp-sized parking lot was built on the steep side of a hill and as I slid into it I wondered if I'd ever get out again. Mercifully, my brakes did their bit and I was able to stop before I hit anything. After claiming a quarter of the lot's space as my own I retrieved my luggage from the trunk. It was dark, it was late and I was buzz-eyed from driving all day. At that point, if I'd had to desert my car in that lot forever, so be it.

My suitcase weighed me down like an anchor as I hoisted it up the slope of the parking lot back to street level. Where's a Sherpa when you need one? I followed a crackled sidewalk along the rough stone walls of the hotel. I came around a corner and still twenty metres away from the entrance I stopped, dropped my bags and fell in love. Paris was Paris, but this was France. As a young man, when I'd dreamt about what France might be like, long before I'd visited Paris for the first time, it wasn't about scaling the Eiffel Tower or visiting the Louvre—it was this. Cliousclat is what I'd imagined France would be. It's what I wanted it to be.

The rumpled street was dim, lit by the occasional torch or bare bulb, as if electricity had only recently been discovered. I saw shades of apricot and tangerine, scarlet and magenta—the colours of fall, harvest and romance. The buildings were flagstone, none higher than three storeys, and squeezed together like an accordion. They leaned into the street—the threat of falling over already centuries old. Grapevines, thick and gnarled and heavy with fruit, covered entire walls. From somewhere hidden down a winding pathway came the sound of singing and two bocci balls striking one another. At the front of the hotel were half a dozen round bistro tables. A man and a woman, spectacular-looking in the ambient amber light, lounged at one of the tables, drinking wine, laughing and probably falling in love. The air was soft and fragrant as it massaged my skin.

I floated the rest of the distance into the lobby, which was nothing more than a tiny porch with a desk. No one was behind the counter and I looked for a bell to ring. Nope. And I was glad. The sound would be too jarring in this gracious atmosphere. Leaving my bag behind, I poked my nose into a small sitting room off the porch. Empty. Stepping back I noticed a low clearance entranceway opposite the desk that led two steps down into the hotel's eating area. Given the late hour, the kitchen was likely closed, but I decided to take a look anyway. And there, around a heavy wooden table, sat a group of four people who were likely the restaurant staff, relaxing with a litre or two of local vintage after a hard night's work. Or maybe they were just waiting for the laughing couple outside to finally leave. A blonde young woman sluggishly got up and gave me a friendly bonsoir as she brushed past me and headed to the desk. She was petite but curvy and had cornflower blue eyes.

"I'm Russell Quant," I told her. "The concierge at Domaine des Hauts made a reservation for me?" I asked it like a question because I guessed this hotel didn't have a particularly sophisticated booking system and worried I might not be on the list. I certainly didn't want to have to get my car out of that parking lot and drive back down that snaking road.

"Yes," she said after consulting a dog-eared, spiral notebook lying on the desk. She handed me a key with yet another monstrous fob. "Chambre six."

Yes! "Can you tell me if my friend, Harold Chavell, still has a reservation for the day after tomorrow?" I didn't want another rude surprise tomorrow morning.

She repeated the name and referred back to the book. She looked up at me with a sweet face. "Non."

What? Not again! But I had checked, through the concierge, only this morning! "He has cancelled his reservation?" I asked, trying to keep my cool.

"Yes," she said, "because he is already here."

Again I questioned my understanding of the French language. "He is in the hotel right now?"

"Yes. I'm sure he is sleeping. It's very late, monsieur." Was she scolding me?

"That's good. Very good. Could you tell me what room he is in?"

"Absolutely not, monsieur. That is private." Suddenly this small town gal had Ritz-Carlton training.

"But he's a good friend of mine and I'd like to visit him."

"As I said, I'm sure he is sleeping at this late hour. Perhaps you could visit him in the morning? Have breakfast together?"

I could see she was not going to budge and I was too tired to try flirting. On the wall behind her was an old-fashioned mail slot system, one slot for every room. There were only twelve rooms in the hotel. How hard could it be to figure out which one Tom Osborn was in? I thanked her and took my belongings up yet another nasty set of stairs to the second floor and room six.

After sprinkling cold water on my face I plunked down on the bed and pushed buttons on the telephone until I finally succeeded getting a line into Canada. It was 4:00 p.m. in Saskatoon. I first tried for Harold Chavell at his office. A receptionist told me he was away for the day and offered to take a message. Instead I dialled his home number and reached his answering machine. I left a short message, updating him on my progress to date, such as it was. At least he'd know that Tom was indeed honeymooning without him. True, this was not the cheeriest news, but it was news.

I set my alarm for 3:00 a.m. and tried to get some sleep. I woke up ten minutes before it rang. Jet lag is a bitch.

Sneaking down the staircase in pure dark I began to wonder if any staff actually spent the night here. There wasn't even a night-light or illuminated exit sign to aid my progress in the unfamiliar surroundings. The complete silence almost hurt my ears. I cautiously made my way to the front desk and with the help of a dozen or so matches found the registration book I'd seen the young woman use earlier. It didn't take me long to find out that Tom, registered under Chavell's name, was in room twelve. It was so easy I was a little crestfallen. Now what? Shouldn't I have to hide under the desk to avoid a security guard or something exhilarating like that? Not this time. I returned to bed and a good book. I finally dozed off about an hour later.

Perhaps I was overcompensating, but I was determined not to be outrun this time. It was not quite 6:00 a.m. when I found myself in the deserted hallway outside of room twelve. I couldn't very well knock. The guy was probably still sleeping. I put my ear against the door hoping to at least hear him snoring or breathing loudly. Nothing. A quiet sleeper. I headed back downstairs and took a seat at one of the outdoor tables I'd seen the night before in front of the restaurant. It was chilly but refreshing. After too few hours of sleep

I needed the cold to keep me alert. A hot cup of coffee and an English newspaper would have made it perfect. But the restaurant wouldn't be open for another hour or so and I doubted I'd find a newspaper, never mind a non-French version, here in what this morning was beginning to feel like Bedrock. So I wiggled my butt into my seat, sunk my hands into my jacket pockets and made myself comfortable. From where I sat I'd see anyone coming in or out of the hotel. Tom Osborn would have to make an appearance sooner or later.

By 9:30 I was beginning to worry. No one even close to Tom's description had come out of the hotel. This was not good. I waited another half an hour, emptied my third cup of coffee and decided to pay the front desk a little visit.

This time it was an older lady, Brigitte, who greeted me. I smiled and jumped into my best French. "I'm waiting for my friend," I told her. "Mr. Chavell in room twelve. Have you seen him this morning? He hasn't checked out has he?" I crossed my fingers.

She looked down into the book. "No, no, he is still here." She looked over my shoulder and eyed a girl who was arranging a massive heap of dried flowers on a shelf near the entrance to the restaurant. French people are so lovely. She would never have considered screaming out, "Hey, whatsyourname, come over here for a sec!" Subtle eye contact was enough.

The young woman, the same one from last night, came over and smiled at me. Again with those killer split shifts. I learned her name was Sylvie. "Yes, monsieur?"

The older lady described what I was asking in hurried French she probably reserved for fellow countrymen. Who knows what she really said? I kept on smiling. I didn't want to make a big deal out of this. I just hoped Sylvie didn't wonder how I now knew what room my "friend" was in. I explained I had been waiting for him in front of the hotel all morning but never saw him come out. Certainly he wouldn't still be asleep?

"Yes, your friend," she said, flashing those blues at me. "I don't know, but he may have gone out the back door. It leads to the parking lot. Perhaps he drove to Loriol for breakfast. Some people prefer a big breakfast. We don't have big breakfast here. Only café and bread with chocolate. Some toast, marmalade…"

Back door! What back door? "Do you know what car he was driving? Are you sure he hasn't checked out?" I tried to keep the desperation out of my voice.

She cocked her head and looked at me quizzically. "Why would your friend check out without telling you?" Smart girl. I'd have to be more careful around her.

I laughed light-heartedly, or I hoped it sounded that way. I gave the women a jaunty, carefree wave and headed to the rear of the hotel. Indeed, off the tiny sitting room I'd seen the night before was an even tinier outdoor patio with a gate that led directly into the parking lot. There were now several cars, all much smaller than mine, in the lot. It was like a collection of sardines and one big old tuna.

I had no way of knowing which car, if any, belonged to Tom or whether it was missing or not.

Back to room twelve.

The ear against the door trick still told me nothing. Okay, I thought, enough of this. Chavell never said I should sneak up on Tom, just that I should find him and ask him a few questions. And maybe bring him home? Time for the direct approach. I knocked on the door.

Nothing.

Again.

Nothing.

I figured a wee bit of sneaking around might be useful at this juncture. I pulled my precious lock picks out of my jacket pocket. If nothing else, maybe I could find something in his room that would tell me where he was headed next, just in case we should happen to miss each other again. Not that I wasn't confident I was going to nail him right here in Cliousclat, but it's always advisable to have a Plan B. I might even luck out and find a diary or journal that would explain his actions (it's important for PIs to have active imaginations).

As I expected, the lock on the hotel room door was fairly simple and I heard the satisfying click in record time. Possibly a personal best. Glancing about to ensure I was alone I slowly turned the doorknob and pushed forward.

Thud!

I stepped back, speechless.

The chain was on the door.

Someone was inside the room!

My cheeks began to burn. This had never happened to me before. I blurted out the first stupid thing that came to mind. "Housekeeping!"

Not only was it a stupid thing to do, but I inexplicably said it in my version of an old Frenchwoman speaking English!

What was I thinking?

I quickly pulled the door closed and ran away. I felt like a ten-year-old playing the doorbell game. Ring it and then dash away before the door opens. Growing up on a farm, I didn't have much chance to play this game as a kid. I was obviously making up for it now. I locked myself in my room and fell on my bed. Without reason I started to laugh as I tried to catch my breath. Nothing was funny—I was just having a little nervous breakdown.

After I'd composed myself and mentally wrote on a blackboard "Never break into a room that you don't know for a fact is empty" one hundred times, I found a piece of paper and wrote Tom Osborn a note.

> *To Tom Osborn—Room 12*
> *My name is Russell Quant. I would like to meet with you on a matter of some importance. Would some time today be possible?*
> *Russell Quant, Room 6*

I had concluded that if Tom was already on to me he would know exactly what I wanted to meet about. If he wasn't on to me, I didn't want to scare him off by mentioning Chavell's name. I couldn't be sure if he was purposefully trying to avoid me or if he simply hadn't answered my knock on his door because he was in the shower.

After delivering the note to the front desk I decided to heal my battered wits by taking a stroll around town. I wished I had a camera. Everywhere I looked was a postcard. The town rests on top of a hill, vineyards to the north, sunflower fields to the south, the distinctive scent of each mingled in the air. Each ancient building, covered with mildew and dust of many long years, some good, some not so good, revealed its own unique charm. Generations of families have lived in these buildings, worked in them, raised children in them and died in them. I could feel history emanating from these stone edifices.

Cliousclat is a renowned artist's retreat. Painters, sculptors, potters and musicians gather here. Some set up shop. Others come simply for the inspiration of sight, sound and smell. As I walked the crumbling streets I could believe in mystical elves and fairy godmothers. I could believe this was a medieval village and on the other side of the hill, atop a beautiful mountain was a castle with a king and queen and perhaps a dragon. It is a magical place. Magical, but not big. I was done my in-depth tour in under forty minutes and still had nervous energy to burn. I checked in at the front desk on the off chance Tom had responded to my note. He hadn't. I wandered back outside to the rear of the hotel and took advantage of a now near-empty parking lot to retrieve my car. I headed for Loriol and guiltily ended up at a McDonald's featuring "international" burgers. There isn't much to see in Loriol. It lacks the charm of smaller villages and the amenities of a larger centre, so after patriotically feasting on a McCanada burger, I returned to Cliousclat. Hoping Brigitte couldn't smell the back bacon and cheddar on my breath, I asked for any messages. She pulled a lone sheet of paper from my mail-slot. Hooray!

I asked her if I could order a glass of wine to have in the front courtyard. She pulled a jug of red from under the counter and poured while I waited. The glories of a small country inn. I stepped back outdoors with my wine and selected a seat partially shaded by a Cinzano umbrella. I took a healthy sip of the local vintage. Even wine from a jug kept under a desk was remarkable in France. I unfolded the note.

> *Dear Mr. Quant,*
> *I will meet you at 8:00 p.m. tonight at the war memorial near the*
> *east end of town.*
> *Tom Osborn*

The content of the note was about as vague as mine had been.

No mention of Chavell or any indication he knew who I was or what I wanted. I thought about this as I sipped the vin de table. A mischievous thought crossed my mind. Was it possible Tom believed my note to be an invitation for a date, a passionate, French rendezvous? Perhaps Mr. Osborn was not beyond having a clandestine encounter while he waited for his Prince Charming to track him down? I blushed and ordered another glass of wine. I would never act on such an invitation, even if it was proffered, but with a few hours ahead of me until the meeting with my quarry, it couldn't hurt to entertain the idea in my mind—for recreational purposes only. So I sat back with my imagination and welcomed the afternoon sunshine on my face as the aroma of crushed grapes being harvested only metres away played in my nose.

I couldn't maintain a surveillance of the parking lot, the back door, room twelve and the front entrance of the hotel all at once but I tried my best. I'm sure Brigette and Sylvie thought me strange as I ricocheted from one location to another. I was hoping to at least catch a glimpse of Tom before our meeting, but no such luck. At 6:00 p.m. I retired to the little restaurant and ordered a simple and inexpensive meal from Sylvie. The main course was something called *marmite*. I think it was fish. I know it was delicious. I ended off with a *bombe* of ice cream for dessert.

At 8:00 p.m. I was waiting for Tom at the arranged meeting place, *Le Monument aux Morts*. The only light came from a forty-watt spotlight focused on the four-sided war memorial. The monument was dedicated to townsfolk who had lost their lives during World War I, World War II and the Algerian War.

By 8:15 it was dark and Tom had still not turned up. Then the sound of shuffling feet. My stomach contracted. I felt a bit nervous to finally be meeting the man I had chased across the ocean and halfway through France. I called out lightly, "Bonjour?"

"Bonsoir," came back the reply. But it was a woman's voice. Actually it sounded very much like my chambermaid impression from earlier in the day.

From the darkness emerged a stooped elderly woman. She must have been eighty but her hair was jet-black and her dark, liquid eyes danced in the meagre light. She came up to me and thrust a crumpled piece of paper into my chest with surprising force. "Mr. Quant, this is for you," she said in thickly accented French. "I've been asked to deliver this note." With that she turned on her heel and began to move away into the shadows.

I called out to the retreating woman in English, "Where did you get this?" Nothing. I tried again in French.

"The man!" she shouted without looking back.

"What man?"

"The man." There was to be no further conversation. Her figure melted into darkness and was gone.

I opened the note, moving closer to the memorial stone where the light was marginally better. What I read made me swear. I even did it in French. I was being stood up. The note was from Tom, telling me that something had come up and he had to leave right away. It went on to ask if I would meet him in Sanary-sur-Mer on

Monday night. He gave the name of what I guessed was a bar or café. That was it.

"Mr. Chavell?" I shouted into the receiver. Actually the connection was quite good but something about overseas phone calls always makes me want to shout.

"Mr. Quant. I received your message. Thank you. Any more news?"

"Well, actually I was kind of hoping *you* might have heard from Tom."

"No. Unfortunately."

I explained to him what happened earlier with the no-show at the war memorial and the request to meet in Sanary-sur-Mer. "I was hoping you were the 'something' that came up. I can't think of what else it might be. Any ideas?"

Chavell was quiet for a moment, as if processing the new information. "You're right. This is very odd. As far as I'm aware Tom has no contacts in France, business, friends or otherwise… unless…"

"Yes?"

"Unless of course he's met someone."

I knew what Chavell was thinking. I had considered the same thing. Had Tom met another man? Was Tom on his honeymoon with someone other than his intended husband? Ouch! "I've seen no indication of that, Mr. Chavell." I was trying for compassion.

He sighed as if in resignation. "Call me Harold."

"Russell." We were making nice. I wasn't sure if I was ready for that but I couldn't very well continue having him call me Mr. Quant if he was Harold.

"I don't know if I can help you. I can't think of what he could be doing or why he cancelled your meeting."

"Okay, that's okay, Harold," I quickly said. I needed to give this guy some hope. "I just wanted to fill you in. I'm right behind him and I know where he's headed. I'll find out what's going on," I assured him sounding more confident than I really was.

"Yes. That's good."

"One more thing before you go," I said. "After Cliousclat, I noticed the itinerary is a little sparse." I was hoping for another opportunity to run into Tom before our meeting in Sanary. Two days was a long time to wait.

"Yes, I know. We were going to wing it until we reached Sanary. This time of year finding adequate accommodation as you go isn't much of a problem. Actually that was Tom's idea. He wanted to be a little venturesome. I prefer making all reservations before leaving home. I feel more comfortable that way."

So what he was telling me was that between now and Monday, Tom was pretty much a Canadian needle in a French haystack. From his voice I could tell he knew it. "I'll call you from Sanary," I told him.

"Talk to you then."

I sat back on my bed and pulled out my map of France.

Where the hell was Sanary-sur-Mer?

Chapter 5

ANYONE'S GUESS WAS AS GOOD AS MINE as to where Tom Osborn was going to be for the next two days. According to my map, Sanary-Sur-Mer was a town on the southern coast of France. It wasn't quite the Riviera, but close. I studied the region between Cliousclat and Sanary to see if my spidey senses would give me a clue as to where Tom might stop between now and Monday. The only thing I could come up with was Châteauneuf-du-Pape. Chavell and Tom struck me as the type of people who might be wine aficionados. If so, Tom wouldn't pass up a chance to visit this historic village. So that's where I decided to go. The weather was sunny and mild, I was driving a hot car and the fact that I also love fine wines barely entered my mind.

Really.

Châteauneuf-du-Pape is situated between the larger centres of Orange and Avignon. A fourteenth-century papal castle sits high above the town and is the recognizable symbol of all Châteauneuf-du-Pape wines. The pope who built the castle also began the vineyard. Today there isn't much left of the place other than a neat dungeon, a few jagged, rocky walls and a cellar. But it's well worth the walk up for the view and all the little wine shops along the way offering taste tests of their wares. Needless to say, the trip to the top can be time-consuming but fun, the way down—less so. By the time I made my way up and back down the hill, I decided food was in order. I needed something to soak up all the taste tests. I found a sunny table at a restaurant called La Mule du Pape with a bird's eye view of the town's bustling Centreville. I didn't have a clue where Tom Osborn was but there are worse ways of spending a sunny Sunday afternoon in the French countryside.

Monday morning I pointed my Mercedes south and headed for the Mediterranean. I connected to the autoroute à peáge (a toll road) A7, known as L'Autoroute du Soleil, which passes by Avignon, turned east on A8, through Aix-en-Provence, then south again on A52 by Auriol and finally hit A50, taking it all the way down to the coast. It was mid-afternoon when I reached Sanary-sur-Mer. I found a spot to leave the car and spent an hour walking around with a bag of popcorn purchased from a street vendor.

Sanary is a charming seaside town with an active, tourist-oriented harbour surrounded by palm trees and sheltered from the mistral by wooded hills to the north. Every store, restaurant and bar along the waterfront is a shade of complimentary pastel as if arranged by an artist creating the perfect palette. Although intimately near the famed hustle and bustle and haughtiness of the French Riviera, Sanary seems to maintain a low-key, almost lackadaisical atmosphere. As I meandered down the main drag, stealing glances into bistros and boutiques, I could pick out the occasional luminary from the hoi polloi, trying to get away from it all by slumming in Sanary. Incredibly tall, painfully thin women walked as if they barely existed off the runway, with messily handsome men who live in cologne ads. There were old men with young women and even older women with even younger men; middle-aged mothers surgically altered to appear younger than their daughters and daughters made up to look older than their mothers.

To me it was a people zoo. I held back the urge to toss them some of my popcorn.

After checking into a quirky little hotel at one end of the main thoroughfare, I took a walk on the beach and snooped around in the shops. The prices were surprisingly reasonable but nothing caught my eye—at least not sufficiently to make me consider adding to the weight of my suitcase. Before I knew it, it was almost 7:00 p.m. and I was famished.

The place Tom had arranged for us to meet seemed as good a place to eat as any. It looked much like the other bistros on either side of it. It had a wide open front facing the water and small, round tables with multi-coloured linens starting in the dimly lit back area and spilling out onto the street like Smarties poured from a box. If you've ever been to a fancy French restaurant and disliked how close together the tables are—it is authentic. I chose one about midway at one edge of the pack so that I was half-indoors and half-outdoors. It was the perfect spot to keep an eye on the other café patrons and the steady stream of street traffic. I ordered *moules marinières*, which are mussels with shallots in a white wine sauce and appeared to be the joint's specialty, along with a bottle of mineral water. And then, I don't know if it was the heady, salty smell of the sea or too much sun in one day, I ordered a small terrine of *pâté de merle* as my *Amuse Bouche* and sat back to enjoy the view while waiting for my client's errant boyfriend.

By 8:30 I was fairly certain my worst suspicions were coming true. Tom Osborn had successfully led me on a wild goose chase. He had no intention of meeting me that night. Or probably ever. But why? Had he, as Chavell worried, met some man and decided to run off with him? Had he ever wanted to be found at all? Following the itinerary had been too easy. I should have listened to the little bird in my head when I first accepted this assignment: too easy.

I knew now that if I was going to find Tom I was going to have to adopt an entirely different tack. Unfortunately, I had no idea what that would be. But, until I figured it out, I decided to drown my discouragement in a regional favourite, pastis. This was not a particularly professional decision to make at this point in the case, but I was beginning to feel disheartened with the whole experience and needed some lubrication to help swallow my defeat. I figured it all boiled down to not having enough time for a background check on my client and his lover. Still, there was something more at work here and that unknown thing was setting me up to fail.

I needed to rethink my strategy.

But it wasn't going to happen tonight.

Pastis is the drink of choice in Provence. It tastes like black licorice and the secret is to mix the clear liquid with water, making it cloudy and somewhat less lethal. I didn't like it. But I had two before switching to beer.

Although it had no lyrics, the music playing in the café was undoubtedly French. As it darkened, low wattage bulbs and candles created a cozy atmosphere that blurred any visually unpleasant details of the restaurant and the people within. The crowd in the café hadn't changed much since I'd first sat down several hours earlier. I was particularly enjoying a threesome of twenty-some-things two tables over. Two women and a man. Supermodel wannabes. Six impossibly long legs were intertwined beneath the table making it difficult to guess who was with who. Perfect hair, perfect muscle tone, perfect teeth. The pretty people.

At some point during the evening I had noticed a man sitting by himself just behind the glow of these lovelies. He had dark, smoldering eyes, unkempt, nearly black, short hair and a Rupert Everett jaw covered in day-old stubble. I didn't pay attention to what he wore because each time I looked over I was caught in the net of his eyes. He was staring at me as much as I was staring at him. I was sure of it.

It had been a while since I'd had sex, and an even longer while since I'd been picked up in a bar. But the signals were there. Sitting alone. Nicely groomed (in a rumpled, foreign kind of way). Eye contact. Faraway smiles. The occasional licking of lips. Oh yeah. Signals galore.

And so the fever began.

Pastis and beer helped make it clear to me. I was a young, attractive, unattached man sitting in a French café near the azure Mediterranean on a beautiful evening smothered in an atmosphere of amour. Why shouldn't I get laid? The game went like this: I would take a sip of my drink; look over at the man as if I'd spotted someone I knew just over his shoulder—try a little smile—then look out at the sea with a thoughtful look on my face. And he would do the same.

Each time I looked over, he looked right back. There was nothing coy about this fella. After half an hour of this I decided we needed a new game. I was too shy to walk over to his table and obviously he was not the aggressor type either. I paid my bill, which had added up nicely over the course of the evening, stood up, gave him one more meaningful look and left the café slowly. I didn't want Mr. Smouldering Eyes having any doubt about which direction I'd taken. I wasn't sure if the rules were the same in this country, but I was fairly confident that, like music, the universal language of cruising would transcend all linguistic and cultural barriers.

Sauntering down the well-lit street I kept my pace as slow as I could without actually standing still. I didn't want to appear too obvious. There weren't many people wandering about and most of the shops had closed for the night. This would make it harder to orchestrate a chance encounter. I couldn't hear any following foot-steps and didn't dare turn around. The only way to stop and give him time to catch up was to window shop. Unfortunately, the window I chose was displaying women's shoes. I wondered if they carried size thirteen.

"Monsieur?" the deep voice said.

I turned around and smiled at Mr. Smouldering Eyes. At that inopportune moment I remembered I was all talk and no action. What was I thinking? Pastis. I'd have to remember that. No more pastis for Russell. Ever! But those eyes, set deep into a dark, masculine face, were so moist they shone. "Hello."

He talked for about thirty seconds and then looked at me questioningly as if everyone knew Swahili. "Excuse me?"

I think he got the message and slowed down. "I'm sorry, do you speak French?"

"Yes. But the slow version."

He grinned. Nice teeth. "Good. I speak French and Italian but no English."

"Let's stick to French then." My Italian was non-existent. He had the courage to make the first move by approaching me, so I thought I'd return the favour and begin the banter. "So, what are you up to tonight?" Classic line.

"Your name is Russell Quant, yes?"

It took me a second to recover. How did this guy know my name? My head was instantly clear and wary. "How did you know that?"

"I've a message for you."

Not again! Let me guess. From Tom Osborn?

"From Tom Osborn," he said. I'd have to remember to mention to Alberta that I'd become a psychic. "He asked me to wait for you in the café. I could not be absolutely sure whether you were the correct man. I wanted to wait until you left the café before approaching you. I did not want a scene."

I wasn't sure I followed his logic, but, whatever. I was maybe a little more mad at him than I should have been, but this message thing was getting old and Mr. Smouldering Eyes had obviously not been watching me because he found me irresistibly gorgeous. So that was two strikes against him. "What's the message?" I snarled, but, damn it, I was pissed off.

Black-haired beauty pulled a paper from his pant pocket and read somewhat stiltedly: "Tom Osborn tells me you are to say this to Mr. Chavell. You are to say to Mr. Chavell that there are problems in Tom's life that he is not aware of and he therefore wishes to remain in Europe for now while he considers these problems. You are to say to Mr. Chavell that Tom no longer knows what his feelings for him are and that he needs time to think. You are to say to Mr. Chavell that Tom has met some friends and plans to stay with them for the foreseeable future. Mr. Chavell is to stop searching for Tom. Tom will contact him when he is ready."

Tom had obviously figured out I was a detective hired by Chavell. The message contained a lot of information to digest. What problems? What friends? "Who are these friends? Who are you? Are you one of these friends?"

"I can't say. I don't know that information." He seemed confused by my questions.

"Why didn't Tom meet me himself? Why send you? He has no reason to fear me. If he didn't want to return to Canada, there was no way I could force him to."

"I imagine he wanted time to get away."

"From me? Where did he go?"

He shrugged.

"But I represent no harm to him. All Mr. Chavell wants to know, deserves to know, is why Tom did what he did. You haven't answered that."

"I'm sorry. This is all I know."

"Is Tom still in France? Are these new friends of his living in France?"

The man stared at me. Surprisingly I got the sense that he was telling the truth. He didn't know much more than he'd already told me. "Has Tom found a new lover? Is this new friend a lover?"

He shook his head. "I'm sorry, monsieur."

"Is it you?" I was taking a wild stab here. "Are you his new friend? His new lover?"

"No, no, no. It's not me." He held up his hands as if warding off a blow.

"Then who?" I thought that if I caught him off guard he'd spill something. But he looked at me with those alluring eyes and shook his head again. "Can you get a message to Tom?"

"No. I don't know where he is. I expect to never see him again."

This seemed odd. Who was this guy? "How did you meet Tom in the first place? How did you get involved?"

I could see his eyes dart back and forth and his feet made little movements as if he was preparing to take off in a rush if he needed to. The intensity of my questioning may have been frightening him. He had that "what have I gotten myself into" look on his face. "It is my job."

"I don't understand."

"It is my job to deliver messages."

I wasn't sure if I understood him correctly. Was he a courier of some sort or a mailman? "You were paid to deliver this message to me?"

He nodded vigourously. "Yes, yes. That is my job."

So this man didn't know Tom at all. Tom had hired him to wait for me in the café. Tom must have gotten enough of a look at me in Cliousclat to give this deliveryman a usable description. Unless Mr. Smouldering Eyes was lying to me, he wouldn't have any more information than what he'd read off the paper. "Can I see the message?"

He handed me the paper with scribbled handwriting on it. "Is this your handwriting?"

"Yes. From the phone call."

Tom had never even met this guy. He called it in. "Can I have your name?" I didn't think this guy was going to be any more help, but I didn't want to lose track of him, just in case. The man reached into his pocket again and produced a business card. I studied it. Indeed, Mr. Smouldering Eyes Painchaud was in the messenger business. I pocketed the card.

"Would you perhaps like to share a drink with me?" This from him. A sexy smile. He looked like one of those guys who probably wasn't even gay but thought, "Hey, I'm cute, you're cute, let's give it a go."

I smiled back. Also sexily. Maybe my battered ego would escape somewhat intact from this evening. "Thank you, but no. I should return to my hotel and pass this message on to Mr. Chavell as soon as possible."

He reached out and ran his hand down my arm and let it rest near my wrist. I shivered. "And then?" he questioned, his eyes asking more. Okay, maybe he was gay.

"And then it will be very late. But thank you."

With a wink he pulled away, turned and was gone from my life forever!

Melodrama—it's just one of those things you need to pull out of your purse once in a while.

By the time I dragged my lust-sick ass back to my hotel room it was about 2:00 a.m. making it 6:00 p.m. Monday evening in Saskatoon. I dialled Chavell's number. He'd just gotten home from work. I read the scribbled note to him and couldn't help feeling sorry for the guy. I could tell he was taking it hard and having a difficult time believing it to be true. I found myself desperately searching for a way to give him hope.

"I think I'll pay Mr. Painchaud a visit tomorrow. Maybe I can find some way to trace Tom's call. Once I get a handle on these new friends of his, I should be able to pick up his trail again. I just have to start talking to people. A Canadian tourist, especially this time of year, is pretty easy to spot." I was making it up as I talked, making promises I wasn't sure I could keep.

"It's over, Russell." His voice was so low I could barely hear him. Chavell was fresh out of hope and nothing I could say was going to give him any.

"It doesn't have to be, Harold."

"I know, I know. I don't doubt you could find Tom again. But to what end? How much clearer does he have to make it? He left me at the altar. He runs away to Europe. He hides from you. And then he leaves this message. What more does he have to do or say for me to get it through my thick skull that it's over?"

I didn't say anything. What he was saying did make some sense. Tom was not being subtle.

"It's done, Russell. You can come home now. I've found out what I needed to know."

I wasn't certain if I agreed with him. As clear as Tom was about his future intentions, he still remained mute about the real reasons for his actions in the first place. His message said something about problems Chavell wasn't aware of. What were they? If he was my lover I would need to know more. But hey, I'm the curious type. That's why I became a detective.

In the end though, the client is always right. "I'm sorry, Harold." I was.

I heard a dry swallow, then, "You'll send me a bill when you get back?"

"I'll call you as soon as I get home. I should be able to find some flights tomorrow."

And that was it. Tom Osborn was still gone. Harold Chavell was still the confused, jilted lover. And I was out of a job. But I knew I was the lucky one.

Although I was now on my way back to Saskatoon, I couldn't help give in to a pang of homesickness and a need to check on my dog. Wimp. I dialled the phone.

"Hello," came the terse greeting. Errall.

"Hey Errall, its Russell. Just getting home from work?"

"I just walked in the door and I'm late for a dinner meeting thing and *your* fucking dog just puked all over the living room carpet."

"Told you not to feed her people food. Her stomach can't take it."

"Nothing but dry kibble every day is verging on abuse, Russell. Where the hell are you, anyway? Can you come over and clean this up?"

"Sorry—still in France. Where's Kells?" My nickname for Kelly, along with anything that rhymed with Kells or Kelly.

"She's at her studio. Ohhhhhh shit!" I heard the phone drop, a few well-vocalized profanities and then the phone being picked up again. "She just did it again! On my Louis Vuitton briefcase! Listen, I don't have time for this right now. Why don't you call back later. Barbra is fine. Don't worry about her. I guess *I'm* going to have to clean up this crap? I'm wearing a seven-hundred-dollar suit, y'know."

"Appreciate it. Love ya both. Give Barbra a smooch from me. Bye." I hung up in record speed. I allowed a slow smile to fill my face as I thought of super yuppie, Errall Strane, crouching over a pile of dog barf. Good girl, Barbra.

Chapter 6

EARLY THE NEXT MORNING, a little hungover, I began a frustrating day of trying to get home. With a little luck and the time change now on your side, a savvy traveller should be able to get back to Saskatchewan from Europe in the same day. But that wasn't to be the case for me. If I'd heard the phrase "you just missed it" one more time, I'm certain I would have exploded. I ended up having to overnight in Paris in an even smaller hotel room than that in Residence Concorde. I eventually found myself back in Saskatoon at 8:30 p.m. on Wednesday night, a week after I'd left. My mood was not terrific by the time I arrived by propeller plane at the John G. Diefenbaker Airport. To add insult to injury, October had arrived since I'd been away and with the turning of the month, our temperate, crisp, invigorating autumn had retreated into an early winter. There was no snow on the ground but as I traversed the tarmac from plane to terminal, a wicked wind bit into my skin like a hailstorm of icicles.

Waiting for my luggage to be spit out from the sluggish carousel seemed to take forever. But finally, bags in hand and head bowed against the freezing wind, I trudged towards long-term parking, reminding myself why I live here. The RX7 did not look happy to see me, as if wondering how dare I leave it outdoors with all those SUVs and ATVs that think they are better prepared to deal with the harsh weather conditions of Saskatchewan. After I'd stuffed it with luggage the rotary engine turned over easily, not through any dedication to me, but because it was desperate to get back into a nice warm garage. Little did it know I wasn't quite ready to go home.

The runway of lights that began where Cathedral Bluff's gravel road became the smooth pavement of Harold Chavell's private driveway and ended up half a kilometre later at his front door was impressive. My personal rule was to never show up unexpected at anyone's door after 10:00 at night. I had a good half-hour's grace. As I approached the Chavell turnoff, I noticed a small car parked off to one side of the unpaved road. I slowed down, wondering if the driver needed help. It was a yellow hatchback, probably ten or fifteen years old. No one was in it. I guessed the driver had run out of gas or experienced mechanical problems. Although the car was left closest to Chavell's, the driver could have chosen any one of several neighbour's houses to walk to for help. But just in case, I kept an eye out as I turned right and directed my car down the well-lit roadway.

Pulling up to the house's grand front entrance, I glanced around for a valet but it was obviously his night off. Tsk, tsk, tsk. I hopped out of my car, climbed the steps to the front door, hit the doorbell pad and heard yet another in its repertoire of classical excerpts. Who needs a stereo system?

I could tell by the look on his face that Chavell was surprised and maybe a little annoyed to see me standing there. He invited me into the foyer but no further.

"I didn't expect to see you so soon," he said. He was wearing a dark sweater and dress pants. I could smell a sharp-tongued cologne. He looked thinner than I remembered.

"I just got in."

"Well. I do have company. Perhaps we could speak another time?"

What company was he talking about? I hadn't seen any cars other than my own parked in front of the house. Unless…the yellow hatchback parked back on the road? But why park so far away? "I'm sorry to disturb you." I was. Really I was. I hate when people arrive unannounced at my door and expect me to drop everything because they happened to have the time to visit. But, I couldn't ignore my growing feeling of uneasiness. Something was not right about this whole case. I hated giving up and it felt like that was what Chavell was asking me to do.

"I couldn't stop thinking about Tom all the way home. You hired me to find out why he left you and I didn't do that. There's something else going on here and I'd like to find out what it is. But you're right, we can talk about this some other time. Maybe tomorrow?" As I said the words I wondered if Chavell would think I was trying to wrangle a few more chargeable hours out of him.

"Actually, let's finish this right now. I can't go on with this any longer. You did your job—everything I asked. It's clear from what you told me that Tom is anxious to get away from me. For now and maybe forever. I'm confused and distraught…but I have to deal with that in my own way. It isn't easy. However, I don't need any more information from you. I've heard all I care to. You have to understand…this isn't the type of experience I desire or welcome into my life. It's tawdry and disreputable and disruptive. If it's a matter of the bill, just send me an invoice…"

I shook my head. "The retainer you gave me is more than sufficient. In fact I'll write you a cheque for the unused portion."

"No. No, please, keep it. I'm sure this job went far and beyond what you normally do. I appreciate that. And I appreciate your continued discretion. Please keep any extra. It is well worth your efforts."

I like being stroked as much as the next guy, yet I couldn't help but get the feeling that I was being brushed off. What did he mean by saying the whole thing was disruptive? Was Tom's disappearance being relegated to the category of an annoying disruption in Chavell's otherwise orderly life? One more try. "I do think there is more to find out here."

"No, there isn't." His answer sounded pretty final. I looked into his eyes and tried to decipher what I saw. Was this a guy who just wanted to get back to his company or a guy whose heart had been publicly thrashed by his lover and just wanted to, finally, leave it be?

"Can I ask you one question before I go?"

"Of course." Always the gentleman.

"Did you give Tom a half-heart pendant as a gift recently? Perhaps as a pre-wedding present?"

He slowly shook his head. "No."

If he was beat, he was really beat. Chavell gave no indication of being the least bit curious about the pendant or why I'd asked the question. You don't have to tell me twice! Well, maybe twice, but never three times. As far as Chavell was concerned, Tom Osborn was a closed chapter in his life. I wished him goodnight and headed toward my waiting car. I heard the front door close behind me and quickly diverted myself toward the window of what I knew, from my earlier visit, to be the office/sitting room. Lucky me. The drapes were open. Looking comfy on the eggplant couch were two men, obviously awaiting Chavell's return. One was attractive, older, elegantly dressed and, I'd bet my bottom dollar, gay as a garden party; the other looked much the same but about twenty years younger. Neither of them looked like the type to be driving a rusted yellow hatchback. Knowing Chavell might be waiting to hear my vehicle leave, I pulled away from the window and headed for my car.

Having a suspicious mind is a common and useful trait in my business. As I drove away I couldn't help wondering who the men in Chavell's sitting room were and why they were there. Friends? Potential new lovers? Business partners? Relatives? Were they simply enjoying a convivial evening together or was there more to it? Was my imagination getting the best of me or was I just tired from all the flying? I had no easy answer. As I came to the main road I noticed the yellow hatchback was gone.

I pulled into my garage off the back alley behind my house, glad to be home. No matter where I've been or what I've been doing, I always love coming home. Home means peace, quiet, comfort, happiness and warmth among a million other good things. Entering my house without Barbra greeting me with her well-controlled enthusiasm and loving eyes is something I never get used to, but it was too late to swing by Kelly and Errall's to retrieve her now. I pulled my suitcase into my bedroom. It's a large room with en-suite and walk-in closet that takes up the whole north end of the house. French doors open onto a small, bricked pad surrounded by flowerbeds. I decided to unpack some other time with the exception of my toiletries, which I'd need before "some other time." I peeled off sticky airplane clothes and pulled on my bathrobe as I headed towards the kitchen. I thought about a bowl of low-fat granola but settled on a glass of white wine. As I poured, the phone rang. I leaned towards the handset and saw "S. Smith" printed out on the call display. I picked up the handset.

"Was that a wine cork I heard popping?"

I shook my head and smirked. "Uh-huh."

She wore a mustard mandarin jacket held together with clasps that looked like frogs straining to hold hands over her bra-less torso and a pair of matching palazzo pants. Standard Wednesday night fare for Sereena. She curled up in one corner of my living room couch, tucking her bare feet under herself.

I offered her a goblet of the white and settled in next to her.

"Start the fire, Russell," she urged with a hint of feminine wile she knew wouldn't work on me but enjoyed using.

I looked at the black pit that was my fireplace and knew I'd have to go out to the garage to retrieve firewood. "I'm not moving another inch. You start the fire. The logs are in the garage."

"Fuck the fire."

"I thought you'd see it my way."

She gave me a sour look and surly smile. An interesting combination only she was capable of. "So? How was it? Buy anything I should comment on?"

"No time for shopping. Work, work, work."

"Idiot."

"Well, I did get a little tipsy in Châteauneuf du Pape and almost had sex with a French delivery man in Sanary-sur-Mer."

"'Little' and 'almost' are poor adjectives for life's adventures," she told me.

"Are they adjectives?"

"Tell me the story when you've been physically ousted from Châteauneuf for having sex with a delivery man in the town square!"

"But I do that on every trip," I whined.

Sereena was an excellent quipster but our relationship was deeper than that. "How was it?" she asked with a new face. Same words, different question.

I thought about how to answer. "Disheartening."

I spent the next fifteen minutes giving her a rundown of what had happened without divulging too many specific details. I always maintain client confidentiality—even after I've lost the client.

"Your instincts are right," she said. "There is something wrong. Affairs of the heart are complicated things, but not that complicated. I think you're disheartened because everything you found out in France doesn't coincide with what you thought you knew about the relationship in the first place."

She was right, as usual. I didn't know Harold Chavell and Tom Osborn well, but they had planned to spend the rest of their lives together. In fact, they were so serious about it, they had invited sixty of their closest friends and family to watch them commit to that very thing. Tying the knot in the straight world could be a nerve-racking event. To do it as two men was that times ten. They hadn't entered into the decision lightly. Yet now, they had both, in their own way, simply given up on it. Chavell was washing his hands of the whole "disruptive" thing. Tom abandoned not only his life partner, but family, friends and a successful business. That was fantasy, not reality.

I poured us each a refill.

A cloudless Thursday morning arrived almost instantly. I felt no guilt whatsoever showing up at my office well after 10:00 a.m. I parked in one of the four spots behind PWC. Errall's bright blue Miata with black leather seats and Beverly Chaney's sensible sedan were already there. Alberta Lougheed lives close enough to walk to work but that didn't necessarily mean she was in. As a psychic, her hours are even stranger than mine. I entered by the front ground floor door instead of the metal fire stairs thinking I should inform our group receptionist, Lilly, that I was back in the country. However, as I approached her, I realized I wasn't even sure that I had told her I was leaving in the first place.

If anyone had told me what Lilly's last name was when I first moved in to PWC, I had since forgotten it. And now, a year later, I was too embarrassed to ask. Especially since she is the sweetest person I have ever met and she treats us, her four employers, as if we are the most famous people in our respective professions. She looks like a spunky sixteen-year-old but is probably twenty-four or so and I know she has at least two kids and a burly, hockey-playing husband. She is white-blonde, smiley, and has a round, bright face. Although eighty-five per cent of Lilly's workload comes from Errall's law practice and Beverly's psychiatry office (they both really know how to create paperwork), Lilly works for all of us. Her unique ability is making our clients feel comfortable. And imagine the collection of people who end up in our waiting room—people in the throes of being sued, having a mental breakdown, spiritual crisis or, worst of all, my clients. Lilly treats them all with the same sense of respect, grace and patience. And they love her for it. As far as I'm concerned, she is the most important person at PWC.

"Hi Lilly, I'm back." I sidled up to her high receptionist's desk and rested my elbows on the counter.

Biggest white smile ever. "Oh, I was thinking you must be away. You're so lucky getting to travel as much as you do. I'd love to travel. Where were you this time?" Not a hint of guilt over my failure to keep her informed of my whereabouts. Had to love her.

"France. Mostly in the countryside."

"Wow! How was it?"

The waiting room was empty so I felt okay giving her a few details about the trip. She seemed so sincere about wanting to hear it. "Any messages for me?" I asked after I was done.

"I put a few calls through to your office. They probably left messages on your voice mail. And this package was delivered for you." She reached under her desk and handed me a ten by thirteen, sealed, brown envelope.

I thanked her and headed towards Errall's office but Lilly waved me off. "With a client," she said. I'd wanted to tell Errall I was back and arrange a time to pick up Barbra, but that would have to wait.

Back in my office I sat behind my desk and convinced myself that going through my mail should be top priority. A few bills, some junk mail, one cheque from a prior job and finally the brown envelope Lilly gave me. The return address was in Cathedral Bluffs. It was from Chavell. Lilly's "date received" stamp told me it had been delivered the day after my first meeting with him. I opened it and pulled out two lists.

One was a typewritten, alphabetically arranged inventory of Tom's friends and relatives that I had asked for before being thrown on a plane to France. There was also a handwritten listing of wedding guests. A note from Chavell, paper clipped to the top of the thin sheaf, read, "As requested, H. Chavell." The script was tight and pointy and looked as if it had been hastily written. A gentler, flowing hand had prepared the wedding guest list. Tom's? Immediately I was struck by the inconsistency of a man who'd write out this list with such care, and plan for months an elaborate event to celebrate his love for another man, only to discard it all. I knew Chavell wasn't interested in having me continue on this job, but the money he'd paid me would more than cover a little unsolicited overtime. Besides, I didn't have much else to do. Other than type up and close the case file. And I really wasn't in the mood for that. I promised myself I'd give it one day only. If I didn't find out anything interesting by tonight, I'd give it up and begin typing.

I took the lists with me and made my escape through the back door. It was times like this I most appreciated my career. If I didn't feel like sitting in my office doing paperwork I could just leave and no one cared. Not to mention that making money by snooping around in other people's business is usually a great way to spend time. As I headed for my car, I was glad I'd chosen to wear my lined, mid-length, black leather coat. A bit of last night's wind was still in the air and although the sun was blasting its yellow rays all over the place it felt cool.

I knew Tom was a founding partner of QW Technologies. That was as good a place to start as any. Like many of the high tech companies that had sprung up in the city, babies of brilliant entre-preneurs, QW was located at Innovation Place. Adjacent to the University of Saskatchewan campus, Innovation Place is a collection of impressive buildings that house over one hundred different organizations. Once a province dedicated to the sole pursuit of growing wheat, Saskatchewan has been shaken and led by changing times to embrace diversification. Most noticeably and successfully, much of that diversification has come from information technology and agricultural-related biotech ventures. Innovation Place is one of the most rapidly growing and successful university-related research parks in North America. Its role, simply put, is to supply facilities, on a commercial basis, to support the research and development community in Saskatchewan. Driving into the business-park one can almost hear brain cells bouncing against each other, and I'm always amazed by the seemingly peaceful co-habitation of multimillion dollar global enterprises and upstart R&D companies trying to get a break.

I turned off Preston Avenue onto the tree-lined Innovation Boulevard. I drove by buildings that are amongst the most structurally advanced and glitziest in the city. Not bad for a bunch of whitecoats. I pulled into a guest parking lot and got out of my car. The reflection of the powerful prairie sun off the tinted glass of The Galleria building was nearly blinding. I jogged down a set of cement steps into a maturely landscaped bowl, complete with splashing fountain, hoping to avoid spontaneous incineration.

Once inside The Galleria building, one of the main complexes, a helpful security guard, obviously used to people unfamiliar with the maze of the research park, provided me with a photocopied map of the area. Fortunately for me, QW Technologies was one of the businesses within The Galleria and using a highlighter, he traced my route from his desk into the west wing where he told me I would find the QW office. After following the directions down a series of long corridors I found the correct door and walked into a small and sedately decorated reception area with a secretary behind a desk. Behind her was another door which, I guessed, led to the inner sanctum of QW.

"Can I help you?" She had dark hair styled in the late seventies—feathered on top and on the sides but flat in the back where she couldn't reach with her curling iron. Yuck. I could tell she was quite thin, even under a heavy, fuzzy sweater with a wide cowl neck riding up her chin. I couldn't decide if she'd be pretty even with a twenty-first century makeover.

"I was wondering if I might speak with Randy Wurz?" This was Tom's business partner who I'd noticed, along with his wife, was on the wedding guest list.

"I'm sorry, Mr. Wurz is out of town. Do you have an appointment?" Her fingers were still poised over her computer keypad waiting for me to go away.

"I don't. My name is Russell Quant. I'm a private investigator." I flashed her my business card as if to prove my claim. That done, it was time for a bit of lying. "Actually I'm working for Tom Osborn's family."

She gave me the best interested look she could muster at that time of day. "Has something happened to Mr. Osborn? He's on vacation, y'know."

"We're not sure. Mr. Osborn normally stays in very close contact with his family but they haven't heard anything from him in days. They're a little concerned. I'm checking it out." I wasn't sure how much Farrah knew about Tom and Chavell, so I was careful with my words. It wasn't my job to out anyone.

"Oh, well, does Mr. Wurz know all this?"

"I don't know. That's what I was hoping to talk to him about. You haven't heard from Mr. Osborn, have you?"

She shook her head. The feathers swished then settled back into place. "No, nothing. Actually that is kinda weird now that I think about it. Usually he calls in pretty regularly when he's away. Y'know, to see how things are going or talk to Mr. Wurz." She finally relaxed her typing fingers and placed them on her lap.

"I was also hoping to maybe get a look around Tom's office." I thought I'd slip that in and see how she'd react.

"I…I don't think I can do that. At least not till I talk to Mr. Wurz. I wonder if he knows what's happening even, huh?"

"There may be nothing wrong. The family just wants to make sure. They thought I might get a clue to where he might be if I could get into his office." Let's try this again.

"I'm sorry I can't help, y'know. I don't even go into Mr. Osborn's office when he's away. Both Mr. Osborn's and Mr. Wurz's office are locked. And I don't have the keys."

She was a bad liar with bad hair. I wasn't sure searching his office would be much help but I was sure this woman was not about to let me in. "Maybe you *can* help me." Doubtful.

She nodded warily, narrowing her eyes.

"Just what kind of business is QW Technologies anyway?"

She moved her head to one side and opened her mouth into a perfect "o." "Wha?"

"What is it you do here?"

"Ohhhhhhhhh. I get it. I thought everyone knew that, y'know. We make computer games mostly."

"I didn't know that. Anything I'd have heard of?"

"Avenging Angel is the best one. You heard of that?"

I had to admit I hadn't. I still preferred board games to computer games. I left my card with her along with the message to have Randy Wurz call me when he returned. Well, that was strike one. And, as far as I could tell, the office angle seemed like a dead end anyway. I doubted Tom was the type to bring his personal problems to work. However, Randy Wurz and his wife were on the guest list for the wedding. Obviously they were close enough friends to be included in that select group. If the chance presented itself, I decided, it still might be worth my while to have a talk with Mr. Wurz.

It was noon when I drove away from Innovation Place and my stomach told me I was hungry. I used the University Bridge to cross the river and headed toward Colourful Mary's on the south end of downtown. Mary's is a combination restaurant and bookstore owned and run by a couple named Mary Quail and Marushka Yabadochka. Mary is half First Nations Cree, half Irish and Marushka is Ukrainian. A feisty pairing to say the least. Colourful Mary's is Saskatoon's only, publicly admitted, gay-run restaurant, but over the years it has developed a wide range of loyal clientele. Of Mary's gay customers, about seventy per cent are women—mostly because of the popularity of its owners with the lesbian crowd. But in part it's also because a large portion of the bookstore's inventory is of a distinctly female nature. Of the non-gay customers, a whole gaggle of them are little old ladies who live in a nearby seniors' complex. Colourful Mary's is probably as far as they can walk without requiring portable oxygen tanks. They come mostly in the early morning or mid-afternoon to enjoy a cup of tea and piece of Marushka's famous torte. No one is quite certain whether they are even aware of the gay thing. They love Mary and Marushka because they are "such sweet young girls," even though both are in their fifties. I guess it's all a matter of perspective.

The other major subset of the non-gay demographic is the food lover. Marushka cooks like everyone's mother, most notably her own. In addition to some rather standard fare for the less adventurous, Marushka always adds one or two Ukrainian delicacies to the daily menu. From perogies smothered in onions and sour cream to something called goodzeeneh which are pieces of dough covered in beet leaves and drowned in a dill-flavoured cream sauce. Her borscht is renown across the city and wafts of onion, garlic and sizzling butter beckons customers from blocks away. I like Colourful Mary's because Mary, who acts as the hostess (and looks after the business side of things) makes her customers feel as if they've just stepped into her home. You feel cared for but not smothered. I'm also addicted to Marushka's cooking.

When I walked in, Mary laced an arm through my own as if she'd been expecting me and asked if I preferred a sunny table in the middle of chaos or something more discreet, hidden in a dim corner behind a clump of palm trees. I chose the latter. I needed to think. Mary escorted me to a round, wooden table painted barnyard red. Next to it were one bright blue chair and one bright yellow chair. The location was much quieter than the colour scheme. It was near the dessert counter but slightly off to one side alongside a rack displaying the latest editions of *Out*, *Hung* and *Vanity Fair*.

"He doesn't want the balabushkeh!" Mary yelled at Marushka hidden somewhere in the back. She had just placed my order for a ham sandwich and cucumber soup. Rather than a waiter, Mary often takes my order herself. She says it's because my beauty disrupts her male staff. In truth, it gives us a few minutes to gab and gossip.

Marushka's round, cherry-coloured face popped up above the counter where she put up orders for the servers to deliver. "How can you not want the balabushkeh? The dough is so soft, filled with mashed potato and in such a nice, creamy mushroom sauce." Her voice was a melodious, Ukrainian-accented song.

"I know what they are. And I love them," I called back, ignoring Mary's smirk. "But I'm too fat to enjoy them today."

Marushka pinched her ample cheek in a way that looked like it hurt. "This is fat! You are a stick!" With that she was gone, hopefully to make my soup and sandwich.

Mary slipped into the yellow chair across from my blue one. Her strong-boned face and dark eyes glow with vitality and she keeps her black hair short and choppy. She has an almost mysterious look, but Mary is anything but. She's a nice, open, kind person who truly loves people. "You okay? You look a little tired. Of course on you, even tired looks good. Tell me, was it a night of tempestuous lovemaking?" Her chocolate eyes danced above smiling lips.

I laughed. "No. No lovemaking."

"I don't understand it," she said, standing as she noticed a chattering group of twenty-ish gay boys enter the restaurant. "Such a handsome man spending his nights alone. I think it's your job. Get a new one." She rubbed my shoulder affectionately and went off to greet her new customers. I hoped she wouldn't bring one of them over to my table for an "innocent" introduction. She'd done it before.

As I waited for lunch my thoughts drifted to Chavell and Tom. Sereena was right. I needed a better sense of who they were and their relationship before I could put this one to bed. Maybe things weren't as perfect and cozy as Chavell had made it sound. After all, Chavell was considerably older than Tom. That could have caused some problems. Or maybe this was closet rage (a distant relative of road rage). Chavell was well-known in Saskatoon. Yet, I had never heard rumours of his being gay before. Not that I considered myself the most well-informed person when it came to gay gossip, but surely something at some time would have leaked out. Unless Chavell, and therefore his relationship with Tom, was even more closeted than he admitted. Tom, being younger and possibly more hip, was maybe finding it stifling and hard to live with. Maybe he needed to get away from living that kind of half-hidden life. Maybe it made him frustrated and angry enough to leave his lover at the altar. Closet rage.

But didn't all gay people experience that frustration at some point in their life? Didn't all gay people wish they could go somewhere where they could live their lives in the open without worrying about public disdain?

Sure. But generally they didn't disappear without a word to anyone.

Or perhaps there was someone else. Maybe Tom was having an affair. But then why agree to the wedding? Was he forced into it somehow? Was any affair worth running away from your entire life? Maybe. I wouldn't be the best judge.

Or, was Tom the kind of person who really wanted to hurt Chavell and this was what he came up with? Pretend to be in love, agree to a wedding, then leave him at the altar. And then, to make it even more painful, go on the honeymoon without him. Wow. What a scheme that would be. The question was, was Tom Osborn capable of such a thing? And if so, why?

Would Chavell even want to know if this was the truth?

The many possibilities were ensnarling my mind. I was grateful when my food arrived and I made quick work of it. I declined dessert but asked for coffee. I pulled out Chavell's lists. Alongside each name, Chavell had helpfully noted whether the person was "family," "friend" or "business." I considered who would be the most useful in revealing the real truth behind the relationship and behind Tom's character.

A best friend would be perfect, but I had no idea which one of the names with the "friend" notation next to it qualified as best friend. I could call and ask Chavell but I wasn't sure I wanted him to know I was still snooping around. Not yet. The next best thing would be a close relative. Kathryn Wagner was listed as Tom's sister. Her name was also on the wedding list, so the chances were good that she and Tom were close and he may have confided in her. I had a next step.

As I finished my coffee my eye was drawn to a figure standing against the dessert counter looking as if he was ordering lunch to go. At first I could only see the back of him. Long legs. Wide shoulders. Got my attention. From my position beside the magazine rack and conveniently placed foliage I could observe him discreetly without feeling like a leering pervert. Starting at the bottom, he wore black shoes with chunky soles, stylish but not too trendy. Then came the legs. Clad in soft denim that caressed his calf and thigh muscles, his legs went on and on, up, up, up until…damn…a coat. The problem with cold weather is that it often makes judicious ogling a disappointing business. He was wearing one of those light, ski-type jackets that gather at the waist with a drawstring and fall just below the butt. He had the jacket zipped up to his throat and the back of his ears looked a little red. Still cold outside. His hair was dark, stylishly short, but again, not too trendy. The only skin I could see from where I sat was on his hands as they gesticulated while he spoke to the waitress behind the counter. I'm a hand man. Other things are important too, but I love a man with beautiful hands. Not unlike the ones I was seeing now. They were big hands, befitting his six-foot plus frame, with long fingers and perfectly proportioned well-tended nails. The way he moved them indicated strength and dexterity. They appeared soft yet firm. I could imagine those hands cupping a lover's face or sliding down my…whoa…what was I doing! This was a public place!

I forced myself to avert my gaze until certain I'd controlled the fever. Out of the corner of my eye I could see he had finished ordering his food and was now patiently waiting for it. He turned around and leaned against the counter, surveying the crowd.

I was in love.

His face was angular and home to a straight nose, shovel-shaped jaw, high cheekbones, broad forehead and tiny ears. His dark hair was spiky around his face, perfectly mated with thick lashes and emphatic eyebrows sitting low over ink-blue eyes. He had a wide mouth and surprisingly thick lips for a man. He should have been a statue.

His gradual one-hundred-and-eighty degree gaze finally made its way to my table. I was ready for it. Nothing ventured, nothing gained. I looked up as if by accident. His eyes, two magnets, immediately ensnared me.

I smiled and nodded.

He began to smile back then, all hail Beelzebub; a finger tapping his shoulder distracted him. I wanted to snap that finger in two and crush it under the heel of my shoe. I wouldn't really do that, but I could not believe the inopportune timing of the server telling him his order was up. He turned about and gave the smile, meant for me, to a woman with his bagful of food.

I think he glanced at me briefly on his way out but I couldn't be certain. I glared at the server. She acted as if she hadn't just been in the presence of a god. Probably a lesbian. I dropped enough money for the bill on the table, gave Mary, who was busy charming a table of octogenarians, a little wave, and left the restaurant. Out on the sidewalk I glanced back and forth but saw no sign of the statue. I slunk back to my car.

Chapter 7

KATHRYN WAGNER WAS SEVERAL YEARS OLDER than her brother was. Her heavy Slavic accent surprised me until she told me Wagner was her married name and that Tom had changed his name, much to the family's disappointment, from the more difficult Oburkevich. Kathryn was attractive in a round-faced, heavily made-up way. If I had to guess, I would say she had artfully lathered on the Mary Kay cosmetics in the fifteen minutes since I'd called. She had a wide smile and her bright red lipstick had begun to smudge onto square, strong-looking teeth. Her green-grey eyes were framed with green and brown eye-shadow, coal black eyeliner and heavy mascara that had freckled her cheeks. If I didn't know better, I'd say she was made-up for a stage performance. The gay man in me wanted to tell her she'd be more attractive without the Easter egg paint, but I was also a smart man.

The Wagners lived in a pleasant house in Lakeview, a suburban jigsaw puzzle on the southeast side of Saskatoon. I find this part of town particularly difficult to navigate because all the streets have confusingly similar sounding names: Lakeshore Bay, Lakeshore Court, Lakeshore Crescent, Lakeshore Place, Lakeshore Terrace.

And then there was the whole Whiteshore series. City Hall was definitely lacking creativity.

Mr. Wagner was at work at an agricultural parts dealership. One son was at school and the other, only seven months old, was asleep upstairs. Our entire conversation was held in rather loud whispers. We sat on flowered couches in a busily decorated living room. It was the type of room used only for guests. The sofa felt stiff to my behind. I wondered if I'd find plastic covering hidden underneath it.

"I love Tom," Kathryn explained, "but I don't approve of his lifestyle. And Tom knows that. I've always felt it would ruin his life. Hold him back. I think it has. And besides, we're Catholic."

"Were you also fond of Harold Chavell?"

Her eyes bored into me as one severely plucked eyebrow rose up into a furrowed brow. "What do you think? I know they've…known each other for two or three years or something like that, but I've only met him once…no, maybe twice, in all that time. And that, let me tell you, was more than enough. Too old, too snobby, too lah-dee-dah for me, if you know what I mean. And Tom knows—I don't like that man. I told him so, straight to his face."

"But you were invited to their wedding."

She snorted using her painted lips to great effect. "Wedding! What kind of wedding would that be? It's not legal, you know. And it's a sin against the church. I couldn't stand to think of it, and I told Tom that. I told him not to dare invite Mama and Papa. It would kill them. And I told this to Tom right to his face. And he must have thought so too because he never mentioned a word about it to them. I don't know why he invited my husband and me. He said it was because Harold thought family should be in attendance, like for a real wedding. Maybe he hoped it would help us understand. Well, we don't," she said with a dramatic huff and then added, "Until you just told me otherwise, I just assumed he went through with it."

"So you didn't attend?"

She made another interesting noise with her mouth, something in a high pitch that sounded like a cross between an owl and a nasty crow. "Absolutely not. We stayed home. And I told Tom that. I said, Tom, I love you, you're my brother, thank you very much for the invitation, but I am not coming to this...this event."

"So you haven't heard from Tom since then?"

"No."

"Are you surprised Tom would just disappear like that?"

"Welllllll...now that you put it that way, it isn't like Tom at all. He was always pretty good about staying in touch, especially with Mama and Papa. I know they mentioned the other day they hadn't heard from him in several days. But what was I going to tell them? Tom is on his honeymoon with another man? Maybe he'll call later? I didn't think much of it. I just assumed he would come back from France and, well, we'd go on from there. The wedding thing wouldn't change a thing as far as I was concerned. He's my brother. I love Tom. He knows that."

I was pretty certain Kathryn would be content to discuss this further, but that didn't mean I'd get much new information. She loved her brother, didn't care for Chavell, and didn't even know Tom was missing. I suspected she was right about one thing. Tom would contact their parents eventually. But, until then, I was considering this strike two for the day. If I wanted to find out what kind of man Tom Osborn really was, I'd have to go elsewhere. "Do you know any of Tom's close friends?"

She shook her head and grimaced until her crimson mouth looked like a flattened figure eight. "I don't think I'd know about those type of people, if you know what I mean."

I nodded and began to rise.

"There is one girl, come to think of it. He mentions her fairly often. Colleen something. Last name sounded Presbyterian or Anglican or something. You know the kind of name I mean? Maybe English? I know Mama and Papa hoped she was more than just a friend, even though she isn't Catholic and is quite bossy. Tom brought her to a few of our family dinners. Last time we saw her I think was for my own birthday party last year. We had a barbecue. And food like you wouldn't believe! I think Mama was measuring this girl up for a wedding dress. Tom is getting to the age where he needs to marry, if you know what I mean? Anyway, that's all I know. Colleen something. She was nice I suppose—but bossy. I wonder if she knew?"

"If she knew…?"

She looked at me as if I might be simple-minded. "You know. About Tom and his type. That may have been what broke them up. I never saw her again after my birthday party."

I forced a smile and got to my feet. "Thank you for your time. I appreciate your help. This is my card. If you think of anything else that might be useful or if you or your parents hear from Tom, I would really appreciate it if you would call me."

She looked at me a little suspiciously. I think it was beginning to dawn on her that I might be on Chavell's "side" and possibly one of his "type." "We'll see," she said.

Back in my car I pulled out the lists and looked for the name Colleen. There was a Colleen Arber on both. Looked promising. I dug around behind the driver's seat and found the City of Saskatoon phone book I always kept in the car just for this purpose. I had reasons to be distrusting of directory assistance. But that's another story. I activated my cellphone and called the number I found listed next to Arber C.

"Hello." A woman's voice.

"I'm calling for Colleen Arber."

"I'm sorry, Colleen's at work. Can I pass her a message?"

Darn! "Actually I was hoping to talk directly to Colleen."

"Well, she's usually home by six. You could try back then."

I was hoping for something more. "You wouldn't have her work number?"

The woman hesitated then asked, "May I ask who's calling?"

"My name is Russell Quant. I'm a private investigator and a

friend of Harold Chavell's." Bit of a lie there, but I thought it might be helpful. "I'm trying to track down Tom Osborn."

"I knew it!"

"What do you mean?"

"Well you know Tom didn't show up for the wedding, right?"

"Yes. That's why I'm looking for him. No one seems to have heard from him since."

"Exactly. Colleen and I are getting worried. Harold told us Tom went to France without him, but that just doesn't seem right. He wouldn't just leave without calling. Unless something was very wrong."

I was beginning to think the woman on the phone would be just as informative as Colleen Arber. "Are you a good friend of Tom's?"

"Yeah, sure. But Tom and Colleen go way back. They are best friends. I'm sure she'd want to talk to you about this. She works at Dutch Growers. You can find her there."

I thanked the woman and set out to find Colleen Arber.

Dutch Growers is a massive greenhouse and nursery easily recognizable by the full-size, functional windmill, the base of which is the front entrance of the retail area. I parked in a nearly empty parking lot. October is definitely low season. Outdoor gardeners have already harvested their vegetables and prepared shrubs and flowerbeds for winter and declared themselves retired until spring. As soon as I stepped into the large, sunny building the first thing I noticed was the smell of fresh mint, dill and tulip bulbs. It's always spring in Dutch Growers land no matter what time of year it is outside. I took a grateful whiff and proceeded into the store.

As I passed through the craft area I realized I had not only forgotten to ask the woman on the phone her name, but also how to recognize Colleen. I wasn't winning any awards as a detective. I blamed it on jet lag. I dragged myself away from a beckoning display of clay pots after promising myself to return at a later date and proceeded to the rear of the store where the indoor greenery was housed.

"You must be Russell Grant," a sinewy, brown-haired woman with sharp features said to me from behind a thick stemmed philodendron.

I rounded the overgrown houseplant and held out my palm. "Quant, Russell Quant."

She pulled off a glove and shook my hand with a strong grip. Her palm was tough as leather and her skin a tanned hide. "Sorry, I guess Norma got that wrong."

Apparently Norma had called ahead and told Colleen to watch out for me. "That's okay."

"I want those over by the figs, Kristie!" She yelled over my shoulder, startling me. "They'll drop all their leaves before supper if you let them stay there. Come on, you guys! You know better."

I looked over my shoulder at a group of worker ants following Colleen's bellowed instructions.

"Sorry about that," she said, her intense eyes focused once again on me. "This isn't the perfect time to talk. We're rearranging the greenhouse and starting to move some of the outdoor plants today. It's gotten a lot colder a lot quicker than we'd expected. I wouldn't even take the time but Norma said it was about Tom. I want to help if I can."

"Yes, thanks. I was wondering if you could tell me a little about Tom, how you know him and what you know of his relationship with Harold Chavell."

Every so often her eyes would dart away to assess the activity of her minions but she seemed intent on answering my questions. "Tom and I have been friends since our clubbing days in the eighties." I wasn't sure what that meant but I let her continue. She was either talking about going to nightclubs or else a primitive form of hunting. "We've been through everything together. New relationships, good relationships, broken relationships, new friends, old friends, dying friends, career ups and downs, family problems, you name it. We made it through together. Tom is a great guy, Mr. Quant. I think you would like him. Everyone does. He's not only cute as a button, but he is genuinely nice and sincere. He really cares about his friends. And he is smart. He's one of the few gay men I know who put his dick aside long enough to make something of himself. He went to university and then started QW and now it's a big success. Despite all that, Tom has no ego whatsoever. He's just a regular guy. That's why I love him so much."

Well, you couldn't ask for a more glowing review than that. "What about Harold Chavell. What do you think about him and their relationship?"

She smiled. It was amazing how it softened her craggy face. All of a sudden I had a much different opinion of this woman. Mostly I was less afraid of her. But the smile disappeared as quickly as it had developed when she caught the eye of another worker and silently but forcefully made a hand signal that communicated something I couldn't decipher. This woman could train recruits at an army base.

"To tell you the truth, at first I wasn't too excited about the whole thing. It took me a while to warm up to Harold. He's so different than Tom. More standoffish. And inflexible. And rigid. Or at least that's how he seemed at first. But, I suppose, someone like him doesn't get to where he is by being a pushover. After they were together about a year, I began to realize that maybe I'd read the man wrong and tried to make more of an effort to get to know him. Once we both let down our guards, I really came to understand and respect him. You might even say I like him. They have a good relationship. I just can't understand what could have made Tom take off like that. And to not even call me! It doesn't make any sense, Mr. Quant. I'm glad Harold hired you. I know there is something wrong. I can feel it."

"So if something had happened to make Tom change his mind about getting married, you think he would have told you about it?"

"I don't kid myself that Tom tells me absolutely everything just because we're best friends. But something like that? Yeah, I think he would have told me."

"When was the last time you saw Tom?"

"The night before the wedding. There was a small get-together for friends at Harold's house. A rehearsal party I guess it was." She gave me a look. "Were you there?"

I had told Norma I was a friend. Lies always catch up to you. But in my job you had to take the chance and run until they did. "No, no I wasn't." Not very convincing.

"I was Tom's designated driver that night. He didn't drink much but I drove him back to the apartment anyway. It was kind of a joke, making Tom and Harold spend the night apart. It was an early night. We stopped at Earl's Lounge on the way for one last singles drink and then I took him home. I went up for a quick chat, some coffee, nothing heavy, and then I left. It must have been around eleven. Through all of that, he didn't say a thing to make me suspicious he was getting cold feet. If anything, he could barely wait for Saturday to come. He seemed pumped. He said he'd make it to the ceremony on his own. I offered to pick him up but he joked about Norma and I needing all the time we could get to coax ourselves into dresses and make up. He said he'd be fine on his own." She looked away for a second. She was too tough for tears but I saw a look of concern and maybe some guilt in her eyes. "I didn't get that there was anything wrong. I guess we should have gone to get him."

"If he was intent on running away I doubt that would have made any difference," I told her softly.

She nodded then looked away again. "I'm sorry. I have to get back to work. I don't have anything else to add anyway. But let us know if…when you find him."

"One more thing?"

"Yes?" She was beginning to sound a little impatient.

"What kind of vehicle does Tom drive?"

"A black Jimmy."

"Do you know where it is?"

Her eyes tightened as she thought this over. "No. I just assumed it was at the apartment. In the parking lot behind the building."

It was probably one of the collection I'd seen there. "I'm sure you're right. I just thought I'd ask."

I handed her a card and watched her march off.

Strike three?

So far the only thing I had learned was that Tom seemed to be a great guy loved by his sister and best friend. I was beginning to get more of a sense of who Tom Osborn was and what he might or might not be capable of. According to these two sources, Tom Osborn had every intention of going through with the wedding. Yet something changed his mind. Something made him run. Something made him cut off communication with family and friends.

It was getting late and I had three strikes under my belt. But hell, I never liked baseball anyway. Still parked outside Dutch Growers, I studied the lists one more time. Now that I knew Oburkevich was Tom's real last name, I looked at the roster with a different eye. Father Leonard Oburkevich was on both lists. Was he an uncle? Would a priest attend a gay wedding?

Curiosity got the better of me. I had to find out.

Letting my fingers do the walking, I searched the Yellow Pages under the heading for Ukrainian Catholic churches. There were only four. In no time flat I found Father Oburkevich at Saints Peter and Paul Church on 11th Street. The woman who answered the phone offered to put Father Oburkevich on the line but I made some excuse and hung up. Whenever possible, I find meeting people in person is much preferable to a phone conversation.

Saints Peter and Paul Ukrainian Catholic Church and its rectory are two of the most unique buildings in Saskatoon. Not only because they're far from traditional in design, but also because they appear so hopelessly out of place. On the corner of the block sits the rectory, a two-and-a-half storey edifice consisting of two side-by-side octagonal structures with domed roofs attached to a Fred Flintstone-looking garage and seemingly inspired by a Greek island resort with its whitewash and bright blue panels. Next to it, across a paved parking lot where I was parked, is the church. This dirty-white monstrosity resembles a giant, headless worm with its mounding sections sliced lengthwise and left sitting on a bed of grass. Was it a misunderstanding with the architect?

It was late Thursday afternoon so I was betting the priests would not be in church. But what do I know about what priests do on Thursday afternoons? I approached one of the rectory entrances and hesitated. I was stumped. Is a rectory like a church or like a home? Do you just walk in? Or do you knock? I knocked.

An elderly lady answered the door. She squinted at me from behind thick, wire-rimmed glasses and chipmunk-like, overly rouged cheeks. "Who is it?"

"Good afternoon, ma'am. My name is Russell Quant."

"We don't give out food or money here."

I looked down at my appearance. Did I look like a beggar? This was a fairly sedate and respectable neighbourhood as far as I knew. I was surprised she would expect a panhandler at her door. "I'm looking for Father Len Oburkevich," I said as sweetly as I could.

"You won't have any better luck with him, young man. No food. No money."

I decided she must be in need of a new eyeglass prescription. Otherwise I'd really have to rethink my wardrobe. "No, I don't want food or money. I'd just like to talk with Father Oburkevich."

"You planning on getting married?"

Huh?

"You here to discuss preparation for marriage?" Her tone was barely more welcoming now that she suspected I was a future groom looking for guidance. I could see the old-lady-powder that had shaken off her cheeks and neck onto her dress collar. I showed remarkable restraint by not offering tips on her appearance and listened politely as she continued. "There's another class beginning tomorrow. Do you want me to put your name down? It's at seven-thirty. I'll need your intended wife's name too."

I was beginning to lose faith I would ever get through to this woman when a tall, thick-bellied man with a full beard appeared behind her. He was wearing a navy, short-sleeved shirt fastened at the neck with a white collar. Thank goodness. "Father Oburkevich?" I asked hopefully.

"That's all right, Olga, I'll talk to the man," he said as he gently directed her with a big hand on her frail shoulders towards the staircase behind them. I wondered if she'd ever make it all the way to the top without him. He turned to me with a hearty smile. "You're not here for food or money, right?"

I smiled back. "No. And I'm not getting married either."

He winked and stepped aside to let me in.

The chill was beginning to turn my nose red. "I didn't know there were panhandlers in this area."

"Most of them don't live here, they just come here from other parts of the city. They make a circuit of all the churches, hoping for the best. Sometimes they get lucky. Father Shaddock is a real softy. Gives them cookies." His gentle voice was full of patience and understanding and good humour.

"Thank you for letting me in, Father Oburkevich, I just need a few minutes of your time."

"Actually I'm Father Hryniuka. Can I help you or do you need to see Father Len?"

How many priests lived here? "Oh. Well, I'd really like to talk to Father…"

"You can call him Father Len. Everyone does. He's in the church if you need to see him." I must have looked uncertain because he then added, "He's not saying mass. I think he's working on a sermon. He likes to write in the church. Gives him inspiration. Me, I like a big desk, a bright light and a glass of scotch!"

I thanked the hearty cleric and made my way across the parking lot to the church. The wind was picking up again and I was certain I could see the occasional snowflake flutter by. I scaled the church steps and heaved open the heavy door where the worm's head should have been. I walked through an empty foyer and opened a second set of doors. Incense. The husky scent threatened my stomach but just as quickly made itself comfortable in my nose and soon I hardly noticed it. I saw a single head in a pew maybe two-thirds of the way up the left-hand side of the dimly lit church. It was quieter than a gay bar before midnight. Although no signs were posted I found myself walking half-speed. I wasn't trying to be quiet, and actually hoped the priest would hear me so I wouldn't startle him, but my rubber-soled shoes made no sound. I stopped one pew back from where he toiled over his sermon.

"Excuse me," I said.

The priest turned and gave me a beatific smile.

I froze.

I stared at the collar around his neck, the white of it a blindingly bright beacon in the murky light.

I couldn't speak.

Father Len Oburkevich was the statue.

I could tell by the look on the priest's face that he recognized me too but couldn't remember from where. Should I tell him we were checking each other out at Colourful Mary's just a couple of hours ago? But something gave me the suspicion that the way I had noticed him was not the same way he had noticed me. Maybe it was the white collar, I don't know. I said nothing. I was trying to build up a new supply of saliva in my mouth.

"Hello," he said, gracefully sliding out of the pew and turning to face me. "You look familiar."

I hate to admit it, but I blushed. "Hello, Father. My name is Russell Quant."

"Quant? Hmmm, no, I don't think I know that name. Oh wait a minute, I saw you this afternoon at the restaurant!" He smiled his Greek god smile with a satisfaction known only to supreme beings of exquisite beauty.

"Oh really?" I said, playing stupid, as if the last thing I'd be doing is looking at another man in a restaurant. In reality, everyone knows it's one of the official sports of the Gay Olympics and I was always open to a little training.

"Yes, yes, at Colourful Mary's, I was waiting for my lunch order. They have the best Ukrainian food in the city. Don't tell anyone," he said, winking at me and rendering me breathless over what he might say next, "but it's as good as my mother makes."

I laughed and agreed. I could barely keep on my feet standing so close to this man. He seemed to radiate a glow that drew you closer to him. His eyes shone and he placed his hands on his slender hips rather than piously clasped together over his crotch, as I'd expect of a man of the cloth. I could smell the gentle fragrance of his cologne. He wore a black shirt with the ever-present collar and those nicely fitting jeans I'd admired earlier.

They're right. Denim *does* go with everything.

"What can I help you with, Mr. Quant?"

"Call me Russell."

Another smile. I liked making him do that. "Russell then."

I gave myself a mental slap in the face before continuing. Not only was this man involved in my case, but he was also a priest for Pete's sake! "I'd like to speak to you about Tom Osborn. I understand he's a relative of yours?"

"Please, sit down," he said, indicating the pew he'd just vacated. His face showed sudden concern. I plopped down in the spot still warm from his body heat and he moved in next to me. "Tom is my brother. Has something happened? Are you with the police?"

I don't know why I automatically assumed Father Len Oburkevich would be an old uncle or distant cousin. Now that I looked at him, I could pick out obvious similarities between the two men. "I'm a private investigator. I was hired by Harold Chavell."

"Is this about Tom not showing up for the ceremony?"

"You knew about that?" Of course he did. He was invited.

"Yes. I was there. Did Harold hire you to find out what happened? Do you know where Tom is?"

"Yes. And as far as we know, Tom is still in France."

Father Len shook his head and looked away. "Tom, what are you doing?"

"I take it you haven't heard from him?"

"No." His attention was back on me.

"Before the ceremony, did you have any idea something might be wrong?"

"Not at all. He was very excited and happy to be taking this next step in his relationship with Harold."

"How did you feel about that? I know the Catholic Church does not particularly embrace gay relationships."

"That's true." He hesitated and I was beginning to think he wasn't going to answer the question. "But Tom is my brother. I love him very much. As long as he and Harold have a relationship built from love, that cannot be a bad thing." He gave me a lopsided grin. "That is my position, not that of the church."

"Do you have any idea why Tom would have done this?"

Again his head moved from side to side. "I've thought about it since the day he left and I've talked to Harold about it. I can't think of anything to explain his actions. However, even though I'm a priest and Tom and I are close, he is not in the habit of confessing to me."

"I see." Another dead end.

"Do you think Tom is in danger?"

I was surprised at the question. Was he in danger? Is that why he ran away? Is that why he blew me off in Sanary? "I don't know."

"Is there anything else I can do to help?"

There was nothing. This case seemed to be going nowhere. Maybe Chavell was right. Tom's actions didn't seem to make sense to anyone who knew him, but it wouldn't be the first time someone did something no one expected. And maybe Tom meant to keep his reasons a secret. "No, thank you, Father."

"I'll pray."

Now there's a comment to help you remember who you're talking to.

We shook hands and I tried not to rush out of the church.

Outside the horizon was dimming and it smelled like snow. I sneered at the sky. It was too early in the year for the white stuff. If it snowed now, it would be a long winter. And the kids would have to wear coats over their Halloween costumes. I hate when that happens.

I decided to call it quits on the Osborn case. If not for good, at least for today. All I wanted to do was go home and snuggle with my dog in front of a roaring fire.

I groaned. My dog wasn't home and the firewood was in the garage.

Errall and Kelly live in a great two-storey house on Pembina Avenue. It's built on a hillside with a partial view of downtown and a rolling, woodsy backyard that Barbra loves to investigate. I first met Kelly in high school, too many years ago to count. Back then we weren't best friends, but we knew each other and liked one another well enough but just moved in different circles and had no idea the other was gay. After graduation we pretty much forgot about one another but reconnected several years later at a gay dance in Saskatoon. We've been best buddies ever since. I like Kelly because she reminds me that there is calmness and serenity and simpleness in the world. A visit with Kelly is like taking a relaxation pill. Kelly is a potter and woodworker, an artist of growing fame, particularly for her spectacular gaily-painted bowls and plates. She owns and manages On Broadway, a small retail gallery in the artsy Broadway Avenue area that features many Saskatchewan artisans along with her own work. I was glad to see Kelly's face when the front door opened.

"Kells Bells, how are you?" I asked as we hugged and simultaneously moved inside the house.

"Terrific. You've come for the beast? They're in the backyard. Brutus will hate to see her go. He loves having his sister here. Want some coffee or something to drink?"

I followed Kelly into the rustic kitchen at the back of the house. She is maybe five-foot-two and has an athlete's build, stocky and muscular. Errall is fond of saying Kelly looks best in nothing but a sports bra and boxer shorts. She keeps her wiry, reddish-blonde hair short. Her face is small but her eyes and mouth are big and wide. It gives her a sort of cutesy, Teletubby look that she hates but everyone else finds adorable.

"I don't want to interrupt if you're busy getting dinner ready or something."

"I do have to get to a pottery workshop I'm teaching in a bit, but I was just finishing eating. You can keep me company. Want a taco?"

We each hopped up on stools around the kitchen island where Kelly's half-eaten plate of food was sitting. "No thanks. You eat."

"There's fresh coffee," she said as she dug into her refried beans.

I helped myself and settled in again around the island. "Where's Errall?"

"Work. Big surprise. She's really been killing herself lately. A couple of big cases going on."

We spent the next half-hour talking about nothing like friends can do. Afterwards, as I prepared to head outdoors to retrieve Barbra, we spied both dogs through the window. Except for Brutus being about an inch taller, they were twins standing shock-still under a large ash tree, heads quirked to the right watching with childlike curiosity as the first leaf of autumn fell to the ground.

Chapter 8

FRIDAY MORNING WAS ONE OF THOSE MORNINGS that makes you shake your head at the wonder of Saskatchewan weather. Whereas the night before seemed on the brink of snow, Friday began with a brilliant sun in a powder blue sky unblemished by a single cloud. I drove to work with the top down revelling in the twenty-two degrees Celsius temperature. When I entered PWC I tossed Lilly a cheery hello and headed up to my office.

I hit the message button on my answering machine and listened as I made coffee. In addition to a message from my buddy, Anthony, I was interested to learn from two other calls that the seeds of my little investigation from the prior day had actually sprouted shoots.

The first was a message from Randy Wurz, Tom's business partner. It was short and sweet and professional, giving me a number should I still want to contact him.

The second was from Colleen Arber. This sounded a little more interesting. "Mr. Quant, this is Colleen Arber, Tom's friend from Dutch Growers. I've come up with some information you should hear. You said to call. Ahhh…how about this, work isn't good, so how about we meet at the band shelter in Kiwanis Park at 9:00 p.m. tonight. I'll be there anyway so if you can't make it that's okay. I'll be hard to reach by phone. Hopefully we'll see you there. Oh, by the way, Tom's Jimmy *is* in the parking lot behind his apartment building."

I poured myself a mug of coffee and stepped out onto the sun-splattered balcony. Kiwanis Park was right across the street from my office, but the band shelter was a few blocks away on the other side of the Bessborough Hotel, which blocked my view. I sat on a deck chair and let the sun beat some colour into my cheeks. What I was really doing was debating a dilemma. Should I let this case go, as my client had suggested, or should I keep going as my gut was telling me to?

The phone messages from Randy Wurz and Colleen Arber bothered me. They probably wouldn't lead to much, but even so I couldn't very well call them up and say, oops, forget it, I don't need your help anymore. And I had already bent the truth with these people yesterday, having pretended that Harold still had me on payroll.

As the sun's rays warmed me, I ran familiar scenarios through my head and added a new one. Suppose Tom Osborn had recently tested positive, couldn't bring himself to tell Chavell and therefore decided not to go through with the wedding. Possible? No matter what the real story was, I realized the bottom line was that Chavell didn't want to know the truth. If he did, he wouldn't have quit so easily. What was I expecting to achieve by continuing with this? It wasn't my wedding that had been ruined. Even if I found out what really happened, would Chavell appreciate it? Maybe he'd announce to all that I was the best private investigator in the world? Not likely.

I left my spot in the sun and went back inside to fix another coffee and return to my desk. I pulled out the papers I'd need to write up and close the file. But my head just wasn't into it. My mind continued to whir with indecision. I finally decided on a compromise. I would do nothing further to actively pursue clues in the case as I'd done yesterday. That meant no more interviewing family or friends or making inquiring phone calls. But, I would follow up the leads I'd already cultivated. It was unprofessional to let a lead dangle after you'd asked for help. I could sell that to Chavell if he ever caught wind of what I was doing.

Besides, I wasn't charging him.

I grabbed the phone receiver and dialled the number Randy Wurz had left on his message.

"Randy Wurz," came the brisk reply. I could tell from the number and the poor reception that I'd reached a cellphone.

"Mr. Wurz, this is Russell Quant."

"Oh, Mr. Quant. Glad to hear back from you. If I lose you I'll call you back from a pay phone. I'm in my car on my way home from Regina."

"Sure." Regina, the capital city of Saskatchewan, is about a three-hour car ride south of Saskatoon. "Business trip?"

"Yes. I've been away for several days, but my secretary reached me yesterday and told me about your visit." I bet she did. "Terrible news about Tom. I can't believe it. I'd be glad to do anything I can to help."

It sounded to me as if the QW receptionist was making things out to be a little more dramatic than they were. I thought I'd better diffuse the situation. "Oh, there's nothing to really worry about. I hope I didn't give your secretary the wrong impression. We know Tom's in France. Mr. Chavell would simply like to find a way to contact him. I understand Tom is in the habit of checking in with you whenever he's away from the office. Have you heard anything from him in the last two weeks?"

He hesitated as if thinking about it, then answered, "No. Nothing."

"Is that surprising to you?"

"Well sure, but my wife and I were at the wedding. I just assumed he wanted to keep a low profile for a while. It was a pretty embarrassing evening. For both of them. I had no idea he had broken off contact with everyone though. I didn't know he was actually missing."

"Well, as I said earlier, he's not missing, just…out of touch."

"I'd say that's understandable under the circumstances, wouldn't you?" Without waiting for an answer he said, "My secretary said you wanted to have a look in Tom's office. I don't know how it will help but I told her it would be okay to let you in. She keeps a spare set of keys in case we lose ours. I'd let you in myself, but after I get back into town I'm in meetings away from the office for the rest of the day."

So, the secretary *did* have keys to the offices. Wasn't she the sly one? "I appreciate that. Thank you."

"Absolutely. Anything else I can do, you just let me know. Tom and I go way back. We went to university together. I've been worried about him ever since the wedding was called off. Anyway, I'd appreciate it if you kept me up to date with what you find out, Mr. Quant. We'll talk soon."

The connection ended. I wasn't sure if his cellphone cut out or if he'd hung up on me. No matter, I got what I wanted.

I cleared the line and dialled Anthony Gatt's number. Although my Uncle Lawrence was single at the time of his death, Anthony, I suspect, was the love of his life. They had parted amicably some years prior to the fateful trip that claimed my fabulous uncle's life and had remained the best of friends. After Lawrence was gone, Anthony became my Auntie Mame. He is sometimes friend, sometimes father, sometimes mentor, sometimes protector. Anthony has been thirty-nine years old several times over and judging by how he looks, he'll pull it off for many more years. He is tall, dashingly attractive in a Robert Redford-Great Gatsby kind of way, and has a vocabulary to kill for with just enough of an English accent to sound well-educated but not patronizing.

Anthony spends his days overseeing his high-end menswear stores called gatt (small "g") with outlets in Saskatoon, Regina and, oddly enough, the chic Whistler Ski Resort in British

Columbia. His goal is to dress the prairie man as if he regularly shopped the runways of Paris and Milan. At night, Anthony is a leader of Saskatoon society, throwing extravagant parties in his penthouse apartment, some gay, some not, some a daring mix of both. He is involved in one way or another with the opera, symphony and several theatre groups, and known for his financial generosity, is a sought after guest at every fundraiser in town. He is the only person I know who owns more than one tuxedo.

Anthony's partner in life is the stunning Jared Lowe. In his early thirties, Jared is in the twilight of a successful modelling career. When barely a teenager, Jared won a talent search contest sponsored by a local modelling agency and soon found himself carried off on the wings of a fairy to the glittering world of international fashion shoots. Anthony met Jared at a fabulous party in some fabulous place and they began a fabulous long distance relationship that neither took seriously—until they realized they were in love. Despite the glamour and excitement and fame, Jared's fondest wish has always been to return home to roost forevermore. So for him to find a lover who not only lived in Saskatoon but also could, at least temporarily, survive equally well in the fast-paced world of modelling, made a coupling with Anthony Gatt a perfect combination.

Although neither admits it, I believe Anthony and Jared do more for allaying homophobia in Saskatoon than a thousand gay pride parades. They do it not by raising placards or pushing their lifestyle into people's faces, but by simply being there, where you wouldn't necessarily expect a gay couple to be, co-existing with the "normal" crowd and fitting in perfectly. Often, by the time anyone gets around to discussing the possibility that they might be a couple of homosexuals, it just doesn't matter anymore.

"Russell! How terrific of you to call!"

I hate people with call display, even though I have it too. I like my calls to be a surprise. "Actually, you called me. I'm returning your message."

I could visualize Anthony's winning smile as he swivelled about on his fine leather chair in his penthouse home office with the commanding view of the South Saskatchewan River. "Yes, that's right, I'd forgotten. How are you anyway, dear boy? I haven't heard from you in days. Heard a rumour you'd been in France. Did you look up Sophie?" Anthony knows someone glamourous in every country in the world.

"I didn't have the chance. Working you know. How are you? How is Jared?"

"Ask him yourself. He's flying in for tonight."

Oops. I was getting that nasty feeling like I'd forgotten something. "Tonight?"

"I was calling to inform you of the proper attire for the evening, but apparently I have to inform you of the entire event. Again!"

Now I remembered. Anthony was throwing a "welcome to the city" cocktail party for the new artistic director of one of the local theatres. Normally I could get away with not attending, but lately Anthony was claiming astonishment at my consistent lack of male companionship, and he was a stalwart supporter of the idea that in order to find a mate you had to step out on occasion. I had only agreed, several weeks ago, when he assured me there would be no blind date waiting for me next to the punch bowl. Been there, done that, got dumped. "Is that tonight?"

"You remember the address?" Smart-ass.

"Goodbye, Anthony." I hung up the phone before asking what I should wear. Knowing Anthony, it could be anything from formal to pool-party chic. Oh well, if I didn't fit in I'd just have to leave early. Besides, I could always count on my wonderpants.

When I stepped into the reception area of QW Technologies later that afternoon, the secretary gave me a wary smile of recognition. "Hi," I said, returning it and wishing the world was the kind of place where I could give her some much needed advice on her retro hairdo. Somebody had to tell her. But, come to think of it, I was ripped at her for not letting me into Tom's office the last time I was there. Sure, it was her job, but she didn't have to be sneaky about it, pretending she didn't have a key. Maybe she deserved bad hair. "I spoke to Mr. Wurz this morning. He said you'd be able to let me into Mr. Osborn's office now."

"Oh sure," she readily agreed, as if she'd forgotten our earlier conversation.

"I hope he told you where the key was." I couldn't help myself.

She gave me a funny look and led me through a door into the back. Apparently the entire decorating budget had been spent on the reception area. The rest of the office was pure Home Hardware, inexpensive but utilitarian. The secretary passed by three doors, unlocked a fourth at the end of a hallway and then went away without offering me coffee, water or a "see ya later." Something told me she was beginning to catch on to my snide remarks and astonished stares at her hair and wasn't liking me much. I closed the door and began to snoop.

Tom's windowless office was small and without much furniture. It was as neat and impersonal as his apartment. The walls were bare except for a corkboard heavy with pinned up notes and articles, all pertaining to computer stuff. His desk drawers and filing cabinets were, surprisingly, unlocked. Trusting guy, I guess. Or maybe he simply had nothing to hide or keep safe. I snooped through files and found little of interest. I checked his "in" basket and found several unpaid invoices from a place called TechWorld. I remembered the name from when I'd checked the phone in Tom's apartment. I made a mental note to see what I could find out about TechWorld and moved on.

I booted up his computer and was able to get into his documents folder without a password. Not everyone protects their computer files with passwords and although this made it simple for me, it raised doubts in my mind about whether I'd find anything important. The folder was labelled "QWHD" and contained five files. I opened each of them and scanned some rather dry reading material and spreadsheets. Nothing was striking me as significant. I did notice that several of the documents made reference to information that could be found on "QWS," "MSHD," "TWHD" or "NavyHD." I was sure "QW" referred to QW Technologies and I guessed that "HD" was short for hard drive, but the other letters meant nothing to me.

I opened his e-mail and was halted by a request for a password. Finally, some safeguarded information. I clicked on a button that told the e-mail server I'd forgotten my password. It then asked me what my mother's maiden name was. I pulled out my cellphone and dialled Kathryn Wagner's number. She couldn't quite figure out why I'd want her mother's maiden name, but she finally revealed it, just to get rid of me. Budnyk. I typed it in. Voila! Tom had received 137 new e-mail messages since he'd last read them. After several minutes I'd only gotten through a handful and realized I'd have to order in food if I intended to read all of them. I'd be willing, but I didn't know how long Ms. Sassy Pants Secretary was going to let me stay. I decided to focus on the ones that were obviously personal in nature. There were two desperate messages from Chavell but it was a third message that caught my attention.

> Tom,
>
> *Thanks for agreeing to see me. I know you're uncomfortable about what I have to say. But it's important. You can't go through with this until we talk.*

Go through with what? The wedding? A business deal? A new haircut? There was no name at the end of the message. I scrolled down hoping this was a reply to an original message attached below. No luck. The sender's address was TWirp@hotmale.com. "TW" in big letters, "irp" in small. TWirp? Was it an acronym? Did the "TW" have any relation to the "TW" in "TWHD"? TechWorld? Were they initials? Someone with the last name of Wurz or Wagner perhaps? I had no idea what "irp" could stand for. Whoever TWirp was, he or she had had a meeting with Tom. I checked the date and saw the message had been sent late Thursday, the night before the rehearsal. Tom and TWirp could have met any time after that and before Tom's Sunday departure. I jotted TWirp's e-mail address down on a piece of scrap paper and stuck it into my pants pocket.

I hurried through a few other messages and although none of it was compelling, I took notes on what I found. Most of them were repeat messages from a handful of acquaintances wondering where Tom was. Obviously not wedding invitees.

I was about done when Charo stuck her nose into the room. "I'm getting ready to lock up. You about done? Mr. Wurz called. He was surprised to hear you were still here."

Now what do you suspect she was trying to tell me? I had one more thing to do though, so I had to stay on her good side. "Oh wow. Time really goes by fast. I'm real sorry to keep you waiting, especially on a Friday night. Perhaps I could meet you here tomorrow morning, say around seven or so? I can finish up then. I don't want to keep you waiting tonight."

She looked at me as if I was an alien. "Saturday?"

Yes, it is a day of the week, I wanted to tell her. Instead I smiled sweetly and pretended to get ready to leave. "Or Sunday would be okay too. I know Mr. Wurz wants this to get solved as soon as possible. It'll just take me a few minutes more."

She wasn't totally buying my act, but she wasn't taking any chances either. "I'll give you ten more minutes. Then I gotta get outta here, y'know. I'm meeting my friends at Champs."

Like I needed that information. And I could imagine the stories she—the new Erin Brockovich—would be telling after a few too many Labatt Lite with her friends. Big smile again. "Great. That's all the time I need." I kept on smiling like a cheeky monkey until she left the office As soon as she was gone I felt in my jacket pocket for the key I had taken from Tom's apartment. I still had not found the lock that matched it and this room held many good possibilities. His desk, several filing cabinets, a dusty suitcase behind the door.

No go.

Taking one last look around the room I admitted defeat. Except for the e-mail from TWirp, Tom's office had not been communicative. I placed the key back in my pocket and left the room. As I headed back to the front I passed by the other doors. The first two were locked and I guessed at least one of them had to be Randy Wurz's office. The third door opened into a washroom. I glanced at my watch and judging I had at least two minutes grace before being hunted down by Heather Locklear (the Sammy Jo years), I ducked inside, closing the door behind me. It was a bright, antiseptic room with the requisite bathroom facilities, sink, toilet, cupboard. I opened the mirrored cupboard doors above the sink to see what lurked behind them. As it turned out, nothing much but a collection of skin care products, hair spray, room deodorizer, Aspirin, eyewash solution, hydrogen peroxide, calamine lotion, Polysporin and rubbing alcohol. The bottom cupboard held a refuse container that had recently been emptied. As it had in Tom's apartment, the question ran through my head: Had I not found anything simply because there was nothing to find, or had I missed it?

Or…had someone already taken it?

It was after seven and already dark when I pulled into my garage. I heard a single, low "woof" from Barbra as I approached the back door of the house. She greeted me with a wagging tail and as much subtle excitement as a laid back Schnauzer can muster. Never a mood. Never a headache. Never a bad day. Barbra was always happy to see me. And no matter what anyone said, I know my coming home was the high point of her day. And come to think of it, it was usually one of the better parts of my day too.

As was our habit, Barbra submitted to a quick pat on the head before running off to her favourite pee spot. I barely had the chance to knock back a couple ounces of cold juice straight from the cardboard container before my dog indicated her desire to be let back in with a staid scrape of her delicate paw against the door.

Usually she spent a few minutes sniffing around but not today. I let her in and noticed a tiny cardboard tube fastened to her collar. Had it been there a few minutes earlier? It must have been. Inside was a note. It read, "I've been fed and played with and why aren't you ready yet? Hungry? Don't know what to wear? Go next door. Love, Barbra."

I recognized the writing. And the odd sense of humour.

Anthony Gatt.

Although the message attached to my dog was from Anthony, the invitation was to visit Sereena. Standing on her stoop I held up the cardboard vial when she answered my knock with an innocent look. She smiled with her mouth. It was the best I could hope for. I have never seen her smile with her eyes. Something in her past doesn't allow it. "My life has been arranged?" I said.

"Only a very small portion of it and doubtlessly for your own good," she told me as she sashayed her way to the kitchen. I followed.

Sereena's distinct and unique flair is on full display in her home. Each room is an ever-changing work of art. I know that if I ever spent more than six months away I'd never recognize the place. Sereena seems to care little about blending one room's look into the next. She regularly and unrepentantly mixes periods and paint colours into bizarre cornucopias that defy contemporary mores. The result is sometimes disarming, sometimes spectacular, and always unmistakably "Sereena."

I particularly loved the current kitchen. It reminded me of Santorini, one of my favourite destinations in the Greek islands (and, incidentally, the church on 11th Street). All bright white, blue and red. We sat in an austere nook of rough-hewn stone where she'd already laid out white wine chilling in a clay pot and bowls of herbed tomato, dark-skinned olives, chunky feta and hunks of torn bread. I wondered if she ever ate Chinese food in here. Or would she have to change the decor first?

"This is great, Sereena. But why?" I asked, dipping a piece of bread into a plate of oil, balsamic vinegar and minced garlic. I had a party to go to later, so I veered away from the garlic as much as possible.

"You're so suspicious. Have you always been?" Nice ploy. She was in a duelling mood.

"Not suspicious. Just curious. It's not everyday my neighbour takes my dog for a walk, feeds both of us, and then plies me with wine." Not everyday, but often.

She cocked her eyebrow. "When I ply someone with wine, the last thing they're doing is talking about it."

I laughed. "I believe that." She was wearing a simple muumuu-style dressing gown of icy blue silk. The colour emphasized the steel in her eyes. She knew this and used it to great effect.

"Anthony's party tonight. He knows how busy you are right now with this case you're sort of on. But he thinks it's important you take some time to enjoy yourself as well. I agree with him. You should go to this party. Strike that. You will go to this party."

Now I was suspicious. "Is he setting me up again? Is there going to be some unbearable blind date scene to get through? If there is, I am not going!"

"You should be so lucky. There's no one left in this city willing to go out with you, Russell Quant. You've turned them all down."

"That is not true!" It wasn't. I hoped it wasn't.

She poured me more wine. "Just go to the party, Russell. All you have to do is take a shower, slip on this shirt and…"

"What? Slip on what shirt?" I saw the wrapped package sitting on a nearby chair. "You're going to clothe me! You bought me a shirt?"

"And pants."

I was shocked. "B-b-but, why…I can't believe you did this…"

"Not me. I have better charities to waste my money on. It was Anthony."

"I take it Anthony doesn't trust my taste in clothes?"

"He said you should consider it an early birthday present." She looked at me as if assessing my ability to withstand her next comment. Apparently I passed the test. "He also said that if you showed up in 'those black pants' he would strip you naked in front of all his guests."

Those black pants? Could he have meant my wonderpants? He didn't like my wonderpants?

By 9:00 p.m. the temperature had dipped dramatically from the pleasant daytime high. There would be one doozy of a frost over night. I quivered inside my black leather coat with the fur lining as I walked toward the band shelter to meet Colleen before heading to Anthony's party. I left my car nearby on 20th Street where, strangely enough the block between Spadina and 4th Avenue had nose-in parking but only on one side of the street. Kiwanis Park was pretty much abandoned on a freezing October evening. I knew that much later it would come alive with cruising cars and young men tough or desperate enough to brave the cold in the hopes of finding some action. Unfortunately, I realized, I would fit right in. Anthony had selected a rather form-fitting costume for me. Shudder. After trying it on and tossing it off just as quickly, I was forced to wear it when I realized my black wonderpants, the official pants of social gatherings, were still balled up at the bottom of my suitcase. Even wonderpants couldn't survive that. I really had to unpack soon.

The slacks were a dove grey and some sort of crushed velvet material that seemed anxious to highlight every crevice of my lower body. They were tight around my lower waist and upper thighs, then flared out. The matching sweater was also grey, kind of fuzzy, V-necked and tight. I wasn't a fashion nerd, I knew that what I had on was in all the magazines and likely featured in the window of gatt, but I still missed the familiarity of my black pants. Surprisingly "crushed velvet" and "kind of fuzzy" clothes were not as warm as the words suggested. As I stood in the lighted area near the hulking, white band shelter that was nothing more than a domed platform, formally known as the Vimy Memorial, and shaking like a vibrator, I seriously considered returning home to change into something that was made of fleece. Then I saw two lights approaching me. Cyclists.

Two women dismounted and joined me in the minimal protection of the band shelter. They each wore paunchy jackets and leg warmers and looked toasty warm.

"This is my partner, Norma Epps," Colleen introduced the other woman.

Norma was a dark-haired, fit-looking woman with the reddest lips and cheeks I'd ever seen. It wasn't cosmetics or exertion from biking—she just had naturally bright colouring. She shook my hand enthusiastically. Whereas Colleen was standoffish, her lover was much more willing to be friendly. Another case of opposites attracting.

"Hi. We spoke on the phone. I was the one who told you where to find Colleen."

"Yes, of course. Nice to meet you, Norma. I appreciated your help."

"No problem."

Colleen spoke up. "Sorry about all this cloak and dagger, meet you at night in the park stuff. It wasn't until I told Norma what I'd suggested to you on the phone that she pointed out how weird it might have sounded."

I shook my head to be polite. "No, really, it's okay. I'm glad you called."

"It's just that at work it's too busy to talk and Norma and I go biking down here almost every night."

"Somehow Colleen thought meeting here at nine o'clock on a Friday night is a normal thing to do. But, only if you're a cyclist," Norma explained.

I smiled and nodded. "Good bike paths here." It was getting cold. "You said you had some information?"

Colleen shifted gears just as efficiently. "Yes. I don't know if it's important, but I thought you should know. After we spoke, I decided to take a look around Tom's apartment. We have an extra key. He has no plants or pets, so we've never really used it, but he wanted us to have it in case of an emergency."

I hadn't wanted Colleen to start doing her own detective work, but from the little I did know of her, I should have expected it. "Did you find something?"

"Yes. His bike is missing."

"Tom was into biking too," Norma explained. "We often did the Meewasin Trail together and usually a few long distance trips in the summer."

I bobbed my head, unsure of the importance of the information.

"I know you were wondering about Tom's whereabouts the day of the wedding," Colleen said. "And I know for a fact that when I dropped Tom off the night before, the bike was in his apartment. Now it's gone. He must have ridden his bike somewhere on Saturday, or before leaving for France on Sunday, and didn't go back to his place."

"Or he did go back but didn't bring the bike with him," Norma added.

This was interesting news indeed. But what did it mean? Had Tom ridden his bike over to a friend's house and had the cohort drive him to the airport? But certainly he hadn't hauled his luggage by bicycle? Or did he go somewhere by bike and for some reason return by some other means? Regardless, this could mean someone other than Colleen was the last person to see Tom.

"Are you sure about this?"

"Absolutely," Colleen told me. I hadn't known her long, but I trusted that when she said something, she meant it. Nothing much left her mouth without being well thought out. "Tom is a fanatic about his machine. He babies that thing like it's a pet. He never leaves it outdoors. It was expensive—a Trek 5200 road bike. What a beauty—bright blue, handmade in the US, an OCLV 120 carbon frame—that's Optimum Compaction Low Void carbon—one hundred grams lighter than the 1999 Tour de France winner—it's the world's lightest, strongest frame material. Anyway, my point is, he wouldn't just leave it somewhere without a very good reason.

I think if you find that bike, or who has it, you might find answers to some of your other questions."

"You could be right." I was getting quite cold by this point and stamped my feet to encourage blood flow. I looked forward to finding warm respite soon, but apparently our meeting wasn't over yet.

"We talked with Harold," Colleen said with little emotion. But there was something powerful going on in her eyes.

"Oh?" I said lightly. I knew what was coming.

"Harold has no idea what you're doing, does he?"

I met the woman's searching eyes with what I hoped was an innocent look. "Why do you think that?"

"We didn't tell him." This from Norma. She obviously wasn't the game playing type.

I looked at Colleen questioningly. What was going on? If they talked to Chavell and found out I wasn't working for him, why not tell him? Why protect me?

"It seems to me that you're looking out for Tom," she said, answering my question before I asked it. "Trying to figure out what happened."

"Yes," I told her, "that's true."

"If it isn't," she said darkly, "we'll have something to talk about."

I wasn't sure if I'd just received a threat or simply a serious warning, or even which of the two I'd prefer. I thanked the women and watched them pedal away.

I had all these clues, the missing bike, the key that unlocked nothing, the half-heart pendant, the mysterious e-mail message and the fact that Tom doesn't seem to be the type to just up and run away. Each on their own seemed trivial, but together they painted a picture I couldn't figure out. Yet. All I really wanted to do at that point was go home, warm up and think about what I'd just heard. But duty called. Anthony and Jared live in the penthouse suite of the Radisson building, a mere two-minute walk from where I stood. I convinced myself I should at least make a quick appearance.

And maybe, if I was lucky, I could get away with keeping my coat on and no one would have to see my outfit.

Chapter 9

A BLACK-SKIRTED, WHITE-BLOUSED WOMAN offered to take my coat at the door. Her badge told me her name was Betsy and that she was on loan from The Saskatoon Club, a private business club only a few blocks away. I pretended to debate and finally told her I'd keep my coat on for a while until I warmed up. Although I knew the fur lining might make me hot in no time, the black leather was an okay match with my party boy outfit and gave me that covered up feeling I like when I step into a crowd of strangers.

It was after nine-thirty and by the noise floating into the foyer from spaces beyond it was obvious the party was in full swing. I spent a minute in the relative calm of the entrance evaluating the artwork and colour of the walls. Nice. I studied the clothesline of halogens and wondered if Betsy would ever leave the foyer long enough for me to make a break for it. I hate parties. No. That's not entirely true. I enjoy parties once I'm in the throes, drink in hand and safe in the company of someone I know. So I guess what I hate is entering parties. When I throw a party I fear no one will come. When I attend a party I fear I'll find no one to talk to. Neither has ever happened as far as I can recall.

I poked my nose around a wall and surveyed the crowd milling about the living room. I could hardly see beyond the well-dressed throng to the incredible view outside the wrap-around windows. This won't be too bad, I thought. Really big parties are okay. Even if you don't know anybody, who's going to notice? And, the best part, you can usually leave without causing a stir. The worst are medium-sized parties where everyone notices when you come in and when you leave. Probably because the party is so boring they have nothing else to do.

"Oh for chrissakes!" A woman's voice.

I could feel my protective jacket being yanked from my shoulders. I swirled around and saw Sereena. Although I'd been with her only a short time ago, she had given me absolutely no hint that she too would be attending this party. As far as I knew, she was staying at home to eat ice cream and watch a Bogart movie. Fat chance.

I looked at Sereena in mock anger and made an unattractive noise in protest over losing my jacket. Sereena's hair was piled luxuriously on top of her head, stray tendrils trailing down around her face. She wore a near-transparent turquoise shift held up by invisible fishing wire straps. She was a box of dynamite. And I could see in her flashing eyes that she might explode if I insisted on keeping my coat. Without another word she turned on impressive stilettos and ferried my leather away.

"Nice ass, Quant. Is it getting bigger?" Another woman's voice.

Again I swirled around. I was getting dizzy. It was Errall. Tall, dark, intense, with features so sharp they could cut ice. Errall Strane is almost six feet tall with shiny, chestnut hair, flawless skin and eyes so blindingly blue it almost hurts to look at them too long. She is smart, driven, quick-witted and a workaholic. She and Kelly have been together for seven years. Kelly is my friend— Errall is someone who sleeps with my friend. At least that's how our relationship began and remained for quite some time. Errall and I see the world in different ways. This leads to quarrels and nasty looks. But now I find her interesting and often helpful to talk to. To use a weird analogy, Kelly is my comfortable pair of ten-year-old loafers that slip on with ease, Errall is the spit-and-polished, shiny, black, lace-up Oxfords that click when I walk and feel a little tight around the instep. I prefer the loafers, but sometimes nothing will do but a pair of Oxfords.

"Don't get me going on these clothes. From gatt." I grabbed the wineglass in her hand and took a healthy sip of a woodsy Merlot.

She cocked one of her well-shaped black eyebrows and extended a fluttering palm towards my sweater. "It works, Russell. I never knew you had definition. Look at those triceps!"

"Stop it!" I brushed away her hand and surreptitiously glanced at my arm. "You look terrific tonight, as usual," I told her. Errall wore something silver, sleek, sleeveless and high-necked.

She leaned in close and whispered, "Makeup dyke."

I chuckled. She wasn't a particularly with-it lesbian. "I think they're called lipstick dykes."

"Yeah, whatever." She was already busy surveying the room. Looking for potential clients to schmooze no doubt.

"Where's your better half?" Actually I consider Kelly her better three-quarters but decided to keep that to myself.

"Let me take you to her," Errall said, weaving a long, thin arm through mine with the impressive triceps. "I think I saw her with Jared, hiding in some corner, pretending they hate parties."

On the way we helped ourselves to more wine off a passing tray and Errall greeted a few thousand of her closest friends and business acquaintances. I thought I recognized one of the waiters. Indeed we found Kelly and Jared laughing about something in a dim corner, six shooter glasses sitting empty nearby.

Errall shot her lover a look. "I guess we're taking a cab home tonight?"

Kelly ignored the comment and rushed over to give me a welcoming hug.

Next came Jared. I embraced him and, as always, marvelled at the existence of something so beautiful. His precise facial features appear sharp from a distance but are softened on close inspection by the sheen of his impeccable olive skin. His hair, a mass of loose and boyishly unkempt curls, has a unique copper tint that sets his golden green eyes ablaze. But despite the incredible wrapping paper and corny as it might sound, Jared's heart, deep within his muscular chest is his most attractive feature.

For years I have suspected the worst: that I am in love with him. But I've never allowed myself to discover the truth.

At different times since I'd first met Jared, I toyed with the idea of telling Anthony. If for no other reason but to alleviate the weirdness I feel when the three of us are together. Somehow I thought it might make it easier if Anthony knew and absolved me of all guilt. He is a pretty understanding guy in that way. In my less generous moments I've wondered if Anthony might not just give me Jared like he would a sweater I've fawned over. I know Anthony loves Jared. But he also loves his sapphire pinky ring and beaching in Minorca.

"When did you get back?" I asked as I pulled back from our hug and we exchanged smiles. Suddenly I found myself flexing and sucking in and sticking out the different parts of my body brazenly shown off by my new duds, wondering if Jared would notice. Bad, bad, bad boy!

"Just a couple of hours ago," he told me, his skin still aglow from whatever sun-drenched location he'd arrived from. "I'm glad to see you. You look great."

"Oh, yeah," I said with little conviction. "What are you two up to?"

"Kelly and I were just planning a little dinner party for next month. We need an event more low-key than this where we can actually talk and visit without a million people hanging around."

"I want to catch Councillor Manning before he leaves," Errall said as she extricated herself from the group. "Don't you three hide out here all night." I saw her and Kelly exchange winks before she strode off.

"That's a great idea," I said. "Count me in."

"Great," Kelly said, "because it's at your place. And you're cooking. And providing the booze. And entertainment."

"Tell me again what you two contribute to this whole thing?"

Kelly beamed, slightly intoxicated. "Planning expertise."

"I think I want to be part of the planning committee. Jared, you around for a bit this time?"

"Unfortunately no. I'm out of here on Monday."

"Where to now?" I liked the fact that I always had to ask. Jared was not one to volunteer details about his glamourous life without some goading.

"Actually New York for a bit. There's a lot going on there right now. How about you? You on a case? Kelly was telling me you just got back from France. You're getting to be quite the international spy, Mr. Bond."

I aimed a light punch at his mighty biceps. "Someone has to keep the world safe from the domination of evil in all its horrific forms!"

Kelly scrunched up her doll-like face and nudged her body into Jared's. "I think we need another drink before we hear anymore of this."

Jared agreed with a grin and nod. "Anthony has been looking for you."

"We've been telling him you were in the bathroom with a waiter for the past hour," Kelly joked.

I gave her a sour look. "Which one?"

"The one off the kitchen."

She and Jared broke into gales of laughter. The kind that was heavily inspired by alcohol.

"Ha, ha. I meant which waiter, not which bathroom." I felt I needed to explain.

"All of them." More laughter.

I stepped away in mock disgust. "I think I'll go find Anthony now. I've decided I don't like this conversation."

"Come back soon!" Jared called as I rejoined the salmon run upstream.

"Send over a waiter!" Kelly shouted, holding up her empty glass. "If you can spare one!"

I spent the next few minutes circulating the room without seeing another person I knew. I ate snacks off silver trays and drank another glass of wine. I was considering making an unobserved exit when I finally caught sight of my host. Anthony saw me at the same time and we slowly headed towards one another. I covered more distance than he did because constant interruptions from party guests delayed his progress.

"I love the toggery!" Anthony said to me as he placed an arm warmly about my shoulders. "What taste! What style! What an unerring eye for what's now and what's wow!"

I smirked. "Anthony, you picked out the clothes."

"Ohmygosh!" He feigned surprise like a pro. "You're right! I'm so embarrassed to have gone on like that!"

"You're just pissed off more people didn't hear."

"They will before they leave," he said with a mischievous smile. "Make sure you circle the room a few times so everyone can get a good look. I'm so glad you made it. Are you having fun? Did you see Jared? Have you eaten?"

I was about to tell him what a droll party it was and that I was off to find something better to do when I caught sight of a familiar face over Anthony's shoulder. "What is she doing here?"

Anthony turned his head ever so slightly. "Of whom are we speaking?"

"Next to the bar," I said, "wearing the red disco dress and Adrienne Barbeau hair."

Anthony considered the woman. "I believe she came in with Randy's group."

"Randy Wurz?"

"Yes. QW Technologies, as well as Randy and his wife personally, are big donors to the theatre."

I couldn't believe my luck. "Is Randy Wurz here?"

Anthony nodded and eyed me carefully. "Yes. I suppose you'll be wanting an introduction?"

"Could I get my coat back first?"

Without another word, he directed me by the elbow across the room to a small group of four men hurriedly discussing business before their wives caught them. Randy Wurz was not quite six feet tall with an average build, light sandy hair, green eyes and a small but noticeable mole on his jaw. He looked like a man who took care of himself and was particular about his appearance. He had an expensive and precise haircut, wore a pricey, conservative suit with matching belt and shoes and glistening cuff-links. The embedded diamonds looked real.

As we shook hands I noticed he'd recently had a manicure and wore a multi-carat, diamond pinkie ring on his right hand. To match the cuff-links I guess. His smile was a testament to cosmetic dentistry.

Once Anthony made the introductions he skillfully managed to move the two of us away from the group without being overly transparent and then left us. Randy Wurz seemed as surprised to see me, as I was to see him.

"I understand you were able to take a look around Tom's office today?" he said. "Did you find what you were looking for?"

"Yes, thank you. I appreciate your help."

"Anything to help out. Still no word from Tom?"

"No. I know a party isn't the greatest place for it, but I was wondering if I could ask you a couple of questions about that."

He looked around as if thinking up an excuse, but finding none he said, "Sure, of course. What would you like to know?"

"I know Tom was one of the founding members of QW Technologies so I assume he was an important part of the business' day-to-day operations. Is that going to be a problem the longer he stays away?"

"Well naturally my first concern is for Tom, not the business. He and I are good friends as well as business partners."

"How long have you been partners?"

"We started QW as soon as we graduated from university. We began just wanting to have some fun making computer games. We had some pretty nice successes and the business took off. Tom is Mr. Technical and I'm Mr. Marketing. So we make a good team. Tom in particular spends a lot of time on research and development. While he does R&D, I'm out there peddling our existing products. Works out pretty well for both of us."

"Was Tom working on anything important before he left? Something you'd expect he'd want to get back to pretty quickly?"

Randy shook his head as he thought over his response. "Not really. He was working on a couple of small projects, but nothing major. Nothing that was anywhere close to moving off the drawing board. You have to understand, Mr. Quant, the computer game industry changes faster than you can toggle a joystick. A lot of what Tom works on is trying to second-guess what the consumer will want—not today or tomorrow but the next day. So, by its nature, many of Tom's R&D ideas are pie-in-the-sky kind of stuff. But hey, you never know until you try. That's why we hit it big in the early days with Avenging Angel—up until then, no one had seen anything quite like it. And given time, we'll do it again. Tom's a genius."

I realized Randy hadn't answered my first question. "Is the company in trouble with Tom gone?"

He laughed uneasily. "You sound like one of my customers, worried if we can still meet our commitments. Like I said, Tom spends a lot of his time on R&D. I handle the real stuff—making sales, overseeing production, making sure sales orders are filled. I run the business. QW is okay for now."

"For now?"

"Like I said, in this industry, things change faster than you can say microchip. It's a turbulent world out there. We have to keep pace."

"You're worried then?"

"Nah. Tom just needs some time to get himself together. I'm sure he'll be calling soon. Generally he's a pretty level-headed guy."

My ears pricked up. Generally? Had there been times in the past when Tom Osborn had shown hints of behaviour that was not level-headed? "You mean he's done something like this before?"

I could feel the space between us grow cold. Randy Wurz pulled back slightly.

"Oh no. Nothing like this…exactly."

Was this man was trying to tell me something without actually saying the words? Was he uncertain whether he could trust me? I had to tread carefully. "No, of course not. But sometimes he gets upset about things? He needs to get away from work for a few days?"

"He gets anxious," Randy said, obviously growing uncomfortable with the conversation. I guessed he was wondering what the line was between betraying his friend and helping him. "About personal stuff."

I nodded. "He talks to you about that sort of stuff?"

He made a funny movement with his head that wasn't a shake or a nod. Maybe it meant "sort of." I didn't get to find out because at that moment a sparkling creature in a low-cut gown nuzzled Randy's side like an impatient cat.

"You two aren't talking business I hope!" She said it as a half-serious, half-joshing warning. It was the wife. It's hard to explain exactly how she pulled it off, but she wore her party dress in a way that conveyed without doubt not only how expensive it was but that she certainly hadn't bought it in Saskatoon. I checked her neck to see if she'd accidentally left the designer tag untucked. She hadn't.

"No, not at all," Randy quickly told her.

He introduced us and they glided away soon after under the guise of having to refresh their drinks. I didn't think Randy Wurz wanted to go any further with our talk. He was probably feeling guilty about revealing the confidences of a friend. I was anxious to hear those confidences. Damn cat. This was the first indication I'd had that perhaps the relationship between Chavell and Tom Osborn was not quite as rosy as I'd been led to believe. It was not so far-fetched that Randy Wurz would know something Tom's family or friends did not. Sometimes it was easier to confide in a third party outside your inner circle. Randy would have been the perfect candidate if Tom needed to unload. He was someone Tom had a long-standing friendship with and someone he trusted.

So what did this mean, I wondered.

I was standing in the middle of the lively room when another thought hit me in between the eyes.

Anthony.

Why did he immediately assume I'd want an introduction to Randy Wurz? He hadn't even asked why.

As the beautiful people of Saskatoon bustled around me, I tried to recall our conversation. Had I said anything to lead him to guess the importance of QW Technologies to me?

The pieces began to fall together. Harold Chavell said he'd been referred by an acquaintance. Someone who'd assured him I could be counted on to recognize the special sensitivity of the case. Anthony Gatt.

Harold Chavell and Anthony Gatt? Very possible. Now that I thought about it, it was quite likely these two men would know each other. Actually, given the similarity of their lifestyles and social standing in a community the size of Saskatoon, it was near impossible that they didn't.

I found Anthony deep in conversation with a local newscaster and the dean of the College of Commerce. He saw the look on my face as I approached and extricated himself from the duo with practiced aplomb, diverting me into a private nook behind an oversized salt-water aquarium.

"You're vexed with me," he said with alarming insight. "Yes, I suggested Harold give you a call about finding Tom."

The frothy head was blown right off my latte. "You know Harold Chavell and Tom Osborn?" I asked as I watched the colourful reflections of exotic fish swim across Anthony's face.

"Yes, of course. For years."

"Why didn't you tell me you knew them?"

"Would it have made a difference?"

I didn't appreciate the smirk on his tanned face. I was happy to see a strand of flaxen hair askew at the back of his head. I didn't tell him about it. "I would have liked to have known, that's all. I appreciate your recommending me for the job. I just wish you'd have told me. For one thing, it would have saved me a lot of trouble trying to find out who Chavell and Tom really are."

"I can't help you there. Jared and I know Harold and Tom, but only the public façade. That's all most people know of them. Not many people get any closer. They are very private in that way."

"But you're two high-profile gay couples making it in the straight world."

"Oh crap on that. We know they're gay and they know we're gay, but so what? It doesn't make us anything more than nodding acquaintances. Just because you see someone with the same coat you're wearing doesn't mean you start having drinks together. It just means that you have the same good taste. That's all. In fact, the only time we've ever traded on the discrete knowledge of our shared sexuality was when Tom disappeared. Chavell called me hoping I could suggest an investigator. He didn't want to use his regular lawyer or advisors. This was extremely private. I knew you'd keep it that way. You and I didn't need to discuss it."

I nodded. "No. I suppose not."

"Our connection to and success in the straight world is a tenuous one at best. We succeed at it because we play by their rules most of the time. Or at least we make them believe we are. We can escort a man to ritzy social events, refer to ourselves as 'we' and 'us,' make no excuses for leaving at the same time, and hold our heads high— just as long as we remain scandal free. But, one nasty homosexual imbroglio and we lose more ground than for a thousand straight divorces. And that's our story. Harold and Tom have even more to lose because many of their circle supposedly don't know they come as a pair."

I nodded my understanding and an irritating thought entered my mind. Was this why Chavell asked me to stop looking for Tom? Had it suddenly occurred to him that he could avoid scandal by simply ignoring what happened? I hoped not.

After I got home I gratefully slid off the second skin that was my outfit and deposited it on the dry-clean pile. And that was being generous. My first intention was to throw it in the garbage. It was late but I knew I wouldn't be able to sleep. I had to ease myself down from the high-octane infusion of Anthony's party. I shrugged on my bathrobe and went to the kitchen, Barbra at my heels. A glass of water for me, a dry biscuit treat for her. We went into the den that doubles as my home office. It's a small, square room hidden down a hallway from my bedroom. I've filled it with bookshelves, a big desk, a couple of heavy leather couches and best of all, a gas fireplace that ignites with a flick of a switch. Barbra loves this room. Like many dogs, she's fond of small spaces and she adores the instant heat of the fake fire. I turned it on, and as is her habit, she stretched out before the grate and immediately fell into a snore-filled slumber. I plopped down into my comfy desk chair and opened my e-mail. The inbox had only one message in it. It was a joke of the day from a friend in Regina. Delete. I was about to close the program but instead I hit the compose button. There was one more person I wanted to talk to. In the To space I wrote "TWirp@hotmale.com" In the empty message screen I typed:

> Dear TWirp,
> I know about your meeting with Tom Osborn. Let's meet to discuss.
> A friend,
> R

I reread my brief message once and hit Send before I could change my mind. This was a big part of my job, throwing out a fishing line without being sure what I might catch, if anything at all.

I stretched out on the floor alongside my dog and read a chapter of a novel by firelight before eventually heading off to bed.

That night, while Saskatoon slept, more leaves turned from green to shades of orange, maroon and yellow. Some simply froze to brown.

Normally I don't go to PWC on weekends unless I'm on a case. And even then, I tend to work from home. Although I wasn't officially on the Chavell case anymore, a mind game of information racquetball drove me out of bed and into my office on Saturday morning. I wanted to make notes and flowcharts and update character descriptions. I still felt I had a puzzle to solve and suspected someone in Saskatoon was the missing piece. It was a frustrating process. I barely knew the questions, never mind the answers.

Generally weekends around PWC are quiet, so I was startled later that morning by a knock at my door. Alberta barely made it in during the week, never mind the weekend, but Errall and Beverly occasionally had clients in on Saturdays and sometimes Sundays.

"Looking for Dr. Chaney's office or Errall Strane?" I asked the man I found on the other side of my door.

He was tall, square, with hair just a touch longer than a brush cut. He wore a light brown trench coat over a suit and carried a serious briefcase. He looked like a football player dressed for church. "You're Russell Quant?" he asked in a surprisingly cultured voice.

"Yes."

"Could I have a few minutes of your time? My name is Clark Shiwaga. I'm Harold Chavell's attorney."

Oh, oh. Chavell must have found out I was still prying. I moved aside to let the man into my office and closed the door. Had Chavell sent over his brute of a lawyer to rough me up? Or maybe I watch too many cop shows.

"Would you care for something to drink, Mr. Shiwaga?"

He shook his blocky head.

"Please, take a seat." I indicated the chair in front of my desk. I fixed myself a cup of coffee and took my place. "How can I help you?"

"Late tonight or early tomorrow morning the media will carry a story about a body pulled from the bottom of Pike Lake."

I stared at the man. I didn't understand why he was in my office on a Saturday morning, in his lawyer drag, telling me this story about a body. "Yes?" Not a snappy reply.

"I'd like to have your assurance that you will not reveal to anyone, for the time being, what I'm about to tell you," Mr. Shiwaga said.

Seeing as Chavell no longer employed me, I didn't owe him or his legal eagle any assurances. "I'm not certain I can do that. Not without more information about what you're thinking of telling me." Suppose this body had been murdered and he was about to tell me who the killer was? Caution was important here.

"Your *temporary* silence is to protect the family. The next of kin has not yet been notified."

"Whose next of kin?"

It seemed forever before he answered my question. And when he did, I was speechless.

"The body in the lake, Mr. Quant, is that of...Tom Osborn."

Chapter 10

THE NEWS STRUCK ME LIKE A SPEEDING FREIGHT TRAIN. "Did you say Tom Osborn? Are you telling me it was Tom Osborn's body they found in Pike Lake?"

Clark Shiwaga nodded. I could not read the look on his face. He didn't appear prepared to elaborate.

"How can that be? Tom Osborn is in Europe."

"Not anymore."

"Why are you here, Mr. Shiwaga?" No use beating around the bush.

"Mr. Chavell would like to hire you. I have a cheque to retain your services. Same amount as before. Is that appropriate?"

"What is it exactly I'm being hired to do?"

"Last time he wanted you to find Tom. This time, he wants you to find his killer."

He was murdered! "He was murdered?"

"Yes."

"Are you sure?"

"Yes."

"How? How do you know all this if it hasn't even been made public?"

The big lawyer studied his hands for a while, pausing before he answered. "I have contacts."

"Contacts who just happened to know that your client would be interested in this information?"

"Yes."

This didn't jive with what I'd heard from Anthony last night. According to him, Chavell had called him for suggestions on a private investigator because he specifically didn't want to involve his own lawyer. Yet here was that lawyer sitting before me and acting as if he was in on the whole thing. How to phrase this delicately? "I was under the impression Mr. Chavell did not use his business advisors in personal matters." Hopefully that would get the point across.

Shiwaga seemed a bit put off by this. "I handle all of Mr. Chavell's legal matters. Business and personal."

So much for tact. It rarely works. "Do you know Mr. Chavell is gay and that Tom Osborn was his partner?"

"Yes." The answer came quickly.

"Does Mr.Chavell know that you know?"

"Yes. However Mr. Chavell believes most other people do not have that information."

"But he is incorrect in that belief?"

Shiwaga's eyes never left mine as he nodded slowly. "To a certain extent… yes."

"So once the Pike Lake body was identified, your contact knew you and your client would be interested?"

"Will you take the job?" he asked without answering my question. I knew the answer anyway.

"There's one big difference from the last time Mr. Chavell hired me. The police weren't involved. Now they are. It's their job to find the killer. I used to be a policeman in this city and I can assure you they will undertake a complete and thorough investigation."

"Yes, I'm sure they will. However, there are some…special circumstances here."

"Such as?"

"It is only a matter of time before investigators from the police and media get wind of the relationship between the victim and Mr. Chavell. My client is concerned that suspicion will fall quickly upon him when that happens. Not only is that suspicion unfounded, but it would be…cataclysmic to Mr. Chavell's reputation in this city. You already have all the background information. You respect the sensitivity of the matter. You know the people involved. Certainly some of the work you did for the former case will help you here. And, you know Mr. Chavell is innocent."

"I don't know that, Mr. Shiwaga."

He acknowledged this fact with a curt nod. "Mr. Chavell greatly valued his relationship with Tom Osborn. Above all else, Mr. Quant, he wants to ensure everything possible is being done to find out the truth about what happened to Tom. Mr. Chavell knows that with the police involved your freedom to investigate will be restricted. He knows this may all come out to the public eventually no matter what you or I do. But if that happens, he wants someone who is looking for the truth while the police are being blinded by erroneous assumptions or simple homophobia or both. Certainly you can understand that?"

I nodded.

"Then you'll take the case?" he asked one more time. The man held out an envelope that contained another retainer cheque. I felt a twinge of guilt. But that didn't last long. Finding Tom Osborn's killer was not going to be a walk in the park. I took the envelope and set it down on my desk without opening it.

"How was he killed?"

Shiwaga's shoulders relaxed. He took my question as a yes. Which, I guess, it was.

"I don't have that information."

"When was he killed?"

"I don't have that information."

"Was it last night? Two days ago? Three? Your contacts must have given you some idea."

"They didn't."

"What *do* you know?"

"I know Tom Osborn is dead."

Some contacts.

Clark Shiwaga rose, indicating an end to our meeting. I followed suit and shook hands with the lawyer. I caught him glancing around my office and sensed he did not approve of the decor. I guessed that, as attorney for one of Saskatoon's richest men, Clark Shiwaga was not used to doing business in a less than pristine environment. I was about to say something but instead showed remarkable restraint and graciously showed him out.

Clark Shiwaga hadn't been much help. All I knew was that Tom Osborn was dead and my client's head might find itself on the chopping block for it. I had to have more details before I'd be able to efficiently work this case.

"Kirsch," the voice answered the phone.

"Kirsch, it's Russell Quant."

There was a slight pause. He'd been waiting for the call. "Back from Italy already?"

Bugger. He knew very well that it was France. "France."

"Oh right. That's pretty much the same thing though, right?"

I tried to stifle a groan. He loved to play the redneck with me. "Pretty much." If you let on that he was getting your goat, you were lost. "I'm looking for some information on a body pulled from Pike Lake yesterday."

Again the hesitation. "Body?"

"Darren, don't screw with me. We both know what I'm talking about."

"In that case we both also know that information has not been made public yet."

"Do you know who it was?"

"Mmmm."

Darren Kirsch, I hate to admit, is no dummy. I had no doubt that as soon as the body had been identified as Tom Osborn he'd have remembered our conversation. He knew I'd gone abroad to search for Tom. He just hadn't counted on my knowing about the murder so quickly. And fair enough. If it weren't for Clark Shiwaga, I probably wouldn't have heard about it until after the weekend, along with the rest of the TV audience. "You hungry?" That would take him further off guard. We've never eaten together.

"Uh, nah…"

"One o'clock. Colourful Mary's. Downtown." I hung up.

I was confident he'd show up. He wasn't sure how much I knew, but he knew I knew something. He couldn't risk the chance of missing out on information about a fresh murder case. Inviting him to a gay-owned restaurant was just my way of tweaking his nose for being such a prick.

I spent the rest of the morning fattening my file on the now re-opened, new and improved, Chavell case. Upgraded from "Errant Lover" to "Murder." This was a definite step up from "The Case of the Missing Casserole Dish." Before leaving for the restaurant I checked my e-mail. I was hoping my message to TWirp would elicit a quick response. It hadn't.

It was a few minutes before one o'clock when I walked into Colourful Mary's. The Saturday lunch crowd was noisy. Most of the customers were off for the weekend and happy to loll about over fruity teas and dessert rather than having to dash back to work at five minutes to one. A dreary autumn drizzle and mushroom soup sky cloaked the diners in the cozy, warm space. I shook the rain pebbles off my black lambskin jacket and scanned the room. A couple of familiar faces but no one I really knew. Good. Mary was showing a group of university students around the bookstore. One or all were probably thinking of doing a psychology paper on homosexuality. Always a trendy subject. I caught her eye and she nodded toward the rear of the restaurant.

Darren sat alone in a small booth, nursing a jar of juice. He looked uncomfortable and perplexed. Good. Just as I'd hoped.

Darren Kirsch is the archetype City of Saskatoon policeman. I generally dislike stereotypes, but in this case it's hard to deny. I know. I used to work with these guys. Every other policeman in Saskatoon is six foot plus with a top heavy, muscular body, short, dark hair, neat, dark moustache, deep-set, stern eyes and a snarly nose. Most have either been hockey players or football players or brought up on a farm. It's uncanny. And Darren has "the look." But as I appraised him now, I saw there was something more. It was his eyes. They weren't as harsh as I've always thought they were. Maybe it was because he didn't know I was around. They seemed soft and almost innocent and, archetype or not, he is cute. Cute, cute, cute and as het as a muscle car.

As I slid into the booth, the innocent look on Darren's face disappeared rather quickly. He was no pushover. I wanted something from him and he wanted something from me. And neither of us was ready to give it away.

"Like the place?" I asked. "Come here often?"

"No, but I bet you do," he said.

I frowned. "Why would you think that?"

The grimace on his face was priceless. "Before you got here, I thought I'd take a look in the magazine rack for an auto mag. I found one called *Hot Rod*."

I almost choked on my tongue. I valiantly fought to keep the corners of my mouth from turning upwards. "Not what you were looking for?"

"Not quite. But I bought you a subscription as a birthday present."

"Thoughtful of you."

"Uh-huh." He took another sip of his juice and surveyed the room with a practiced cop's eye. He shifted uncomfortably on the pumpkin-coloured leather booth.

"The food is actually quite good here."

"I already ordered for both of us," he said to me as if we'd been married for fifteen years.

I wasn't sure I'd agree with his choices but I didn't want to argue this early in the meeting. "Great."

"How do you know about the body, Quant?" He'd obviously exhausted his ability for small talk. So much for getting to know one another.

"It was on the news," I lied.

"Tomorrow's news."

"Uh-huh." Damn. He caught me.

"How do you know?" he repeated.

"Alberta Lougheed, who works out of the office next to mine, is a psychic. She told me." Playing cute with Darren was a risk. The look on his face told me I'd best try another tack. "I heard it from a client. Well, actually my client's lawyer."

"Who's your client?"

"Who's the body?"

Darren looked away while a waiter filled our water mugs and took my drink order. I took the time to consider my next move. It was obvious we were heading for an impasse. I wanted information about Tom's death. Darren wanted information on who my client was and why I'd been hired to find Tom Osborn in the first place. I knew I couldn't tell Darren about Chavell. If I did, he'd be the cop's number one suspect in no time. I couldn't reveal his identity. But I had nothing left to offer.

"Darren, I know the body was Tom Osborn."

He nodded. "You know a lot, don't you? Name's the same as the fellow you were looking for in France. Did you find him?"

"No." There. I'd given him something. Now it was his turn. "Can you tell me what happened? I understand it wasn't a simple drowning."

"No it wasn't, and that's why I can't tell you anymore."

At this rate, this conversation was going to be over before our food arrived. I hate silent meals. "Darren, I know you'd like to know who hired me to find Tom Osborn. But I can't tell you that. Not yet, anyway." If the police found out about Tom and Chavell on their own, I could certainly tell Darren a little more then. "I guess what I'm saying is that I can't offer you anything right now, but I'd appreciate anything you could tell me about how Tom Osborn died." All I had to appeal to was our professional relationship, which to date wasn't much, and the possibility of useful information later on. Cops and private eyes, it was a give and take deal. But right now, I needed to take without giving. Not a position of strength.

Darren remained silent while our lunch was served. I looked on in surprise as Marushka herself brought out plate after plate of doughy triangles, some stuffed with potato, others with cabbage or stewed fruit, and floating in cream and butter, along with thick slabs of meat so tender they barely kept their shape.

"Now this boy knows how to eat!" she proclaimed as she patted Darren's shoulder and waddled away.

Darren began filling his plate without a word.

"Was there any country in particular you had in mind to feed when you ordered all this?"

He shook his head, reddening at the ears. "I couldn't understand what she was saying most of the time. I told her to make enough for two."

I snorted. Enough for two in Marushka language means enough for two herds.

Then he said, "He was found by two elderly Pike Lake residents on a walk."

Pike Lake is a small oxbow lake twenty minutes southwest of Saskatoon. It's surrounded by a couple of rows of cabins hidden amongst bluffs of spruce and aspen trees, a modest beach and a camping area. It's a popular weekend retreat for city folks who want to get away but don't want to drive north to one of the more scenic lakeside resorts that Saskatchewan is known for.

"I thought Pike Lake is closed this time of year," I said.

"There are a few permanent residents out there. Anyway, the body had floated to the top and got caught in some brush by the side of the lake. The autopsy results won't be in for a while, but we don't need 'em to determine cause of death. He didn't drown. He was shot in the back of the head."

I lost my appetite. Shit! Shot in the back of the head. What a cowardly act. I shook my head as I imagined Harold Chavell hearing this grisly news. I could barely stomach it. Chavell must have been inconsolable.

Darren continued. "Interesting thing, there were rope burns around the ankles. Looks like the body had been weighted down with cinder blocks but somehow came loose. Guess the murderer didn't get his Boy Scout's badge for knot tying. Anyway, whoever killed him went to a lot of trouble to ensure the body was never found."

I shook my head in disgust.

"This is all speculation right now, Quant. I'm just telling you what we've seen so far. Nothin's been proven."

"I understand." Darren needed to cover his ass.

"Do you think your client committed the murder?"

The question was so unexpected I asked him to repeat it.

"Your client. Is he the murderer?"

Our eyes met over the steam of piping hot sausage. I didn't like what I saw.

"Harold Chavell," he said easily. "Is he our shooter?"

I tried my best poker face, but it was too late. Darren already knew about Chavell.

"I've given you information, now you give me something," he said in a rough voice. "Why did Chavell hire you? What did you find out? Did you meet with Osborn before he was killed? Did he come back to Canada with you?"

Suddenly I'd become a bigger part of the police investigation than I'd ever considered. Fortunately I wasn't easily intimidated by police interrogation techniques. Especially when the policeman in question was now chomping on perogies. "How did you find out about Chavell?"

"Once we identified the body we began contacting family members."

Kathryn Wagner. I wouldn't doubt Tom's sister would point her ruby-coloured fingernail at Chavell as a suspect as fast as she could. "I already told you why Chavell hired me. Tom had gone missing in France and I was hired to track him down. But like I said, I never found him. I came back to Canada alone. I never even spoke directly to Tom."

"Harold Chavell is still your client?"

"Yes."

"You're working this murder investigation then?"

"Yes."

"You'll follow appropriate protocol when dealing with police on this matter?"

In a murder investigation, everything is a police matter. Did Darren really want me to promise to be a good boy? I'd get nothing accomplished. "I think we can be helpful to each other," I said.

"You haven't been much help to me today," he said as he tossed down his fork and wiped his lips with a napkin. "As I see it, I've been the one giving out all the help and you...well, you've just been having lunch."

"I've told you everything I know right now."

I could see by the look on his face that he wasn't buying that line. "I'll be expecting to hear from you." With that he slid out of the booth and stood up. He caught sight of Marushka shyly peeking at him from behind the kitchen door. She did this with all new customers who'd ordered the Ukrainian full meal deal. He gave her a thumbs up sign. She smiled and disappeared.

"You'll wait for the bill?" he asked without offering any currency from his own pocket. I watched him stride from the restaurant followed by more than one set of admiring male eyes.

I had walked the several blocks from my office to Colourful Mary's to meet Darren. But the earlier drizzle had now settled into a sodden downpour making a long walk undesirable. I used that excuse to stop into several shops along the way back. When I arrived at PWC forty minutes later I wasn't any drier than I would have been otherwise, but I did find a great piece of Mel Malkin raku and a pair of slip-on Skechers. I stopped at my car long enough to deposit my shopping bags in the trunk and proceeded inside.

"Tracking down some felonious ducks?" Errall, in a killer pin-stripe suit and wide-collared shirt, stepped out of her office. "Why don't you come in for a visit while you dry off," she suggested. "I've some great news."

I followed our house attorney into her office. Errall's workspace is much different from my own. It takes up nearly one half of the main floor and is divided into three connecting areas. There's the desk area, the client meeting area and the research area. The room is smartly planned, impressive and, I think, somewhat cold.

"Look at this." Errall sat behind her desk and tossed a magazine across its expanse in my general direction.

I picked up the copy of *Western Living* magazine and gave her a "what's this about" look.

"Page seventeen," she told me.

I sat down on the chair opposite the desk, mopping wet hair out of my eyes. *Western Living* is a magazine dedicated to gracious living in western Canada. It features beautifully shot ads for numerous hoity-toity shops—many located in good old Saskatoon. Had Kelly coughed up the dough for an On Broadway advertisement? I found page seventeen but saw nothing. Again I looked at Errall and shrugged.

"The interview. Read the interview."

I studied the page again and saw an article about Margeaux Clemence, an up-and-coming Calgary interior designer. Scan, skim, scan, skim…ah hah! I found it. And I quote, "It's the little things, not immediately noticeable, that can really make a room sing. I call them secret treasures. Two of my favourite ways to add character and cachet to a room are a Norma Cilante tapestry and a Kelly Doell wooden bowl or platter. They are one-of-a-kind items and simply beautiful. They grab the eye without trying."

Wow, I thought to myself, my friend is famous. I grinned from ear to ear as I reread the complimentary words.

"Pretty big stuff, huh?"

I glanced up at Errall and saw for a moment what Kelly loves about this woman. She was radiant with pride for her mate. "This is amazing!" I enthused. "I've got to call her right now."

"Actually I just got off the phone with her. How about joining us for sushi and too much sake tonight at the Bessborough?"

"I'd love it. Is she pretty excited?"

"She is so jazzed. She may never make it down off the ceiling. Now, I want to hear about France and your case. It sounds intriguing."

Since moving into PWC, Errall has acted as my business and personal attorney. That arrangement of legally bound confidentiality allows me to talk freely with her about my clients. And I was definitely at the point where I needed someone to talk things over with. It's at times like these where my relationship with Errall becomes something much different from our usual state of agreed-upon acrimony—something neither of us cares to inspect too closely.

I spent the next ten minutes bringing Errall up to date on the basics of the Chavell-Osborn case up to and including the recent discovery of Tom's body at the bottom of Pike Lake.

"So let me see if I have this right," she responded following my soliloquy. "Off you go to France, blah, blah, blah, you come back empty-handed and then, poor old Tom ends up dead in Saskatoon."

I didn't quite agree with her description of my time in France but generally she had it right. "Yes. At some point after I had my final contact with him, Tom boarded a plane for home—who knows why—and meets up with his murderer."

"When exactly was that?"

"What?"

"Your last actual contact with Tom Osborn in France?"

"Wellll…I suppose he could have been anywhere when he arranged for the messenger in Sanary-Sur-Mer, so my last real contact with him was at La Treille Muscate in Cliousclat…"

Errall nodded vigorously. "Okay, and the last thing that puts him there is the note he left in your mail slot, right? So he could have left Cliousclat and been on his way back home as early as Saturday noon, right?"

It was possible. Everything after the note was more than likely a ruse. "Tom would have had to drive to a larger centre, perhaps Orleans, but from there it would have been easy to catch a plane with connections back to Canada. He could have been back in Saskatoon on Sunday or even late Saturday." I didn't get back to Saskatoon until Wednesday night.

"But why?" she mumbled half to herself as she mulled this over, then said, "Maybe he really did need some time to himself and that's why he was in France. But when you showed, he decided the gig was up and came home," Errall theorized. By the look on her face I knew her brain was abuzz with possibilities. "And Harold Chavell told you that he never heard from or spoke to Tom after Tom had left for France?"

"That's right," I said.

"Could he be lying?"

I had to seriously consider this possibility. Was my client lying to me? Was my client a murderer and using me for some sort of corroborating alibi? "I suppose so, but Errall, why would he hire a detective to find someone he wanted to kill? That's just too obvious."

"Maybe that was the point." Errall narrowed her eyes until they were two blue beacons. "Being too obvious is sometimes a pretty clever ploy; too obvious for anyone—including a jury—to believe it could be true."

"Alright, but if Harold convinced Tom to come home in order to kill him, why would Tom then send me on a wild goose chase, unless…unless it wasn't Tom who arranged for the messengers at all, but…"

Errall was right there with me. "…Harold pretending to be Tom! He could have easily made the necessary calls from Canada. Or had an accomplice do it. He needed to keep you in France per-petuating the lie he'd so carefully manufactured while he was doing the dirty deed!"

My blood began to curdle as Errall and I concluded our grisly fairy tale gone bad. One that left me with a conniving client who'd committed murder and was using me as his unwitting accomplice.

Was Harold Chavell the type of man who could kill his own lover? He certainly did seem to give up easily after I called him from Sanary. If our suppositions were true, by that point he'd have no further need for me in France. Tom was already dead and under several feet of water in a Saskatchewan lake. And I'd established the fake alibi of Tom's disappearance. He took me off the job because he thought it was over. I had played my role exactly as he'd designed it. But then the body was discovered. And he immediately put me back on the payroll.

It made sense. But that didn't make it true.

When I returned to my office, the first thing I did was check my e-mail. Finally. Success. There was a message from TWirp.

> Dear "Friend,"
> I don't know what meeting you're referring to.
> There is nothing to discuss.
> Where's Tom?

That was it. I read it several times in order to squeeze as much information out of the few words as I possibly could. The last line was the most interesting. "Where's Tom?" Apparently TWirp had no knowledge of Tom's death—or else he or she was playing with me. This was now a murder case and I didn't have time to screw around. I decided to push TWirp and see if it paid off.

> Dear TWirp,
> By now you'll have heard of Tom Osborn's death. I know the two of you met before he died. I know he was unhappy with what you had to say. As far as I can figure it, you're either the murderer or you'd like to help me catch the murderer. It's your choice.
> Russell Quant
> Private Investigator

My note contained some lies and half-truths. Using my name was a risk. But sometimes in my business you had to use lies and risk to get anywhere. I clicked Save Draft. I'd send it as soon as news of the murder hit the airwaves. TWirp could be a big help to me. Or, TWirp might hunt me down and kill me.

Chapter 11

LATER THAT NIGHT I MET KELLY and Errall at Stovin's Lounge in the Bessborough Hotel for sushi and sake to celebrate Kelly's new found fame. It was one of those nights when everything serious in your life gets tossed aside in favour of gaiety, and you're simply happy to bask in the warm company of friends. Halfway through our second bottle of rice wine, Anthony and Jared showed up, post some splashy event or other, and together we laughed the laugh of the carefree until three cabs showed up to take us home.

When I first opened my eyes on Sunday morning I was gratified to see the weather co-operating with me. It was definitely a stay inside day. Exactly what I needed. Although it was 8:30 a.m. the sky was still inky and a turbulent wind slashed through the trees. It looked miserable out there. An Amur Maple near my bedroom window scratched at a pane already trembling from the blustery weather. I looked down at the foot of the bed where Barbra was curled into a tight ball. I heard the comforting sound of the furnace cutting in and snuggled deeper under my quilt.

As I luxuriated in my nest, the events of the past week and a half washed over me. It was difficult to believe I'd met Harold

Chavell only twelve days ago. I was tired and needed a break. I was still jet-lagged from my trip to France for Pete's sake. Once I gave myself the permission to take the day off, a sense of well-being overcame me. Yet, instead of closing my eyes for another dose of sleep, I had this sudden urge to jump out of bed and do all those lazy, permissive things that make a day off so special.

I shrugged into my favourite pair of faded blue, threadbare sweats, let Barbra out the back door and put on a pot of coffee. I considered a quick trip to the gym. But then it wouldn't be a day off, would it? By the time Barbra wanted back in I had poured her kibble, topping it off with one of those soft dog treats that look like a T-bone steak, and fixed myself a tower of Pop Tarts. I pulled a comfy blanket out of the linen closet and took root on the den sofa in front of the TV and fireplace. I read; watched a couple of movies; dozed; pet my dog; and ate unhealthy food. I did not let the thought of Tom Osborn or Harold Chavell enter the house. All in all, it was a cozy, wonderful day.

Bright sunshine and chipper air signalled a return to work on Monday. Throughout the city, trees emblazoned with bright autumn plumage belied the evidence of abandonment laying about them in deep, crunchy piles. I spent all of that day and most of Tuesday contacting the rest of the people on Chavell's lists. It was a rather discouraging couple of days. Everyone was still in shock over the news of Tom's death. And everyone seemed to have the same story. No, they hadn't seen Tom before he'd left for France. No, they did not hear from him while he was there. No, they did not see him after he returned and before he was murdered. No, they had no idea who could have killed him. I was getting nowhere fast. And to top it off, TWirp was ignoring my latest e-mail. I had either scared him or her off or else made a silent enemy.

By mid-Tuesday afternoon I had hit a wall. There were a few people left to contact, but they were either out of town or screening their calls. I needed to refocus my efforts. I considered the possibility that someone was involved who was not on either of these lists. Someone Chavell didn't know about or didn't think to include. Although more often than not, people are murdered by someone they know, there are exceptions. Maybe this was one of them. Maybe I was looking in the wrong place.

For every case I work, I keep a file labelled Herrings. In it I place information I have yet to follow up on or don't really know what to do with. Generally these are the bits and pieces I pick up or hear about during a case that usually mean absolutely nothing. But, instead of allowing them to burrow around in my brain, I let them go, knowing I've put them someplace safe where I can revisit them whenever I needed to. If I ever needed to.

I opened the Chavell-Osborn Herrings file and pulled out a piece of paper and began making phone calls. I hit pay dirt in about twenty minutes.

"Yes," the woman on the phone answered after my description of the sketch I held before me. It was my rough depiction of the half-heart pendant I'd found in Tom Osborn's apartment. "We do sell silver, half-heart pendants. They're called Joined in Love. Absolutely stunning pieces. Signature Jewellers are the exclusive distributors of the Joined in Love collection in Saskatoon. There are also rings and…"

"Yes that's it, ma'am. Do you sell many of them?" This had to be it. Not only did the pendant match the description, but she also confirmed the Signature Jewellers jewellery boxes are unmarked and burgundy with cream-coloured silk interiors.

"No. They're a very unique item. Not too many available…" I think what she was saying was that they were expensive or else not popular or both.

"Well I'm interested in a sale that took place recently. About two or three weeks ago." I was taking a wild guess at when the pendant was likely purchased.

"Is there a problem with your purchase?" She was beginning to sound a little less exuberant.

"Not at all. It's just that I recently had a birthday and received the pendant as a gift through the mail. Unfortunately, whoever sent it must have forgotten to include a card and there was no return address on the package so I don't know who to thank."

"Oh dear, that is unfortunate. Let me see…" I could hear the clicking and clacking of computer keys and some movement of paper, then, "Yes. This might be it! I remember now. We sold one set almost three weeks ago. Would that be about right?"

My hopes soared. "Yes indeed. Could you describe the man to me?"

"Oh, it wasn't a man who purchased the pendant, sir. It was a woman. An elderly woman. I remember it because I had to count out the cash. She paid in small bills. Very irregular."

You've got to be kidding! My soaring hopes crashed to the ground like a kite out of wind. Either Tom Osborn was having an affair with a grandma or I was skipping down the wrong path.

An elderly woman answered the door and for a crazed moment I wondered if this grey-haired, spectacled vixen had purchased the Joined in Love pendant for Tom. "Good afternoon, ma'am."

Her eyes squinted as she looked up at me. She had shrunk to less than five feet but made up for it in girth. A hairnet covered most of the steel-grey hair gathered into a loose bun at the nape of her neck. She wore a once lovely summer dress of pale blue with tiny yellow and white flowers. I suspected she purchased her reading glasses from the drugstore for sixteen ninety-five, hoping for the best improvement in sight that that amount of money could buy. "Afternoon? It's darn near five o'clock! Supper time! Whaddaya want? How'd yeh get in here?"

I wasn't about to admit to her how I'd nefariously gained entrance into the sanctum of her apartment building. I didn't think she'd approve. After all, she paid good money for the security offered by the building and there was no use making her doubt her safety. "My name is Russell Quant. I'm a detective working on the Tom Osborn case." I hoped that told her enough.

"Terrible news, that was. Not safe anywhere these days." Had she been reading my mind? Although I had only heard her voice, I was certain this was the same woman who'd chatted up the visitor outside Tom's apartment while I was inside, about to wet my pants.

"I was wondering if I could ask you a few questions."

"Yeh weren't interested in what I had to say before."

My ears perked up. "How do you mean?"

"Right after they found the body. Yeh cops were here talking to us. Gathered us all downstairs in the common room. Eight o'clock at night, too! Don't yeh know respectable folk are bound to be in bed by that time? Anyway, yeh said yerd be by to talk to each of us separately. Never saw hide nor hair of yeh since. Now yeh come by at supper time!"

"Sorry ma'am. Is there a better time I could come back to see you?"

She pulled back from the door and motioned me in. "Nah, yeh my as well come in now. Get it over with. Come on. In with yeh. I knew a woman once, name of Marguerite Quant. Know 'er?"

I smiled, shook my head and squeezed by her Buddha belly into the front hallway of her home. Mrs. Coyle lived across the hall and down a bit from Tom's apartment. The layout was identical but in reverse. Other than that, they were as different as two apartments could be. I guessed Mrs. Coyle had moved the contents of a fairly large house into the apartment without giving or throwing away a thing. Except for the pathway needed to traverse from one room to the next, every piece of floor space was covered with furniture or boxes, and every surface was utilized to display neatly arranged knick-knacks. I could see she tried her best to keep her possessions in order but the sheer volume was overpowering. Many of her things were tiny: porcelain animals, commemorative teacups and glass figurines. I imagined the poor woman spending her days moving from shelf to shelf with a cloth trying to stay ahead of the dust. The apartment smelled of lemon Pledge and herbal tea. Not unpleasant really.

"Sit down at the table," she instructed.

I did as she told me and was dumbstruck as she placed a dinner plate, cutlery and a matching cup and saucer in front of me. "Oh. This isn't for me I hope?"

"Yeh hafta eat." She was too busy in the fridge and at the stove-top to pay much attention to me.

"I, ah...I really...no thanks, Mrs. Coyle, I'm not hungry. I just have a few questions for you and then...or maybe I'll come back some other time." I made a move to stand up.

"Sit back down," she said without turning around. "Don't get yourself tied in a knot. Yeh gotta eat."

I noticed she hadn't set a place for herself. "What about you? Aren't you going to join me?"

"I ate 'bout an hour ago. Yeh'll eat and I'll talk."

I was beginning to understand why the cops didn't pursue a statement from Mrs. Coyle. I tried to think of another excuse to leave but nothing kind came to mind. The china and flatware before me were old. The plate looked so thin and worn, I thought I'd see right through it if I lifted it up to the light. The edges were greying and little spider-web cracks marred the delicate rose and leaf pattern. I was anxious to turn the plate over for more information. Had Mrs. Coyle served me on her Sunday best? Or had she found this at a garage sale? Within minutes she forked a deep fried cutlet onto my plate along with a scoop of instant mashed potatoes and a healthy glop of golden-coloured gravy. She filled my cup with lukewarm water, threw in a tea bag and sat down opposite me, the chair wheezing under her considerable bulk. I eyed the cutlet suspiciously and wondered if it was the same one that she'd offered the blonde man who'd been knocking on Tom's door.

"Do yeh wanna say something first or should I just tell yeh what I know?"

"Well, I'm interested in whether you knew Tom very well, when the last time was you saw him, whether you've observed anything suspicious..."

"Got it." She used a soup spoon to squeeze the tea bag in her cup against its side, making the water a medium brown. I did the same. "That Tom, he was a nice fellow. Didn't know him too well. Just hellos in the hallway, he'd hold the front door open for me now and then, that sort of thing. I asked him to come over to play canasta one night but he didn't have the time. He wasn't home too much from what I saw."

That coincided with my belief that Tom's apartment was not his full-time home. "I was wondering..."

"Mr. Quant, yeh can ask me all the questions yeh want, but there's only a thing or two I know yeh might find useful, so let me get to it." She gave me a steady look. I had never come across anyone quite so direct when it came to providing evidence. I nodded my head and dug into my cutlet. I needed a sharper knife. "On the Friday night before he disappeared, he was dropped off here by some woman. I remember that 'specially 'cause like I sez I'm usually in the bedroom by eight...not always t'sleep, but in my room...anyways, that night I couldn't sleep 'cause of...well I guess I don't know why not...but I couldn't sleep and I caught sight of that gal dropping him off. Think she came up for a spell too. The whole thing was odd. As I sez, he wasn't here much and especially not on weekends. Almost never saw him on weekends. I'd seen her with him several times before though. I'd say they were close friends. I may have overheard her name once. Colleen maybe it was."

I had to hide a grin. I was beginning to realize Mrs. Coyle was an observant neighbour.

"After that no one else came to see Tom 'cept for someone in a silvery-brown looking truck on Saturday morning. And maybe someone in a little yeller car after that. Not sure 'bout that one. One of my shows was on. Hard to keep track of things when one of my shows is on. I think Tom went out sometime in the afternoon but I don't know where. Never saw or heard him again after that. But like I sez, he wasn't usually here much on weekends anyway, so I didn't think much of it. That's it. That's what I know."

I confirmed the Saturday she was talking about was the Saturday of the wedding. The silvery-brown truck I concluded had to be a pewter-coloured Jeep or similar type vehicle. "How do you know the owner of the silvery-brown truck was visiting Tom?"

"I saw it pull up in front of the building at eleven o'clock in the morning and then right after, heard a knock on Tom's door. Later, 'bout eleven-fifteen, I hears someone leaving Tom's apartment then see that same truck pull away. Whoever was in it visited Tom I'd say."

I nodded. It sounded like a fair conclusion. "And possibly someone in a yellow car visited Tom after that? About what time?"

"Woulda been about twelve noon."

"Did you see or hear when the yellow car left?"

"My shows were on!" she said, as if defending herself.

"And about what time after lunch did Tom leave the apartment?" I was betting she could answer to the minute.

"I'd say around two-thirty, two-thirty-five maybe."

"And you're certain he didn't return after that?"

"Well he musta. When I went out later I saw his truck in the back parking lot. I jus' didn't hear him come back in. Heard him leave, but didn't hear him come back. Like I sez, never saw him again after he left at two-thirty-five."

This was surprising. Eagle-eyes-and-ears Coyle missed Tom coming home, yet he evidently did return with his truck at some point that day. I knew from Colleen—and now Mrs. Coyle—that Tom's Jimmy was in its parking slot. But perhaps he never came back up to the apartment. Or maybe he hadn't used the truck at all. From her apartment, Mrs. Coyle can see street parking in front of the building, not the tenant parking lot in the rear. She only knew Tom had left because she'd heard him leave his apartment. But where did he go at two-thirty? And how? With his bike? Did someone pick him up? Had he packed his bags and gone to stay with a friend? A lover? Perhaps whoever it was that drove him to the airport the next morning? Or could he have taken an earlier flight? Maybe he left Saskatoon on Saturday night. Or maybe Mrs.

Coyle was wrong, and Tom did spend Saturday night in his apartment.

"Did anyone try to visit Tom on Saturday night?" I wondered if Chavell or someone else had attempted to find him after the wedding was cancelled.

"If it was after eight o'clock, I couldn't tell yeh. I was sleepin' with my earplugs in." Earplugs? It made sense actually. How else would an insatiable snoop get any sleep?

"What about Sunday morning? Did you see or hear Tom or anyone else?"

"Nobody. I'da told yeh already if I had."

"What about when Tom came back from France? Probably on Saturday or Sunday of last week. Did you happen to catch when he got home?"

She shook her head, looking at me like I might have a hearing disorder. "Like I sez, I never saw him again after he left on Saturday. He never came home again. Ever."

As far as I knew, the cops had yet to determine time of death. Perhaps Mrs. Coyle was right. I imagined someone meeting Tom at the airport, waiting with him for his luggage and then, taking him away to be killed. Maybe he never made it home. "Is there anything else you can think of that might be of use?"

She looked at me with an odd look on her face. "If there was, why wouldn't I have told yeh already?"

Okay, stupid question. I quickly downed the last bite of my cutlet and waited for it to clunk to the bottom of my churning stomach. I left a card with Mrs. Coyle, thanked her for her help and dinner, and left.

I spent an hour or so at the airport with pictures of Tom and Chavell (just in case) hoping for someone with a good memory for faces. It was a long shot but I wanted to try pinning down the time of Tom's return from France. After ticketing agents I talked to security guards, parking lot attendants, retail salespeople, wait staff in the restaurant and finally the bartender. Nothing. I returned home feeling a little dejected.

I had taken out some chicken in the morning and planned on having a stir-fry. Although Mrs. Coyle's skinny little cutlet and suspicious mashed stuff hadn't filled me up, I wasn't sure my belly was willing to accept anything but fresh fruit or some nice veggies. I decided to wait and see. I put on a country-boy-inspired, red-and-black fleece jacket and a pair of Nike running shoes and drove Barbra to the dog run just south of the city limits. The dog run is a scruffy piece of land on the river where dog owners can unleash their pets and let them run free. Every time we visit I wonder how we escape without a big canine, free-for-all but somehow it always turns out fine. Everyone, owners and pets alike, are always on their best behaviour. Although Standard Schnauzers are energetic dogs that will take as much exercise as they can get, Barbra isn't one of those dogs who goes mad with robust enthusiasm when let free in the wild. She loves it for about forty minutes then she'll run up to me with a look on her face saying, "Tell me again why we're out here when there's a nice comfy sofa at home?"

By the time we got back to the house it was dark and cold outside. As we stepped into the warmth I revelled in that wonderfully invigorating feeling of having been out in the fresh, clean air. Barbra immediately went to lie down in front of the fireplace in the living room. That was my cue to make a fire. So I did. Once my dog was satisfied, I checked my machine and was surprised to find Darren Kirsch tersely leaving a number where he could be reached. It had to be important. I couldn't recall him ever phoning me at home before. I still wasn't hungry so I washed some green seedless grapes, put them in a bowl, poured a glass of Merlot, took a spot in front of the fire with my goodies and returned the call.

"Hello." I recognized the deep female voice as belonging to Darren's wife, Treena.

"Hi Treena, it's Russell Quant."

"Russell! Why don't I see you anymore? You really should come for dinner soon." From our little visits at parties and cop get-togethers in years gone by, I was pretty sure Treena had caught on to the fact that I was gay. But for a smart gal, she hadn't caught on to the fact that her husband and I were not close.

"I know. I'm sorry. Just keeping too busy I guess."

"You're just like Darren." I hope not! "Let me get him for you."

After a moment I heard the phone being picked up again. "Quant."

"Hey Darren. Your wife just invited me over for dinner," I said, a devilish glint in my eye.

There was silence at the other end of the phone while He-Man figured that one out. Finally he said in his dry tone, "Do I have to be here?"

"Ha. Ha. You called?"

"Yeah. You sitting down?"

I didn't like the sound of that. "Mmhmm. What's up?"

"Just thought I'd let you know. We've made an arrest in the Tom Osborn case."

I took a big gulp of my wine. Something told me I was going to need it.

"It's Harold Chavell. We've arrested Harold Chavell for the murder of his lover."

I don't know why my immediate reaction was anger. Although I wasn't about to admit it to anyone (least of all to myself), since my talk with Errall, I had slowly begun to convince myself that my client was indeed guilty. But if that were so, why was I so angry that the police had arrested him? It just seemed too neat and easy.

"Damn it, Darren! Why did you do that? Because they were gay lovers? Because they were two men who wanted to get married? Because one man dumped another man?"

Darren said nothing for a moment. He was smart enough not to fuel my fire. Then he said in a calm, steady voice, "Because Tom Osborn's body was found floating face down in Pike Lake near a cabin owned by Harold Chavell. And because we found the murder weapon—registered to Harold Chavell—at his house in Cathedral Bluffs."

The news stunned me. Harold Chavell owned a cabin at Pike Lake? Was *that* where Tom really lived rather than the Main Street apartment? I assumed he lived with Harold in Cathedral Bluffs. Why hadn't anyone told me about the cabin? And what about the gun? Would Chavell have been so confident that he wouldn't have even bothered to dispose of the murder weapon? Maybe originally— when everyone still thought Tom was lost in France—but after the body was discovered? Why wouldn't he hide or dispose of it? Something was not right here. More and more, I was coming to doubt the scenario imagined by Errall and myself. Harold Chavell was not a murderer. Suddenly, in a moment of unexplained clarity, I was certain. My client was being framed.

Chapter 12

TOM'S FUNERAL WAS AT 10:00 A.M. on Wednesday morning. Harold Chavell was arrested for his murder on Tuesday. He certainly wouldn't be attending the service. But I was interested in who would be. It may sound a little heartless, but funerals are a perfect place to spot potential suspects. And, I have to admit, after chasing him halfway around Europe and back, I felt a bit of a connection to Tom Osborn. I wanted to pay my respects to this man who remained a mystery to me.

The sun was out in full force, but every day now it took a little longer for the morning air to defrost. I arrived at Saints Peter and Paul Church forty-five minutes early. I parked my car on the street opposite the church's front entrance from where I could easily watch the mourners as they entered. Even this early, the church's parking lot was nearly half full. And more interesting, one of the vehicles in the parking lot was a pewter-coloured Land Rover. The same vehicle Mrs. Coyle spotted outside Tom's apartment? I would have to find out who owned that baby.

A crowd was turning up to mourn this man's unfortunate passing. I could see a number of people had a head start on their crying before they even entered the sanctuary. It appeared Tom Osborn was loved and would be missed. I was dreading the Ukrainian Catholic funeral service. They have a reputation for being highly emotional affairs.

From my vantage point, I watched the guests arrive, many of whom I recognized: Randy Wurz turned up with his peacock of a wife; the big-haired QW receptionist; some of Tom's neighbours including Mrs. Coyle; Clark Shiwaga; Colleen and Norma; and, surprisingly, I spotted Darren Kirsch running up the steps at ten to the hour. What was he doing here? He had his shooter behind bars. Or did Darren also have doubts about Harold Chavell being the murderer? I was about to get out of my car and follow Darren inside when two immaculately clean, black sedans, followed by a hearse, pulled up to the front of the church. It was the cortège.

As if choreographed, all the vehicle doors opened at once, expelling the family. I recognized Kathryn Wagner, trying to comfort a young child pressed against her thigh. Beside her was a thick-bodied man with thinning hair who I took to be her husband. Father Len, looking worn and distressed, was graceful in simple, long black robes. He kept a protective arm wrapped around an elderly woman whom I guessed was his mother. Another man remained slightly behind the pair, a rumpled hat in his strong, farmer's hands. There was no doubt that he was the father of Tom and Father Len. He looked just like his sons, only thirty years older. His deep-set eyes seemed on the verge of spilling cobalt blue ink. No parent should have to attend his child's funeral. Of all the sorrowful faces, his was the most stricken. Although it made no sense, I wished I could rush over and give him a hug. Boy, what a wuss I am! The funeral hadn't even begun and I didn't even really know Tom Osborn, but the sight of his bereaved father brought me close to tears. I couldn't help but wonder where Harold Chavell would have fit in with this group. If at all.

I waited until the procession of casket and family had entered the church before I followed at a discreet distance. I was too late to find a seat in the main hall of the church so an usher directed me to a side room where we could observe the service on a monitor. I saw Darren at the back of the room and squeezed in next to him.

"Wow. Popular guy," I said quietly.

No response from the big lug.

"I hope you brought your hanky. Ever been to a Ukrainian funeral before? They're the saddest. I've no idea what they're singing but the music is so mournful it wouldn't surprise me if afterwards we all rushed to the University Bridge like lemmings and jumped off."

He mumbled something that sounded like "mmhmphf."

"Why are you here anyway?" I whispered.

He glanced at me, then away. "I just wanted to see who showed up."

"Like the real murderer perhaps?"

He gave me a pained look. "Can it, Quant."

"That's the only reason I can think of for you to be here. But let me give you a little advice." I felt like needling him a bit. "When you're on a stakeout, it helps when you don't arrive late. I saw you running in at ten to."

He turned and gifted me with a Cheshire grin. A smile from Mr. Kirsch is a rare thing. "And I saw you pulling up to the front of the church about half-an-hour before that. Nice car. Rotary engine, right?"

Damn. He had beaten me. Where had he been parked? I didn't see him at all. I put a finger to my mouth and whispered, "Shhhhhh! This is a funeral."

As expected, it was one of the saddest funerals I'd ever been to. The songs, most sung in Ukrainian, sounded like sullen death marches. Babas wailed in their pews and four eulogists mined every tear in the house. Sad and long. I've attended my share of funerals and I've found that some cultures are quite reserved when it comes to expressing sorrow at memorial services—even going so far as to give them joyful sounding names like "Celebration of

Life" or "Beginning of a Glorious Journey." Ukrainians seem to have a need to get it all out right then and there. None of this weeping in our remoulade six months later while on vacation in the Caribbean. Not a bad idea really.

At noon, when it looked to be almost over, I gently prodded Darren in the ribs and took my leave. I wasn't bored or trying to be insensitive, but I wanted to be back in my car before anyone else left so I could see who owned the pewter Land Rover. I didn't have long to wait. The truck was driven away by none other than Clark Shiwaga, Chavell's lawyer. Well. I'd catch up with him later.

I was greeted at the door of Kathryn Wagner's home by Hank, her husband, who directed me to food and booze laid out in great abundance on two massive banquet tables. It was a dizzying display, set on linens decorated with colourful Ukrainian embroidery. The house was crammed with people chattering away as if it were a cocktail party. Not knowing what else to do, I headed towards the buffet. Through gesticulating limbs and bobbing heads I caught a quick look at Tom's father, standing shock-still in the centre of the living room, not even pretending to pay attention to the mournful ramblings of the oversized women who surrounded him. The eye of the storm. At the bar I poured a 7Up for myself and a potent rye and Coke. Using my elbows as protection, I struggled through the crowd to the side of Mr. Oburkevich. He looked at me blankly. I said something inane and pressed the drink into his calloused hands. He took a sip. He looked at me again and nodded his thanks. As I moved away from the ruined man I caught sight of his son, Father Len, watching from across the room.

I found myself drawn to a group of five men. They were gay. How did I know that? It was pretty easy in this crowd. The men were unusually pretty. Even those who weren't physically gifted looked attractive because they emanated that thing that said they cared about how they looked. They wore more jewellery and of better quality than Kathryn's. And the hair. Always a giveaway.

Stylish and shiny. They smelled nice. They were barely touching the too-sweet, bubbly wine in their glasses—obviously accustomed to something better (or pretending to be). And, my best hint of all: Kathryn Wagner was staring daggers at them. My conclusion: A courageous group of Tom's friends who dared the wrath of his homophobic sister by showing up. Just what I was looking for.

Although I'd never do this at a gay bar, and many would tell me I should, I unabashedly approached the clique and held out my hand to the one nearest me. "Hi, I'm Russell Quant. You must be friends of Tom?"

A mink-haired man accepted my hand, without much choice really, and introduced himself and the other four. Two Dougs, a Kent, a Rick and a Bob.

"And who are you?" Doug number one asked somewhat haughtily. They were on the defensive. Fair enough. As far as they knew, I was Tom's cousin Igor who'd come to kick their butts.

"I'm a private investigator." That got their attention.

"What are you investigating? Didn't you hear? They arrested the murderer yesterday. Harold Chavell. Tom's lover." The man said the last two words a little louder than necessary. I think he was deliberately trying to piss off the hostess. By the look of her, he was doing a fine job.

"I'm working for Mr. Chavell."

"Trying to get him off?" the one called Kent said. "Don't you think that's a waste of time?"

I focused on the man who'd been introduced as Kent Melicke. I recognized him. His was the face I saw through the peephole at Tom's apartment. Attractive. A little on the skinny side. Late twenties, early thirties I guessed. He had blonde hair scissored into wisps around his face. He wore tortoiseshell glasses that likely weren't prescription. Perhaps he and Mrs. Coyle shopped together. But whereas she was saving money, he was going for a look. "Why do you say that?" I asked.

"Makes sense to me. That's all."

I studied the man's face. Did he know something or was he simply being dramatic because the role appealed to him? I couldn't be sure. I scoured my memory and did not recall a Kent being on either of the lists that Chavell had given me. I was pretty sure none of the other men I'd just met were either. "Had you seen Tom recently? Before he went to France or maybe after he got back?"

Kent's eyes widened a smidgen. "Are you asking *me*?"

I didn't want to cause panic. "All of you. Any of you. I'd be interested to talk with anyone who might have had conversations with Tom around that time."

"No," Kent told me. "I hadn't seen Tom in a little while."

I looked at the others who indicated the same. It made me wonder. Were these really friends of Tom's? I glanced at the food on the plates of the five. Only Kent's held none of the wide selection of meat available. A vegetarian? I glanced around his neck for signs of a pendant but saw none. I felt a warm palm on my shoulder. It was Father Len.

"Len," Kent said. "I just wanted to…I had to come and express my sympathies. I don't know what to say. I'm just so sorry." There were tears forming in his eyes. The other four men circled about him protectively, their eyes shifting back and forth between the priest and Kent. I began to understand. These weren't friends of Tom's. They were Kent's friends. Here to support him through a tough time.

Father Len nodded and gave the man a kindly look. He reached out and took Kent's hand in his own, holding it rather than shaking it. For a moment I was inexplicably jealous. "I know. I know how you feel, Kent. Thank you so much for coming. Tom would be glad you were here."

Kent nodded, fighting back sobs. He withdrew his hand. "We're going to go now. See you around maybe?"

Len shook hands with the other men, graciously asking their names and thanking them for coming as he did so.

I watched as the gay gang made their way to the front door where they met up with Colleen and Norma who were putting on their coats. Colleen gave me a nod of recognition. I turned back to Father Len and asked, "Who is Kent Melicke?"

"Tom and Kent were lovers several years ago. Before Harold."

It made sense now. The signs were there. I guessed Kent had not been the one to end the relationship. "Some unsettled business perhaps?"

"Not as far as Tom was concerned. But I think Kent believed Tom was still in love with him and would not go through with the wedding."

The crowd was pushing in on us and I knew the priest had many others to attend to. "I think I'll be leaving soon."

"It was nice to see you again. I wish it was under much different circumstances."

I saw the woeful look on his face and wanted to embrace him. Instead I reached out and gave his arm a quick rub that I hoped conveyed a message of caring and sympathy. As relatives and other mourners swallowed him up, I began my pilgrimage to the exit.

I was halfway there, feeling like a football player in a game with no one else on my team, when I saw Randy Wurz. No wife. He was standing alone near a large potted plant wearing a lustrous black suit, Hugo Boss I thought. He looked the way people do when they're in shock. I headed towards him, faking out a few boisterous babas intent on spilling their plates of food on me.

"Mr. Quant," he greeted me with unfocused eyes.

"I'm sorry to see you again under such terrible circumstances."

"The worst," he agreed, doing his best to look miserable despite his perfect hair. "Thank God they've got the bastard behind bars."

"You mean Harold Chavell?"

He finally looked me in the eye as if just realizing something. "Did you have something to do with that? Did your investigation lead to the arrest?"

I shook my head. "No, I'm afraid that credit goes to the Saskatoon Police Service."

He just nodded and made a muffled sound.

"Do you believe Harold Chavell would kill Tom Osborn?"

"Well, yes, I guess I do," he said with a stutter as if he hadn't considered an alternative. "It just makes sense, doesn't it?"

"You're not the only person to think that," I said, remembering Kent Melicke using almost the exact same words.

"You don't think they'll let him go, do you?"

I shrugged. "They will if they can't prove he did it."

"God, I just…" He looked down at his untouched drink. "I just can't believe he's actually dead."

I could see it was time to give the man some room to grieve. I could be sensitive when I put my mind to it. I said my farewell and struggled through the crowd towards the front door. I glanced back once and noticed another mourner approach Randy Wurz. He was a short, dark-haired man with a wide face and pronounced moustache. I stopped and studied the two from a temporary spot of inactivity behind a group of nuns. It took me only a moment to identify the familiar looking man. I'd seen his picture in the local paper several times. Dave Biddle—owner of a company called Quasar. Quasar is a local giant in the communications industry that regularly snaps up almost every award handed out by local and provincial business organizations. I wondered what he was doing at Tom Osborn's funeral. Might be worth following up. Another tidbit for the Herrings file.

A short time later I was sitting in my car in front of Tom's apartment mulling over the last few hours and how the Herrings file was getting so damn full. So far this day had done little but raise more questions. I thought again about Tom's bike. Knowing full well that he wouldn't need it again before the snow flew, Tom may have lent the bike to someone before leaving for France. Or perhaps it was sitting in a repair shop somewhere, waiting to be picked up. I fingered the key I'd found in Tom's apartment. I had gotten into the habit of taking it with me wherever I went. Could it be for a bicycle lock? Where was that bike?

Tom could have ridden the bike somewhere and not returned. Maybe he hadn't used his truck on the Saturday he disappeared at all. I thought about where Tom could easily get to from his apartment by bike. Colleen and Norma lived nearby. Saints Peter and Paul Church was not too far, so he could have visited his brother, Father Len. Innovation Place, where the QW office was located, would be a bit of a jaunt but certainly doable for a serious cyclist like Tom. I could check out the backyards and garages of everyone that knew Tom and lived nearby. But, not only would that take too long, I probably wouldn't find anything for the same reason bicycle thieves are rarely caught. The evidence is too easy to hide.

I laid my head back on the car seat and closed my eyes. What else? What would he do with a bike he babied but knew he wouldn't use for a while…of course! He'd store it! There had to be storage facilities somewhere in his apartment building.

I jumped out of my car and rushed across the street to the front door of Tom's building. I punched in a security number I'd not used before and announced myself as the furnace service guy, there to check things out before winter. I was buzzed in. I found the door that led downstairs. The basement was a good-sized room, floored in cheap but clean linoleum and well lit—all in all, not bad as far as basements went.

Bingo! Four bikes were neatly arranged in one corner, each securely padlocked. I quickly pulled the mystery key from my pocket. Kneeling beside the bicycles I dutifully began on the first lock. It was too big for the key. I moved on to the second. Same story. The third bike had a combination lock and the fourth a fancy digital lock. It was this last bike that caught my attention. Bright blue. And in stylized letters along one shaft: Trek 5200. I remembered Colleen's description of Tom's bike. This had to be it. Another dead end. And the key was still a mystery.

I didn't know any more than I did before I'd gotten here. The damn key was beginning to irritate me. I stuffed it back into my pocket and began heading up when I noticed a series of small doors along the wall that ran beneath the stairs. They looked like oversized post office boxes. Each of the doors was clearly labelled with a number. They seemed to coincide with the apartment numbers. Storage lockers! I raced back down.

I found number 303. My hands were shaking as I pulled the key out of my pocket for a second time. I knew it was going to work. And it did. I swung open the door and peered inside. The space was much too small for a bike but I found a box that at one time held a brand new pair of Sorel winter boots. I pulled it out and flipped off the lid. Inside was an assortment of papers, but the first thing to catch my eye was a 3.5"x 5" navy blue booklet. It was faux leather with gold embossing. I quickly recognized it. Tom's Canadian passport. My luck had just changed! With this I'd be able to confirm the exact date he had given me the slip and returned to Canada. I allowed myself a self-satisfied smirk as I realized the police had obviously missed this little treasure trove and would undoubtedly be interested in my find. Darren would owe me big time. I flicked the pages of the passport carefully noting the immigration stamps.

My heart leapt into my throat.

I couldn't believe what I was seeing. Or rather what I wasn't seeing.

There were no stamps for France. Going to or returning from.

Tom Osborn had never left Canada.

Chapter 13

I GAVE MY HEAD A SHAKE and started from the beginning. Yes, it was a real passport. Yes, it was for someone named Tom Osborn. Yes, the picture matched the photo I had of Tom Osborn. Yes, the date indicated it was his current, valid passport. I flipped through each page, much slower this time. Tom had done a fair bit of travelling in the past three years since he'd gotten this passport—but not to France. I looked through it one more time to convince myself I wasn't missing something. I wasn't.

I sifted through the balance of the box's contents. I paged through tax returns and noticed Tom's income from QW, although not insubstantial, had decreased in recent years. I skimmed through student loan documents, insurance policies, warranty cards and instruction manuals but there was nothing I wanted to spend time on. Nothing that would tell me how my client's dead lover got to France and back without using his passport. Nothing that would tell me who, if it wasn't Tom, I had been chasing after in France.

Had Tom been using a different passport? Perhaps he was travelling under an assumed name? Why? Was Tom Osborn actually an international spy or crime lord on the run, rather than the computer geek he was known to be? Doubtful. And besides, he had used plane tickets purchased by Chavell who would have used Tom's real name. Or had he?

It hit me.

It was a niggling little detail that had bothered me all along but I was never able to pin it down in my mind until now. The messengers. The old lady in Cliouschat and the sultry-eyed man in Sanary-Sur-Mer—neither could speak English. Both spoke only French. Yet, according to Chavell, Tom barely knew any French. But somehow he managed to give detailed instructions to both these messengers? In Paris, absolutely, in Sanary maybe, but in a town the size of Cliouschat, a translator would have been extremely difficult to find on short notice. Someone else had arranged the messengers and the messages. Was it Chavell after all?

The only way the passport made sense was if Tom was never in France in the first place. But that idea made the least sense of all.

It was nearing 4:00 p.m. when I drove back to my office in a daze, my mind reeling with a host of bizarre possibilities that might explain the passport I'd found. By the time I slumped dejectedly behind my desk with a Diet Coke I had concluded one thing. I had learned an important lesson. Never trust a fact, until you've proven it to be one.

I had no real proof Tom Osborn was ever in France. Harold Chavell said it was so and I'd believed him. In my defense, I had no reason not to. The ticket was gone, the apartment was abandoned, his luggage was missing, and most importantly, there was an eyewitness, Solonge Fontaine. The first hours of the investigation were hasty but I still chastised myself for not demanding the time to do my usual background checks before I got on that plane to France. I'd been distracted by the romance of being sent abroad to solve a case. Well, it was spilled milk.

If it wasn't Tom I was following in France, then who was it? Perhaps I was chasing a ghost. I'd never actually seen Tom Osborn. I'd only had hints that he was near. Solonge Fontaine. The clerks at the hotels. The messengers. Could they all have been in on it? Or had they simply been duped as I was? Who else knew the details of the itinerary? Only Chavell? Was he lying to me? Had he indeed sent me on this elaborate wild goose chase as part of a dastardly, clever murder plan? Chavell was certainly bright enough and familiar enough with France to have set the whole thing up. I squirmed as I once again experienced doubts about my client's innocence. But where was the proof? I had none.

I picked up the phone and dialled Darren's number. Since the morgue had released the body for the funeral, the autopsy results had to be in. Tom's time of death could be critical in proving Chavell innocent or guilty. I wondered if anyone was even paying attention to it, especially now that the police had their prime suspect in jail. If Tom had never left Canada, he could have been killed as early as the night before the wedding. Weeks ago rather than days ago. That possibility would open up a whole other group of suspects to the police. Suddenly the clues I had picked up in Tom's apartment before leaving for France (and had stuck in the Herrings file) were becoming more important. The half-heart pendant. The vegetarian meal. Who else had been in that apartment? Were they connected to the murder? Had someone been impersonating Tom Osborn?

Darren was not answering his phone.

I checked my e-mail. Nothing from TWirp. Was I wrong about TWirp? Maybe all I'd managed to do was scare the pants off of some unsuspecting computer friend of Tom's.

It took me a while to get it right, but I finally figured out how to dial the international number for Solonge Fontaine in Paris. I forgot about the eight-hour time difference, but fortunately Madame Fontaine was a bit of a night owl.

"Monsieur Quant, how charming of you to call again. Of course you will slip by for a nightcap?" she said in French.

I smiled at the invitation but doubted its sincerity. "I'm afraid I can't do that, but thank you. You see I'm back in Canada."

"Canada! How wonderful! I love Canada. All those red leaves."

She must have seen pictures of Ontario in autumn. In Saskatchewan, we have some red leaves in the fall, but mostly they're different shades of yellow, orange or brown. "I was wondering if I might ask you a few more questions." And quickly dammit, this is costing me a fortune.

"Of course. Of course. How is my Harold? And did you ever find his little friend?"

Did I just ask permission for *her* to ask *me* questions? "Harold Chavell has been arrested for the murder of Tom Osborn."

I listened carefully for her reaction. At first there was nothing, then a release of pent-up air. After clearing her throat she continued, now serious and without the melody in her voice I'd come to recognize. "How can that be, Mr. Quant? How can that be? I cannot believe that. You must be mistaken. The police must be mistaken. Is he…is he in jail?"

"Yes."

"Oh my." And then she used some French words I wasn't familiar with, but from the tone of her voice I guessed Madame Fontaine was swearing a blue streak. "What can I do? Tell me."

I had come to suspect Solonge Fontaine to be a colourful but ultimately shallow character, yet to her credit she jumped swiftly to her friend's aid. "I need to know about your visit with Tom Osborn."

"But we spoke of this. When we met a short time ago. We spoke of this."

"Yes, I know, but I was wondering if you could describe Tom Osborn to me."

"Describe?"

"Yes. Tell me what he looked like."

"I don't understand. What he looked like? Medium. Medium everything. Brown hair of some sort, I'm sure. Youngish. That's about all I recall." Vague was Madame Fontaine's middle name. I'd have to go about this another way.

After ensuring her she'd been of immeasurable help, I hung up. I looked at my watch. It was closing in on four-thirty. Good. There was a chance Errall would still be downstairs in her office. She had something I needed. I dialled the number.

"Errall Strane, Law Office, Lilly speaking. How can I help you?"

"Sorry Lilly, it's Russell upstairs. Errall's not in?"

"No, she's on her way to a client meeting across town. You could try reaching her on her cellphone."

I did that.

"Russell, where are you?" Errall asked when she heard my voice. "Were you at Tom Osborn's funeral today? Did you hear they've arrested Harold Chavell?"

I ignored her questions and got right to business. "Errall, I know you're busy, but I need some help."

"What is it? You sound odd. Is something wrong?" I heard a blast of her car horn. "Pick a lane, asshole!"

I told her the brief version of what I'd found out.

Aside from the occasional profanity directed at fellow travellers, she listened without comment to my story until the end. "Wow. Now there's a twist to the story I bet you didn't expect. What can I do?"

"You have a scanner in your office, right?"

"Sure. Why?"

"Does Lilly know how to use it?"

"No, but I'm planning to work tonight after this meeting, so I'll be back there in a couple of hours. What do you need?"

"I need you to scan a picture of Tom Osborn and e-mail it to Solonge Fontaine."

"So she can tell you once and for all whether or not she met with the real Tom Osborn?"

"Right."

"But don't you already know the answer?"

"According to the passport, yes, but I want proof. And, if after seeing Tom's picture Solonge still insists she met with him, and we can prove he wasn't there, then we know she's lying and therefore part of the whole scheme."

"If we can catch her in a lie she might be convinced to let us in on the plan and maybe lead us to the murderer." Errall was a bright person. She added cryptically, "Assuming she isn't an accomplice—unwitting or otherwise."

"Exactly."

"Clever."

"Of course. I've told Solonge to expect the picture and wait for someone to contact her about it."

"I can do that. Any idea where I can find a picture of Tom?"

"I have a recent one Chavell gave to me. I suppose I could leave it with Lilly before I go…"

"Don't worry about it, if it's your only one you'll probably need it. When I get back to the office I'll track down a photo from the QW Annual Report or their web site. Give me her e-mail address."

I love efficient people.

Osler Street is in an area called Varsity View near the university. It's a beautiful, heavily treed street with a mixture of old character homes and massive reconstructions that attempted, fairly success-fully, to fit in. Colleen and Norma lived in the former. I pulled up to the white and pastel green bungalow. There were several cars in their wide driveway. Through a large front window I saw a group of people sitting around in a living room. I guessed that perhaps some of the less desirous guests at the wake had found their way back here, to safer ground.

Norma answered the door with her colourful complexion and ready smile and invited me in to the front room. There were about a dozen people. Most of them I'd seen earlier that day either at the funeral or the Wagner's home. Kent Melicke was slouched down in a big easy chair that seemed to envelop his slender frame. He looked up at me but said nothing.

"So we meet again," Colleen said. Her voice had a rough edge to it. Although it was not yet 5:00 p.m. I was certain she was drunk. Looking around the room and surveying the inventory of empty glasses and beer bottles I was pretty certain everyone was well on their way to being unable to drive home.

"Sorry to bother you. I was wondering if I could speak with you alone. It won't take long," I said, knowing Colleen was the last person who admitted to seeing Tom alive. I wanted to shake her up a bit with my news to see if anything interesting rattled to the floor.

"Are you placing me under arrest?" A little belligerence was creeping into her tone. Perhaps this was not the right time. She looked around at her mates and snorted as if to say, "I double dare you!"

"I'm not a police officer," I told her uselessly.

"So what is it? What do you need to ask me? Do it right here. None of us have anything to hide." She looked at the others and snorted again. "At least not when it comes to Tim!"

Some of the others laughed with her, or, perhaps at her. She'd just called her best friend, buried that morning, by the wrong name. Time to lay off the rum, I'd say. Sober, Colleen Arber was a strong, opinionated woman. I respected that. Drunk she was just a blabbering fool. Not very attractive.

"Tom," Norma corrected her quietly. She seemed to be the only one in the room not drinking.

Colleen eyed her partner but continued onwards. "Come on mister private eye man, what is it? What's on your mind?"

To hell with it I thought. Maybe this *was* the perfect time. With a little bit of alcohol lubrication her true reaction, or anyone else's in the room for that matter, might be easier to spot. I began, clearly enunciating every word, "I've come across some information that suggests Tom was never in France. He never left Saskatoon. I just wanted to see if you knew anything about that. You *were* the last person to see him before he left." She didn't have to know about the Saturday visitors spotted by Mrs. Coyle.

Boom! It was like I'd lit a cannon in the room. The wake after its explosion was deafeningly quiet. I studied the faces around the room, especially Colleen's and Kent Melicke's. They were surprised. Were they surprised about Tom never leaving the country, or were they just surprised I'd found out? That was the important question. I wasn't sure if I could answer it. Yet.

"Are you accusing us of something?" This was from Kent who until now had remained quiet and sullen in his cushy chair. I thought it interesting that he took on the shared burden of guilt so quickly. Until now, I think most people in the room assumed I was suspicious of Colleen only.

"No, not at all. I'm just trying to find out the truth."

"I told you the truth," Colleen said. Her voice was suddenly clear, officious and strong as if the alcohol in her body had instantly burned off. "I was the last person to see him."

"How do you know that?"

She frowned. "What do you mean?"

"How do you know you were the last person to see him? How do you know someone else didn't come to see him that night after you left or maybe the next day?"

I saw a quick, uneasy exchange between she and Kent before she answered. "Of course I don't know that. What I meant is that I was the last of our group of friends, the people at the rehearsal party, you know, these people, who'd seen him. I can't speak for anyone else."

I nodded. "You know that for a fact?"

She stared at me, her lips like two bands of steel against her teeth. "It's not like I went around and asked everyone. That's your job, isn't it?"

"Yes. It is." I made a deliberate pass over the faces in the room. Most of them looked a little shocked to suddenly be considered a suspect in a murder. Good. "Well, did anyone else see or talk to Tom after Colleen dropped him off at his apartment on Friday night?"

No one said anything. I was hoping one of them would jump forward and tell me something I didn't already know, but no such luck.

"Would you like a beer or something else to drink?" Norma offered kindly.

I declined and, as politely as I could, made my way out. I was satisfied that I had sufficiently stirred the pot. It was time to let it simmer.

From Osler Street I headed downtown. Clark Shiwaga was one of the senior partners of Bell Brown Shiwaga, better known as BBS. Their offices are on the eleventh floor of the Saskatoon Square Building on the corner of 4th Avenue and 22nd Street. It was now almost 5:30 and I hoped their hours of business extended beyond that time. I circled the block a few times until someone who'd been waiting to pick up his spouse pulled out of the perfect parking spot. I was the only one in the elevator going up. Everyone else was going down. Not a good sign. I stepped off the lift just in time to see who I guessed was the BBS receptionist struggling to lock the heavy, glass, front doors.

"I'm sorry," I said through the space between the doors. "I guess I'm a little late for my appointment. Parking down there is miserable!"

The young woman had dark, almost black, hair and tiny black-rimmed spectacles. Bags under her eyes told me she'd had a tough day. She struggled to pull open the door. "You have an appointment? I don't remember seeing anything in the book. Which lawyer were you booked to meet with?"

I followed her into the main foyer of the office. Yes! I was in! "Mr. Shiwaga. Can you please tell him Russell Quant is here." I was betting my client's lawyer would feel obliged to see me. She motioned for me to take a seat and disappeared behind a wall. I took a seat in the plush waiting area and took in the incredible view offered by floor to ceiling windows. From eleven storeys up, if you squint just a bit, Saskatoon can look like a bustling metropolis. Most of all, I noticed the trees—in parks, down boulevards and along the riverbank. The October sun sashaying towards the horizon gave the streets and buildings a crisp, clean look.

"Mr. Quant." Clark Shiwaga's bulk swaggered into the waiting room. He held out his hand for a manly handshake and directed me into a nearby meeting room.

"Have you come up with something?" he asked as he closed the door and indicated for me to take a seat, which we both did. "Mr. Chavell, as you might imagine, is getting a little anxious."

"Actually I did find something interesting." I let the sentence drop there. For some reason I wanted him to ask for it.

"Oh, what is that?"

Thank you. "Apparently, Tom Osborn was never in France."

The lawyer scowled. He looked genuinely perplexed. Either that or he was a good actor. "What are you talking about? The ticket was gone. Mr. Chavell's friend in Paris confirmed she saw him there."

"I found Tom's passport. He did not travel out of the country. At least not recently. I've arranged to send a photo of Tom to Madame Fontaine. You may recall she had never met Tom before. I believe that when she sees the photo, she'll tell us the man who visited her apartment was someone else."

"Then who? Who was it? And where was Tom?"

"That's what I was hoping you could help me with."

He was silent.

"I know you visited Tom the morning of the wedding." Risk time. I needed to know if the silvery-brown truck Mrs. Coyle saw outside Tom's apartment building belonged to Clark Shiwaga. I needed to know if Clark Shiwaga was more involved in this than he was letting on. I was betting I'd only find out the answer to one of my questions. For now.

With almost no hesitation, he replied, "That's right."

My eyes widened a little. That was too easy. My client's lawyer seemed to be in the habit of keeping things from me and I wasn't in the mood for it any longer. "Why didn't you mention this to me before?"

"I didn't see a need. If you remember, I wasn't involved in this until after you returned from France. When Tom was found dead, our concern was what happened to him after he returned from France, not before he left."

He was right. I hated to admit it. But things had changed now. Depending on when Tom was actually killed, Clark Shiwaga's Saturday morning visit might be important. Or not.

"Then you won't mind telling me why you were there?"

"Tom had some papers to sign before the ceremony."

"Papers?"

"Although the wedding was not a legal ceremony, Tom and Mr. Chavell, wisely I might add, treated it as such. They were putting certain legal agreements in place to protect themselves including a living will and a pre-ceremony agreement—kind of like a prenuptial contract. I was having Tom sign the final documents. Of course he had already agreed to do this."

Typical lawyer. Talk about bad timing. The papers couldn't be signed the week before rather than the morning of the wedding? "About what time was this?"

"Our appointment was for eleven Saturday morning. Tom had already approved earlier drafts of all the papers so it only took us about ten minutes and then I was gone."

So it would seem Colleen Arber was officially off the hook. Tom was still alive the morning after she'd dropped him off. But something else was bothering me. "Harold never mentioned this when we first met. Was he unaware of your visit?"

The attorney shrugged his hulking shoulders. "Apparently so. But he wasn't unaware that the papers needed to be signed before the ceremony."

I had no choice but to live with that explanation. "What state of mind was Tom in when you saw him?"

"Tom was a pretty easygoing guy."

I found it interesting the lawyer called Tom by his first name but still referred to his client as Mr. Chavell. Did they know each other better than he was letting on?

"He seemed just fine. But even if he wasn't, I'm not sure I'd have been able to tell. I didn't know Tom that well."

So much for that idea. Maybe.

"So you didn't notice anything out of the ordinary?"

"Nothing."

"You didn't stay for lunch? Perhaps something from the Blue Carrot Café?"

He quirked his head to one side as if trying to determine the significance of my question. "No. As I've said, it took ten minutes and then I left."

The lawyer was on the verge of objecting to being on the wrong end of an interrogation. But he stopped himself. He knew I was only doing my job and grudgingly gave in to the questions.

"Did you happen to notice a half-heart pendant in a jeweller's box while you were there? Or a gift package of any kind— wrapped or unwrapped?"

Another quizzical look. "No."

"There's one more thing that's been bothering me, Mr. Shiwaga."

He looked at me with surly eyes, unimpressed with my "Columbo" routine. "Oh?"

"Why didn't you tell me about the cabin?"

"What are you asking?"

"The cabin at Pike Lake. The one owned by Harold Chavell. The one near where Tom Osborn's body was found. Why didn't you tell me about it when Chavell sent you to re-hire me?"

Again with the shrug. "I thought you knew."

"Bullshit. You just didn't want to implicate your client any further than he already was."

"And what's wrong with that?"

"A little thing called obstruction of justice. You're a lawyer. Didn't you read that chapter in your law book?"

"Mr. Quant, you are not the police. I don't have to tell you anything."

"But I'd think you'd want to if I'm supposed to be on your side!"

That shut him up.

"I want to go out there. I want to see the cabin."

"Why? The police have already been through it. There's nothing left for you to find."

"If a murder I'm investigating took place in that cabin, I want to see it."

"Harold Chavell did not kill Tom Osborn!"

Our eyes met across the desk like stalemated lasers. "I never said he did."

Shiwaga grudgingly pulled a miniscule electronic organizer from his suit breast pocket and together we agreed on a time to meet at Pike Lake.

"The next time you see Mr. Chavell," I said when our date was arranged, "tell him I'll try to get in to see him as soon as I can. With these new developments I have a lot of things to do."

"Do you think you're on to something that could clear Mr. Chavell?"

I gave the attorney the most confident look I could muster. "I'm on to something that I hope will lead us to the truth."

"Do you doubt Mr. Chavell's innocence?" His tone was rough.

"My job is to discover any proof of his innocence. If there is such proof, Mr. Shiwaga, I'll find it." To show him I wasn't kidding, I walked out without another word. I didn't have to prove anything to this stuffed shirt. And it made for a nice exit.

I ignored the speed limit on my way to Innovation Place. I wanted to catch Randy Wurz at work. Given the time of day, I knew I was pushing it but I'd been lucky so far. As I crossed the University Bridge for what seemed like the hundredth time that day I wondered if Randy may have been too upset to return to work after his partner's funeral and the gathering at Kathryn Wagner's. I used my cellphone to call his office number and, as I'd suspected, reached an answering machine. I tried Randy's home number. No answer. By my watch I saw it was now after 6:00 p.m. Since I was already near Innovation Place I decided to drive through anyway. Perhaps he'd gone into work but wasn't answering the phone. I knew Randy drove a Jaguar because I'd seen him pulling up in it at the funeral. I searched the parking lot nearest The Galleria building that housed QW Technologies. No luck. Randy's car could have been in any one of several other lots but I was betting it was more than likely at home or sitting outside a fancy restaurant. I parked and jumped out of my car anyway and went inside. The security guard was either away from his post or off duty so I went on by and down the now familiar hallways to QW. I tried the door. Locked. I knocked. No answer. My luck had run out.

As I returned to my car a new thought hit me. I remembered seeing a stack of invoices in Tom's office from a company called TechWorld. And when I was in Tom's apartment and hit redial on his phone, I reached TechWorld's answering machine. Whatever this company was, it definitely had a few connections to Tom. I reached into the glove compartment and dug out the Innovation Place map the security guard had given me on my first visit. And there it was. TechWorld. It was listed as one of the tenants of a nearby building on Research Drive.

Deciding to walk, I headed out, map in hand. I noted that the building in question was across the road from another building called The Atrium that was connected by walkway to the east end of The Galleria. So from QW most of the distance could have been covered indoors. According to the map, the building's name was its address and when I found it I saw that it was one of the smaller buildings I'd seen so far, probably only housing three or four separate businesses.

"Can I help you, son?" a cheerful man asked me when I opened the front door. He was in his late sixties and stooped behind a portable night security desk.

"I was wondering if you could tell me where to find TechWorld?"

He gave his grizzled jowls a rub with an arthritic hand. "I could, but won't do you no good. They're all gone for the day, unless you've got a lab booked. If ya got a lab booked, I can help you. But you gotta sign in first."

I wasn't sure what he was talking about but that had never stopped me before. "I see. Can you tell me a little about what TechWorld does?"

"Just a security guard, son. Don't know what half these fancy high-tech places around here really do," he said pleasantly.

I chuckled. "I know what you mean."

"Maybe something over there could help you." He half rose from his well-worn swivel chair and pointed towards the entrance I'd just come through where a chrome rack was overflowing with brochures.

I sauntered over to the rack as if I had nothing better to do. The security guard settled back in his chair, picked up a Zane Grey novel and resumed reading. The old guy was right. I found a vast collection of written material provided by many of the Innovation Place tenants describing what they did, why they did it and who paid them to do it. And among them was a brochure for TechWorld. A quick read told me all I needed to know. TechWorld made its money by renting specially designed laboratory facilities, about a half dozen of them, to research park tenants, particularly those in the high technology sector who needed to perform experiments but weren't big enough (or rich enough) to have their own labs. I made my way back to the security guard.

"You said you could help me if I had a lab booked?"

He put down his novel. I could see by the look in his eyes that he was beginning to suspect I might be up to no good. I had to work quickly before I completely lost him. "Well I'm really here looking for a friend of mine but he's not in his office. I was wondering if maybe he was in one of the testing labs." Before he could say no I added, "My friend is Randy Wurz, from QW Technologies. Poor guy. Just lost his business partner, Tom Osborn."

"Oh yeah, Mr. Osborn. What a shame. He was a nice fella."

"So, can you help me?"

"Sometimes people come in after hours to use the labs for their tests or whatever it is they do in there. I let them in. Some fellas who do a lot of work here have their own key. But just to their own lab, the one they're renting that is. They're still s'posed to sign in though. But I can tell ya without even looking that Mr. Wurz isn't in a lab. It was always Mr. Osborn in there. There was another guy sometimes, but hardly ever Mr. Wurz."

"Mr. Osborn was always in the testing facility?"

"Oh yeah. Recently anyways. QW has a standing reservation for one of the labs—for the last coupla months anyway. Maybe even further back than that."

"But Mr. Wurz hardly came in with Mr. Osborn?"

"Nope. Some other man though. He'd sign him in as his guest."

I shook my head with great sympathy and sadness in my eyes. "I wonder if his guest has even heard about what happened."

Suddenly the security guard was on my side again. "Ya want me to get you the name? I could do that. I just can't let you look at the sign in sheet or let you into the room. It's all confidential like."

I nodded vigorously, full of respect for his protection of confidential matters. "Of course, of course."

I watched as the man pulled a binder out of a side drawer and began flipping pages. "Here we go," he said. "Actually the two of them were together the last time Mr. Osborn was in here himself. Yeah, him and a Mr. Dave Biddle, looks like."

Dave Biddle from Quasar? The man I saw talking with Randy Wurz at Kathryn Wagner's house earlier today? Something didn't seem right. From all I'd just heard, Tom was testing something in one of TechWorld's labs, yet his partner, Randy Wurz, had told me nothing new was on the burner. Did he not know about it? Why was Dave Biddle with Tom in the lab? Did Tom have a secret project that he was sharing with someone other than his own business partner? I asked the security guard to tell me the date of that last visit.

Tom Osborn and Dave Biddle were in the testing facility the day before Tom disappeared.

Chapter 14

LATE FOR MY APPOINTMENT WITH CLARK SHIWAGA, I cleared the city limits heading southeast on Highway Seven towards Pike Lake and floored it. Sunset would be around seven-thirty and I wanted to see Chavell's place in daylight. In fifteen minutes I was slowing down at the entrance of the park. I noticed both tollbooths had signs declaring themselves closed for the season, allowing me free access into the resort. Parked to one side, halfway in the ditch with the motor idling, was Clark Shiwaga's truck. I pulled up alongside the vehicle. The lawyer had a sour look on his face just in case I hadn't already guessed that he wasn't the kind of guy used to being kept waiting. Without rolling down his window, he nodded and motioned for me to follow.

He eased out of the ditch and made a left turn off the blacktop directly into what seemed to be nothing more than a clump of poplars. I followed slowly over rutted gravel with thick brush on my left and, eventually, lakeside cabins on my right. The buildings were difficult to see from the road, often hidden behind gnarled clusters of trees and makeshift fences. In less than two minutes we'd reached our destination. I pulled off onto a berm at the end of the street next to Shiwaga. I fished around in the back of the car for a few supplies and exited. Shiwaga's imposing frame was standing next to my vehicle, waiting. I held up a flashlight. "Thought we might need this," I said brightly. What I didn't show him was the other goody I'd retrieved and slipped into my jacket pocket. My gun. It would get dark soon. I was in an unfamiliar place. Shiwaga was a big guy who I didn't completely trust. And this was a murder investigation. I figured I might need the gun more than the flashlight.

Shiwaga simply growled something about not being out there long enough to need the flashlight and then led the way down a well-worn path through a wall of tall, gangly caragana. Darren Kirsch had told me there were only a handful of residents who maintained homes at Pike Lake year round. From what I saw on the short drive to Chavell's, none of those people lived on the street we were currently on. Most of the cabins we passed had windows boarded over, their water lines likely drained and furniture covered in sheets.

As far as I could tell Chavell's place was the last one on the block, nothing beyond it but more bush and scrubby grassland. I wondered why Chavell would have chosen it. It didn't seem his style. I stumbled along behind the bulk of the big lawyer and immediately on the other side of the caragana we found a rambling cottage surrounded by Swiss stone pines and junipers. Unlike some of its neighbours, the building appeared freshly painted and had recently been re-shingled with cedar shakes. I saw no signs of preparation for winter hibernation. With all that was going on, closing his lakeside retreat for the season was likely the last thing on Chavell's mind. Besides, he was behind bars. Or perhaps it was winterized—the building certainly looked hardy enough.

As we continued on the path down one side of the property squeezing between cottage and trees I found myself enjoying the scent of pine needles and long-dead campfires, the chirp of crickets sounding the approach of evening. Was I a closet camper? I shuddered at the thought. Or maybe it was just the cold.

The path curved around to the rear of the building and ended at a small, wooden deck raised a foot off the ground and the back door. As Shiwaga dug in his pockets for keys I took in the scenery. Not unlike his home at Cathedral Bluffs, but on a much, much smaller scale, Chavell's lot appeared to be long and narrow. Several lines of trees and other indigenous vegetation effectively blocked the line of sight from any neighbouring properties. The lot had a surprisingly spectacular view of placid Pike Lake. The area from the back door deck to the floating dock at lake's edge was a downhill tract that grew steeper as you got closer to the water. The landscaping had a low maintenance kind of look. I liked that.

Shiwaga unlocked the door. It opened into a large, glassed-in porch area lined with overstuffed couches overflowing with cushions. It looked to be a recent addition, not insulated from what I could tell, but it would be a great room to take full advantage of the view. I could imagine Chavell and Tom spending lazy, rainy afternoons in this room reading and snoozing, which, as I understand it, is what one does when at the lake. Although there was still plenty of daylight shining in through the windows, Shiwaga turned on a light and I deposited my flashlight into a pocket.

"So here it is," he said unenthusiastically.

"You have your own key to the place?" I asked innocently (but not really).

"When Mr. Chavell was arrested he gave me all of his keys. For safekeeping." He then added for good measure, "He trusts me."

I nodded in a "yeah, whatever" kind of way. "Can I look around?"

"I'll be in the kitchen." He turned and walked off.

As I watched him leave, I grimly admitted to myself that Chavell's lawyer was probably right. There was likely nothing here to help Chavell's case. The police would have gone over this place like a Hoover vacuum. I wasn't exactly sure what I hoped to find, but if this was where Tom Osborn met his untimely death, I knew in my gut I couldn't ignore it. After another quick scan of the porch I headed further into the dwelling. The next room was a smaller sitting area with two doors—one led into a bedroom and through the other I could see a kitchen where Shiwaga had found himself a beer and was leaning against a counter enjoying it. I decided to try the bedroom first.

I could tell the room was expensively decorated. The massive sleigh bed and matching suite were made of a knotty pine that looked rustic and aged but had definitely not come from a bargain antique shop. In one corner of the room was a cozy area with a loveseat, two plump easy chairs, a couple of shelves (more knotty pine) heavy with books and a fireplace. Thickly woven rugs warmed the hardwood floor, and on a coffee table a remote the size of a dinner plate controlled a battery of entertainment options—stereo, DVD, big screen TV. Even before I saw the framed photographs on the fireplace mantle, I knew Harold Chavell and Tom Osborn had, together, called this place home.

I now knew why Chavell had chosen this out-of-the-way location. A luxurious oasis hidden amongst the anonymity of mediocrity. This was where they lived as a couple, at a distance from the city, at a distance from other people and from their high-powered public careers. This wasn't just a summer cabin. It was a year-round home. During the week, Chavell lived in his ornamental castle in Cathedral Bluffs and Tom in his antiseptic apartment on Main Street, but together they set up house and home, here on Pike Lake. This was where they existed as Harry and Tom, the couple. This was where they'd had fun, relaxed and cooked together, and made love. This was why Tom's apartment appeared so barren. This was why Mrs. Coyle rarely saw him on weekends.

I made my way to the fireplace and studied each picture displayed there. One was of Chavell, looking unusually casual in jeans and a T-shirt, barbecuing something in the backyard, a private smile on his face, a beer in one hand and a basting brush in the other. There was a picture of Tom napping with an equally zonked out Siamese cat perched on his chest. Another photo showed Tom on a summer day running naked from the spray of a water hose and the last one was of both of them in a canoe, on Pike Lake at dusk, looking golden and fit and utterly content.

This was what I had been missing all along. Through all of this, I never had a good sense of the relationship, of how Chavell and Tom really felt about one another. Friends and family gave me details, but, with unknown agendas abounding, I listened to their words with a healthy dose of skepticism. Now it was clear to me. They had wanted to get married. They should have gotten married. Someone stopped that from happening. Now, one of them was dead and the other in jail. I looked again at the picture of the two of them in the canoe. The camera had caught them in a split second of perfect happiness. I whispered, "I'm sorry."

I was yanked from my reverie by a noise. Shiwaga. It was time to move on. I made my way through the sitting room into the kitchen. The lawyer was swigging his beer and looking impatient.

"Find anything?" he asked.

I shook my head and looked around. Like the rest of the rooms the kitchen was artfully done so as not to appear too modern, yet it lacked nary a culinary amenity known to man. Certain that Shiwaga had me on an internal metre which he'd undoubtedly find some way to charge me for, I moved throughout the rest of the cottage, quickly assessing the potential for hidden clues. But the only thing I found hidden in that cabin at Pike Lake was evidence of a life shared by two men who loved one another.

I had to find out what the autopsy report had concluded about Tom Osborn's time of death. That meant Darren. I had been trying to call him unsuccessfully all day. He must have been on the street. It was time for more drastic and irritating measures.

After a quick trip home to let Barbra out and inhale a submarine sandwich, I pulled up to the Kirsch residence on Sommerfeld Avenue near Holliston Park. It's a family-friendly area of older, utilitarian homes, aging lawns and healthy cedars. I had never been to Darren's home before and for some reason I was curious to observe how and where he lived when he wasn't being Oscar the Grouch. Here he was husband and daddy and neighbour. As I walked up the path to the front porch, I saw in the glow of a street lamp, a massive willow tree on the front lawn that had yet to lose any leaves. A rake was leaning against the side of the house waiting to be called into service. I knocked. The door opened and a petite Darren Kirsch looked up at me. His son.

"Hi," I said, "is your dad at home?"

"Who are you?" His seven-year-old voice had a lisp caused by some missing teeth.

"My name is Russell. What's yours?"

Before the kid could answer a young girl stepped into the doorway behind him. She looked a little uncertain as she stared at me. She was too old to be a daughter. Fifteen, maybe sixteen.

"HicanIhelpyou?" The words spilled from her mouth as if she wanted nothing more than to get them out of there. Her arms were wrapped around her skinny frame to ward off the evening chill.

"Hi. My name is Russell Quant and I'm looking for Darren Kirsch. Am I at the right house?"

"Ohyeahheliveshere."

"Could I see him? Is he home?"

"Wellsortabutnotrightnow. I'mthebabysitter."

"It's date night," piped up the more eloquent youngster.

I looked down at the boy. "Your mom and dad went on a date?"

"They just want to get away from us for a while," he said with an infectious giggle. Cute kid. The babysitter I wasn't so sure about.

"Yeahthatsright. ButtheyjustwenttotheDQon8th. I'mjusttheneighbour. Saidthey'dbebackinanhour."

"Thanks. Goodnight."

As soon as they closed the door I jumped into the Mazda, Batman-style, sort of, and pointed it towards the Dairy Queen on 8th Street. It wasn't far and I was betting they might have even walked. I drove what would have been their most direct route but spotted no couple that met their description.

The Dairy Queen on 8th, unlike others in the city, is nothing more than a simple glass-encased booth located on a large lot (a prime piece of real estate) with loads of parking space surrounding it. It serves walk up customers only and is closed throughout the winter months. Like the greening of grass in spring and colouring of leaves in fall, it is a popular belief that the opening and closing of this particular DQ are sure signs of the change in season. It heartened me to see the cheerful lights of the tiny kiosk still blazing well into the dusk of a chilly October night.

I pulled to a stop and surveyed a meagre crowd in fleece jackets and woolly pullovers waiting for their ice-cream treats, refusing to give up an activity best left for summertime. I spotted the Kirsch's immediately. Treena Kirsch isn't a supermodel but she's damn pretty with curly, auburn hair, immense brown eyes and a tiny, fit-looking body. I'd begun to notice Darren showing signs of a slight paunch, but even wrapped up in a thick cotton jacket I could tell Treena keeps herself in fighting shape. She's a normally bright and cheerful person. Some people like that are just irritating, but Treena seems to know how to maintain her effervescence at the perfect temperature depending on the situation. She is a University of Saskatchewan grad with a Bachelor of Education degree, who always expected to and did leave her career behind when the kids started coming. It had been a promotion as far as both she and Darren were concerned. According to Treena, she and Darren each had a role to play and did so without a word of complaint or feeling of guilt. Darren works long, hard hours, cares for the children and provides funds to run the household. Treena works long, hard hours, cares for the children and runs the household. The arrangement seems to work for them.

As I got out of my car and ambled towards the two waiting in line to order, I wondered whether Darren was aware of the wealth of personal information I'd traded with his wife over punch at several year's worth of police social functions. I stopped where I knew they'd eventually have to notice me and pretended to study the outdoor display board that listed the myriad of ice cream treats available to me.

"Russell!" Bingo.

I turned and smiled at Treena Kirsch, ignoring Darren altogether. "Treena! How are you?" I approached.

She gave me a quick hug and pulled back to allow her husband to greet me. He was stuck.

"Quant," he murmured.

"Hey Darren," I said, enthused, playing the part to the hilt. I may have been overdoing it, but so what. "Say, seeing as you're here, buddy, do you have a minute?"

"I mightta guessed."

Treena jumped right in. "You two boys go talk while I order our stuff, but then that's it. This is date night."

I could tell by the look on his face, Darren was wishing she hadn't told me that.

"Date night? Isn't that sweet." I smiled at the happy couple. Darren frowned at me.

"Well you can guess how easy it is to forget about our relationship when there are three rascals running around the house demanding every bit of our attention," Treena explained.

"Absolutely." I motioned towards a wooden picnic bench at one side of the kiosk. "We'll be right over there."

"Do you want me to get yours?"

"Huh?"

"Your ice cream. Do you want me to order it for you?"

"Oh." I'd nearly forgotten my ruse. "No. No thanks. I'm not sure what I want yet. I'll get it later."

"Okay."

I walked over to the picnic table and hoped Darren was behind me.

He was.

It was chilly out but bearable. We stood with our hands buried in our pockets and our jaws set tight.

"I found something you should probably know about," I told him. I thought it would be advisable to start with the "give" part of our give and take relationship.

"Have you been snooping where you shouldn't be?"

"Who decides where I shouldn't snoop?"

"Obviously no one. What did you find?"

"Tom Osborn's passport."

Darren's eyes flashed with curiosity. "Where did you find it? We were all over his apartment and office and Chavell's house and cabin. Nothing like that turned up."

"He had a storage locker in the basement of his apartment building."

"How did you…? Never mind, I don't want to know. What else did you find down there?"

"Not much. But the passport was interesting."

"Exact date of return to Canada."

"No." Now I had his full attention.

"What do you mean, no?"

"There were no stamps for France in the passport, Darren. Tom Osborn was never there."

"How can that be? For Pete's sake, you're the one who said he was there!"

"I was led to believe he was there. But he wasn't. I never actually saw him. People alluded to the fact he was there. I received notes supposedly from him. But I never actually saw him in the flesh."

"Damn! Who would do that? Why? What kind of game is going on here?"

"All very good questions. Just not very original."

He gave me a curdled look. "Are you sure the passport was his?"

"Yes."

"Why the hell didn't you say something sooner?"

"I just found it today and you weren't answering your phone."

He shook his head, deep in thought and began pacing back and forth in front of the picnic table, in and out of the splatter of light from a spotlight mounted on the DQ kiosk. "Time of death…"

Excellent! If he could tell me what I wanted to know without my asking, he'd still owe me one. "Uh-huh?"

"Of course the formal reports from the enquiry aren't available yet, but we do have some information. The body being left in cold water was screwing with the tests. But y'know, we weren't too worried about a precise time of death because we were certain we had the right man. Chavell had motive, the body was disposed of near his property and the murder weapon was covered in his prints and found in his house. We didn't push it any farther."

"And what do you think now?"

He stopped pacing and seemed to concentrate on the question before he gave me his answer. "To tell you the truth, not much different. I still think Chavell did it. Maybe even more so now. He's just one smart cookie. He sent you to France to find someone he'd already killed. How clever is that? If you don't have an alibi for when the murder was actually committed, then simply remove any suspicion that there even was a murder. All he had to do was make it seem as if the victim had left the country and disappeared. And he sets you up to prove it! That's freaking brilliant!"

Inside, I grudgingly agreed. "Whoever killed Tom Osborn went to a lot of trouble to weigh down the body with cinder blocks and dump it in the lake," I argued. "They never expected it to be found. They weren't worried about time of death or an alibi. They never expected to be caught."

"But if the body did get loose—as it did—it makes it tough for us to pin it on anyone because time of death is indeterminate and everyone's alibi is out the window. Could have been anyone. But by having you place Tom in France, Chavell had everyone thinking the murder took place a week after it really did—at a time when he could easily conjure up an alibi. Well I'm not buying it."

"What about the gunshot? Wouldn't that determine time of death? You told me yourself there are year-round residents at Pike Lake. The cabin is lakefront. I was out there and it didn't look to me like there were any neighbours in residence, but gunshots are pretty loud. Someone could have easily heard it."

"I know what you're getting at, Quant. We asked around, and you're right, the properties nearest Chavell's are used only in the summer, so there likely weren't any people nearby. And now, knowing Tom could have been killed much earlier, we won't be able to narrow down the time frame to more than a period of several days. That makes it difficult for potential witnesses to remember anything specific. Chances are someone heard it and passed it off as a wayward hunter or backfiring car. Or maybe the killer used a silencer. At the end of the day, Quant, it doesn't help get your client off—actually it might point the finger even more strongly in his direction if he doesn't have an alibi for the time the gunshot was heard."

"But it might also point the finger at a whole lot of other people too."

He grunted, unconvinced.

I grunted, mad. "I think the police department is scared to consider Chavell might be innocent because they have no idea who else might be responsible. You're desperate for a successful and quick conviction on this one. The Saskatoon Police Service has been going through a thorny time in the garden of public opinion and there've been too many unsolved murders in the last few years. Your reputation is on the line here."

Darren's eyes were flashing again, but this time it wasn't from curiosity. "We have a suspect with motive and ownership and possession of a murder weapon which is covered with his finger-prints and, depending on time of death, no clear alibi. What does that sound like to you?"

"Sounds too easy is what it sounds like." I knew I was making Darren spit fire out of his ears, but it wasn't because of what I was saying. It was because I was picking at the doubt he already had in his mind. "Has your department done any real police work on this case? Or have you simply let it all fall onto the silver platter served to you? Have you any idea what this is doing to the reputation of a respected businessman? Before all of this, Harold Chavell was a name that meant success, now it will forever be tied to a gay murder, no matter the outcome. This city is too small for that to ever go away. He will never have the life here he once had. So you'd better be damn sure you have the right man in jail. Because he's already begun paying the price." I knew the pressures and expectations Darren faced in the department and from a sometimes untrusting public, but I needed him to understand the implications to Chavell before it was too late.

We saw Treena approaching us with two banana splits. He leaned into me. I could feel his breath hot against my chilled cheek. "You really piss me off, Quant," he said.

I nodded.

It was coming up to midnight when I pulled into the garage off the back alley behind my house. It had been a long day and all I wanted to do was crawl into bed. I couldn't believe it was still Wednesday. It seemed like eons since I'd attended Tom Osborn's funeral but it had only been that morning. When I swung open my car door, I knew the day was not done with me yet. Barbra was barking. I knew something was not right. Barbra does not bother with more than a "woof" or two when I come home. And the bark itself was suspect. It was high-pitched, whereas on the uncommon occasion Barbra does bark, from excitement or playfulness, it's a low and rich sound. She was upset or unsure about something. She was seeing something or someone she did not recognize. She was warning me of danger.

I stepped out of my car fingering the pistol still in my jacket pocket from my meeting with Clark Shiwaga at Pike Lake. Thankfully I hadn't had to use it, and I hoped I wouldn't have to use it now. I tiptoed to the rear of the garage and eased open the door that leads into my backyard. At first all I could see were blocky shadows as my eyes adjusted to the dim light. Although my backyard is overhung with frothy birch trees, a protective red oak or two and some spruce, the darkness was not absolute thanks to the garden lights which come on automatically at sunset and stay on until 2:00 a.m. The wattage is low but enough to give the yard an otherworldly hazy glow as if it's being lit from underneath.

The garage door is hidden from the rest of the yard behind a bluff of mock orange bushes, caragana and Russian olive trees. I peered around it looking for intruders. But, to reverse an old saying, I couldn't see the trees for the forest. There was still too much stuff in my line of view. Maybe I'd have to rethink my landscaping next summer. I could still hear Barbra barking. What was she seeing or hearing? Whatever it was, I was blind and deaf to it.

I thought about strategy—the skulker's and mine. I decided it couldn't hurt to check things out from the front of the house. Besides, I was in no rush. I circled back around the garage into the back alley. I noticed Sereena's house was dark. Not home. If she had been I had no doubt my visitor would have been hog-tied and confessing a long time ago. I turned left and walked the full block back to the nearest corner and then up and over to my street. Not a creature was stirring. Lampposts gave off a bluish light. The air was cool and smelled as fresh as new laundry. Two houses in, I saw it. A yellow hatchback. It looked like the same car I'd seen parked near Chavell's property the night I returned from France. Was this the same car? And could this be the same "little yeller car" Mrs. Coyle saw outside of Tom's apartment building? But it was more than the colour of the car that alarmed me. It was the licence plate.

It read: TWIRP.

Apparently TWirp had decided to pay me a personal visit rather than return my e-mail. The car was parked several houses away from my own, so he or she was being careful. Or so they thought. My cheeks grew hot as I considered what TWirp might be doing in my neighbourhood. I doubted it was a coincidence. Did TWirp think I knew more than I did? Was I headed for the bottom of Pike Lake? I realized, too late, that I should have done more to find out the identity of my e-mail pal.

I crossed the street so that I was on the side opposite my house and did a quick walk-by. Nothing. I reconsidered my game plan and decided I'd have better luck sneaking up on my predator in the maze of my shadowy backyard. I retraced my steps to the garage. Again I stared hard into the green abyss. I pulled out my gun. Things were getting serious. I cautiously tiptoed down a brick pathway. Along the way I took fleeting refuge behind large ceramic pots now empty of foliage, wooden arbors and trellises holding up clematis skeletons. Every two steps I stopped to listen for sounds. There was only Barbra's insistent bark behind the back door of the house. I dared a peek from behind an evergreen into the small grassy opening that led up to the deck attached to the back of my house. The first thing to catch my eye was Zeus, a four-foot high cement fountain in the shape of a male nymph who I'd relieved of his watering duties only weeks before. Even in the dark I could see the look on his chiselled face. Not pleased. I was about to move closer when I heard a sound. A scuffling of feet on crunchy autumn leaves that had missed the wrath of my rake. Who am I kidding? I hadn't even begun raking yet. Good thing.

More scuffling. Someone was definitely in my backyard.

It sounded like only one person, but I had no way to be sure. The footfalls had stopped but I could sense a presence. I thought I could hear breathing but it may have been my own. My best guess was that someone was standing near or sitting on the metalwork patio set to my far right. I could have played it safe or gone back to my car and used my cellphone to call the police. But pride and impatience make me do stupid things sometimes.

"Okay, just stop right there," I said. I didn't yell, but spoke in a loud, authoritative voice. I thought it best not to mention to whoever was out there that I had a gun until I was sure that they didn't. No use starting a fight at the OK Corral if I don't have to.

"Who is it?" a man's voice called back.

I had to stifle a laugh. Shouldn't I be the one asking that question? There was something familiar about the voice. I knew this person. "It's Russell. Who's there?"

"It's Kent Melicke," the voice said. "I've been waiting for you."

I put the gun in my jacket pocket but kept my hand on it as I circled the bush that separated us and approached the figure in the sitting area. As I got closer I could see that indeed it was the man I'd met twice earlier that day. Tom Osborn's ex-lover. It was the same man but he looked different. His fashionably-styled blonde hair now looked dishevelled and the tortoiseshell glasses were gone. He looked younger and I wondered if maybe he was still in his twenties rather than in his thirties as I'd earlier surmised. "You're TWirp?"

He looked surprised to hear the name. "Wh...how did you know that?"

I gave my best "I'm a seasoned investigator" look, wordlessly telling him he should know better than to try to fool me. "You really should avoid vanity licence plates if you're planning to break into someone's house."

"I wasn't breaking into your house."

"Then what are you doing here?" I asked, noticing that his arms were shivering at his sides.

"I came to see you. I have something to tell you. When you weren't home I thought I'd wait. But I started to think some of the neighbours might get suspicious if I hung around out front. So I came back here. I was waiting for a light to come on. That dog wouldn't stop growling or barking the whole time."

Good doggie, I thought to myself.

I looked at the man. Quite a few smart-ass remarks came to mind. Hadn't he heard of a phone? Didn't he think a barking dog would alert the neighbours as much as a skulker in the front yard? Ever think of waiting in your car? But I relented. He looked cold. And I was too. I couldn't be certain he wasn't dangerous, but I was bigger than he was, I had a gun and I didn't think he did. I felt safety was sufficiently on my side to invite him in.

It took a few moments to settle Barbra down. She knew this man was the reason she hadn't gotten any sleep for the last while and she would not easily forgive him for that. I fed her some doggie treats to reward her for her heroism.

"This is a beautiful house," he said timidly, eyeing Barbra with mistrust.

"Uh-huh." I was feeling a bit snappish. After all, it had been a long day, it was now well past midnight, and this fellow had pretty much forced his way into my home. But, I wanted information from him, so I decided to make nice. "Would you like some wine or something else to drink?"

"Just water would be great. No ice."

I led him into the main living room and after I poured his water from the tap at the wet bar we sat down. Briefly, I inspected Kent Melicke as a man. Not quite my type, but definitely attractive. He'd taken off his jacket and his tight T-shirt showed off a nicely-toned torso. I couldn't help think about how long it had been since I'd had a strange man over for drinks. Or anything else. For a second, it was oddly erotic.

"So you called this meeting," I said. "What did you have to tell me?"

His thin fingers strummed the rim of his glass as he looked up at me with liquid eyes. "Do you know who I am?"

"I know about TWirp. Now tell me what it means. What does 'TW' stand for?"

He looked unsure of what I was asking, but then caught on. "Oh! That means nothing. Just a slip of the finger when I first came up with my hotmale e-mail address."

"So it really is Twirp with a small 'w'?"

"Yeah."

"Why?" I shouldn't have asked the question. It was doubtful now that it had any bearing on my case.

"Nickname I used to have before I started going to the gym."

It was my turn to be confused. He flexed a not unimpressive bicep at me. "Gotya," I said.

"But do you really know who I am?" He repeated his original question.

This time I knew what he meant. " I know you and Tom Osborn used to be lovers. I know you had a meeting with him shortly before the wedding." I didn't really know the last bit, but I took a good guess.

"Yes. We were lovers. We had a wonderful relationship."

Couldn't have been that wonderful, I thought to myself. Where was this guy going with this? I wasn't in the mood to hear about how they once painted their cozy kitchen bright yellow or bought a puppy together.

"We should have never broken up. I didn't want to, but Tom was so hurt. He couldn't see beyond it to remember how good we were together."

"See beyond what? What was he hurt about?"

"You know. I made a mistake."

Mistake, in gay lexicon, especially when said so cavalierly, can mean only one thing. Kent had fooled around with another guy while he was seeing Tom. "Is this what you came to tell me?"

"No. I came to tell you I lied."

"You screwed around on Tom and you lied to him?"

"I lied to you. Earlier today. At Tom's sister's house when I told you I hadn't seen Tom in a while? That was a lie. Colleen wasn't the last one to see Tom. It was me. I saw him last."

Aha! The meeting TWirp referred to in the e-mail message. This was getting interesting. "You had lunch with him at his apartment the next day. The day of the wedding." I took a chance, but I was sure I was right. It was Kent Melicke who shared the vegetarian meal from The Blue Carrot Café with Tom.

The young man looked at me as if I was the Amazing Kreskin. "How…?" Was all he asked.

I didn't owe him any explanations. "What happened when you met?" I had reason to suspect Tom had been alive up to 11:15 a.m. when Clark Shiwaga said he left after having Tom sign the legal agreements. Mrs. Coyle suspected someone else might have been to visit Tom. Someone in a yellow car. I now knew it was Kent.

"I came over around twelve or twelve-thirty. I wanted to get there early enough to…to…"

"What? Why did you go over there, Kent?"

"I wanted to tell him not to marry Harold. I wanted him to come back to me. To give us another try!" He spit this out as if he had been dying to tell someone the truth.

"Are you saying he didn't show up at his wedding because you asked him not to? Or did he refuse? Did you get angry?" I was baiting this man mercilessly. My jacket was nearby. The gun was close if I needed it. But I wouldn't. I could take this guy. I have muscles too.

"He was very kind. He didn't laugh or get mad or anything. I brought some food with me and we talked about things for a long time. He loved Harold and asked me to understand that. I did. I didn't want it to be true, but I did understand. I guess the news of the wedding just sent me a bit over the edge. Tom was such a terrific guy. You would have thought so too if you'd known him."

He was probably right.

"But I never hurt him. I never could. When I left, Tom was alive and well." Tears glistened. "I'd give anything if he still was. I miss him so much."

Oh crap. Was I going to have to console him? Hug him? "What time did you leave?" I continued my questioning—but in a caring way.

He sniffled but was under control. "Maybe around one-thirty or two."

I considered the options. Either Kent was stringing me a line in order to protect someone else, possibly Colleen or even Shiwaga, or he had been worried I would find out he was in Tom's apartment that day and wanted to come clean with a sanitized version of the truth. Or, alternatively, he was telling the truth and he was simply a heartbroken ex-lover who spent a few, harmless last moments with a man he loved but who didn't love him back.

"Did you give Tom a gift that afternoon?"

"A gift? No, no gift."

"Did you notice a half-heart pendant when you were in Tom's apartment?"

Kent shook his head. "No. I didn't see anything like that."

The half-heart pendant was slowly becoming the one piece of the puzzle that didn't seem to fit anywhere.

There was another loose end. "Were you spying on Harold Chavell?"

He stared at me like a deer caught in headlights. I was too clever for him and he knew it.

"I saw you, Kent." I didn't actually see Kent, but I did see a yellow car near Chavell's property that probably belonged to him. Maybe I wasn't cleverer than Kent Melicke, but I was definitely a better liar.

He looked down, seeming to fold in on himself. "I was there," he admitted in a little boy voice. "At the house."

"Why?"

Now he gazed up at me with a look that was pleading for me to believe him. "After I heard about what happened...at the wedding...I knew something was wrong. I mean obviously, right? Or else why wouldn't Tom have shown up? I began to wonder..."

I got it now. "You began to wonder if your little talk in his apartment had changed his mind after all?"

A nod. "No matter what he said, I know a part of him still cared about me. So I had to go see for myself. That's why I started watching the house. If they were fighting or breaking up or something...I wanted to be there...for him." He shook his head slowly and whispered, as if ashamed, "Just wishful thinking I guess."

"Would you like another glass of water?" I asked, practicing a random act of kindness.

He looked at me with something new in his eyes. "I'd like that."

Chapter 15

I WOKE UP ON THURSDAY MORNING feeling as if I'd had no sleep at all. My eyelids were heavy curtains, my mind a soupy swamp. I eyed the alarm clock with undisguised hate. It was not quite 6:00 a.m. I lay there, still as ice, careful not to nudge Barbra. I knew if I moved too suddenly and woke her, she'd suddenly have to go outside with such pitiful desperation, I'd be unable to resist. And then she'd be hungry and then I'd put on the coffee and before you knew it, the day would have begun long before I wanted it too. As I played mummy, I tried to decide whether I was coming down with something or was simply still pooped out after a trying day. I wished I could stay in bed all morning. But that was not to be. I had the feeling my case was gaining momentum and I was getting closer to finding Tom Osborn's killer. I had definitely shaken up a few people yesterday.

Giving up my dream of a morning of leisure I gently heeled Barbra and watched her eyes open. She pulled herself up to my face and began a mixture of tentative licks and plaintive whining. I pretended to be asleep and she let out a loud sigh and collapsed her furry head so close to my nose I could barely breathe. This dog knew exactly what she was doing.

"Time to go out?" I muttered trying not to ingest any fur.

Her ears perked up at the sound of my voice and she leapt off the bed with the grace of Hyacinth, the animated hippopotamus ballerina from that classic Disney film, *Fantasia*. I pulled back the covers and shivered in the coolness of the room. I dove into my woolly bathrobe and covered my nakedness. I let Barbra out through the bedroom's French doors at the same time sticking out my rooster-haired head for a wake up whiff. It smelled like fall— deep, musky and woodsy. The sky was ruddy as it awaited the sun, an almost startling contrast to the bright tincture of autumn showing off throughout the yard. By the time I retrieved the *StarPhoenix* from the front yard and set the coffee to perk, Barbra was at the kitchen door ready to be let back in, fed and watered. For half an hour we dawdled in the kitchen doing morning stuff, thoroughly enjoying each other's company.

I pulled into the parking lot nearest the building that housed QW Technologies before 8:00 a.m. I was betting Randy Wurz was the kind of guy who started his day early to make up for long lunches, golf games and 4:00 p.m. cocktail hours. I was right. The front door of the office was open but Miss Saskatoon 1979 was not yet in for the day. I dinged the little silver bell on her desk and waited patiently.

The door behind the receptionist's desk swung open and Randy Wurz appeared. "Mr. Quant?" He seemed surprised to see me. I wasn't sure if it was the time of day or whether he simply never expected to see my face again after our brief conversation at Kathryn Wagner's house.

"Mr. Wurz. Sorry to bother you so early in the morning. I was passing by and thought I'd take a chance on catching you before your day got too busy. Do you have a minute? There are a couple of things I want to discuss with you."

I looked closer at the man. The sharpness was gone. His clothes, although pricey, appeared decidedly less than crisp. He looked as tired as I'd felt earlier that morning. I was fine now. Maybe he also needed some coffee and doggie love.

"I am quite busy today, Mr. Quant. With Tom's death, the responsibility around here is all mine now. And really, I don't understand what's left to discuss. Tom is dead. Harold Chavell has been arrested for his murder. What more could there be to talk about?"

"I'm sorry, I know this must be a difficult time for you. Not only losing your business partner, but a friend."

"Yes."

"A friend who may have been murdered by someone other than the man they have in jail." I knew it was an insensitive trick, but appealing to his loyalty as a friend to get his attention was the only card I could think of playing.

"What are you talking about?" He looked genuinely surprised and taken aback, though I'd given him a hint of this at Kathryn Wagner's house. Of course he was probably too much in shock at the time to have heard anything I'd said.

"I'm not convinced Harold Chavell is the man who killed Tom."

His mouth remained open but no sound came out. A good opportunity for me to get to the point of my visit. "I saw you speaking with Dave Biddle at the reception after Tom's funeral. Do QW and Quasar do business together?"

"No," he said, looking as if he was still trying to catch up with what I'd said before. "Biddle's company develops long range, wireless communication software. Nothing to do with video games."

"So are the two of you friends?"

"No...well yes...well not really. Not friends. We're business acquaintances. I'd say Tom and Dave were friends of a sort. They knew how to talk to each other—both techno wizards, if you know what I mean. When Quasar first moved their operations to Innovation Place a few years ago, their offices were right next to ours in The Galleria. Dave and Tom became friends then I think. They'd toss ideas off one another. They both loved to theorize about new technologies no one had ever heard about or tried before. A lot of pie-in-the-sky kind of stuff mostly. Of course Quasar really took off when Dave invented a groundbreaking subway communications system that's now pretty much the industry standard, particularly in Europe. Anyway, Quasar stayed in Innovation Place but moved to a much bigger space in another building on Downey Road. I think Dave and Tom still kept in touch after that. But they weren't as close anymore."

"Did you know Tom and Dave would meet with each other at TechWorld?"

I was definitely rocking Randy Wurz's world. Once again he was speechless as he processed the information I supplied him.

I gave him a break and kept on talking. "Apparently Tom had a lab booked at TechWorld and Dave met him there as recently as the day before Tom's disappearance."

More gaping.

"Were you aware of the TechWorld lab? You told me Tom wasn't working on anything worth moving off the drawing board."

I could see Randy's eyes dart crazily about the room as if they were somehow connected to the part of his brain that was wildly trying to make sense of what I'd just told him. "I did know about the lab," he finally got out. "He was always playing around in there. It was nothing major. He was just fooling around with some new game ideas. He always had something on the go. That's how this business works, Mr. Quant. You've got to keep on trying new things and consider yourself lucky if one out of every thousand bright ideas actually turns into something even potentially marketable."

"I see," I said. Then added, "Does it seem odd to you that your partner might have been working on a project with Dave Biddle and not tell you about it?"

"Good question," Randy said. The man no longer looked tired. There was something else going on in his face. I couldn't decide whether he was upset, confused or something else. I didn't know him well enough to be sure. "Tom and I told each other everything about what we were doing. This doesn't sound right."

"But you've said Tom and Dave were known to use each other as sounding boards on occasion?"

"Oh sure, they talked, but they didn't *work* together. There's no reason I can think of for Dave Biddle to have been in that lab."

"Were you and Tom having any disagreements before he disappeared? Was there any reason to suspect he was working on something without your knowledge or had you sensed that Tom might have wanted out of QW?"

He didn't answer for a count of ten. Controlling his anger perhaps? He didn't seem to be appreciating my insinuations. Neither would I if I were in his shoes. "No. There had been no change in our relationship at all. Actually, Mr. Quant, I question whether your information is accurate. How did you find out about all of this? From Dave Biddle?"

I shook my head.

"Well I certainly need more than your word on this."

"That's what I was hoping you'd say. I was wondering if you could get us into Tom's lab at TechWorld?"

"Absolutely not," he answered quickly. "The equipment and information in that lab is confidential. For QW eyes only."

"Dave Biddle was in there." Gotya!

"Y-y-yessss…"

"Do I look like a guy who knows the first thing about building computer games? You don't even want to know what I think a Game Boy is."

He looked doubtful.

"Listen, if I'm wrong, no harm done. If I'm right, there might be something in there that could lead us to find out who killed Tom."

He was struggling between a rock and a hard place. I'm not sure which one I was. "The police already know who killed Tom. And so do I. Harold Chavell."

Tsk, tsk, tsk. I dislike inflexibility. Time for a little threat. "The police don't know about the TechWorld lab. Yet." It was one thing for me to go rooting around QW stuff, but I was pretty certain Randy Wurz didn't want a bunch of cops in that lab.

After brief consideration he frowned and said, "Let's go."

It didn't take long to convince TechWorld security to allow us access into Tom's lab. Once Randy explained that as the only remaining QW partner he was suspending rental payments on the facility, the young guard was happy to oblige us. He also instructed us to have the room cleaned out before the end of the day. He didn't bother getting up. He had us sign in, gave us a key, brief directions and sent us on our way. The halls were beginning to buzz with the arrival of scientists and technicians and people who did for a living things I could never come close to comprehending. Randy Wurz led the way and we were soon at the door of Tom's lab. He inserted the key and we entered. It was a long, narrow, windowless room with thick, soundproof walls. We looked around and stared in amazement.

Except for a desk, chair and myriad of jumbled cables on the floor plugged in to nothing, the room was bare. I guessed the clean-up wouldn't take us long.

Randy Wurz looked at me almost accusingly. "So what is this all about? Dave and Tom couldn't have been in here. There's nothing here!"

For the moment I was more interested in coming up with reasons why the room had been stripped rather than paying attention to the abandoned partner's whining. "Obviously someone didn't want us to see what was in here."

"What? How can you know that? How do you know there was ever anything in here? Maybe you're making all this up?"

"You can check the sign-in logs yourself," I said, still deep in thought. "Tom and Dave Biddle did meet here."

His shoulders fell half an inch, defeated. "But why?"

I shrugged. A response I'd learned from a big lug of a lawyer.

"You said they were in here the day before Tom disappeared? What were they doing? What had Tom gotten himself into? You don't think Biddle…?"

Wurz didn't complete his thought, but I'd already been considering the same thing. Was Tom killed for whatever had once been in this room? And if so, how was Dave Biddle involved? "Is there any way you could find out what Tom had been working on?"

"I might have been able to if he'd left anything behind for me to analyze, but there's nothing here."

"What about his computer? The one in his office? Could there be something on it that could tell us what was going on in this room?"

Randy thought about that for a moment. "Well, I could take a look at it, see if he left anything on the hard drive or the server. But I think he'd be too smart for that. If he really wanted to keep something a secret, he'd know how. But I'll try."

"Okay. And I'll pay Mr. Biddle a visit."

He stared at me. "I'll go with you. I'd like to be in on that meeting."

"I don't think so. You might be a little too…close to the situation right now. Let's see what I can find out first."

I could hear his breathing get heavier. This was not how he thought his morning would turn out. "You'll keep me informed?"

"I'll call you," I told him.

There was no use hanging around an empty room. We parted ways outside of TechWorld, Randy back to QW and I in search of Quasar.

I already knew Quasar was also located at Innovation Place. When I got back to the Mazda I looked up the address on the Innovation Place map and pointed my car in the right direction. Quasar was located in one of the single-storey, brick buildings on the extreme west end of the development. The building was divided into four large bays each dedicated to a different business with a separate entrance. I opened the glass door with the impressive looking green, blue and white Quasar logo. The attractive woman sitting behind the reception desk had black hair so short it looked like a skin-tight skullcap. Her badge said Jacquie.

"Hi Jacquie," I said as I approached her desk.

She looked up with a professional, detached smile. "Hello, can I help you?" She had a unique accent. Maybe from Guyana.

"Yes. My name is Russell Quant. I was wondering if I could speak with Mr. Biddle."

"Do you have an appointment?" Her voice was friendly but I could tell that she knew, without even checking, that I had no appointment.

"Actually I was hoping to see him as soon as possible. It's rather important and shouldn't take too much of his time. I can wait."

She smiled encouragingly. "Of course. Why don't you take a seat and I'll see what I can arrange."

There was a single loveseat in the small but nicely decorated reception area. Obviously Quasar wasn't used to too many visitors at once. Or, I hoped, Dave Biddle wasn't in the habit of keeping people waiting.

"Mr. Biddle," I heard Jacquie's smooth voice as she spoke into the near-invisible headset microphone suspended in front of her lips. "I have a Mr. Russell Quant here who would like a few minutes of your time." As she completed her request she looked over at me and, seeing me watching her, gave me a pleasant smile.

I watched in fascination as the corners of her mouth slowly turned down while she listened to her boss's reply. Whatever he was saying to her was obviously unexpected or unpleasant or both.

"I see," she finally said tersely, lowering her head and turning it away from my view. "I will do that."

I rose from my seat and approached the desk. "Is there a problem?" I asked.

She tried another smile but it was only a faded replica of what I knew she was capable of. "No problem at all." The mantra of capable executive assistants. "However, Mr. Biddle cannot see you right now. He's expecting a very important conference call and can't be disturbed."

"I can wait." The mantra of capable private detectives.

She did a little better with the smile. "I thought you might say that. Mr. Biddle did indicate that if you needed to see him today we could arrange for an appointment later in the day?"

I drove downtown with the roof down. The air was clean and fresh and each breath was like an invigorating tonic helping to clear my thoughts. I maneuvered into the parking lot behind PWC and entered my office via the back stairs. But instead of sitting at my desk, I found myself heading downstairs. I heard Alberta Lougheed, my upstairs neighbour, call after me but I was already halfway down. Lilly looked up at me as I passed her desk and showed me her shiny bright whites.

"Does Errall have a client with her?" I asked, already halfway towards her office door.

"No. She's in court."

Stopped in my tracks. I nodded dumbly and made my way to the back of the building where I hoped to score a doughnut or muffin in the kitchen. I needed comfort food.

"You look like you could use some coffee." This from Beverly Chaney who was pouring one for herself.

Did I need more coffee? Or did I just look like I did? "Got anything jazzier, like a double chocolate milkshake or better yet, some Canadian Club?"

She chuckled her mothering chuckle. "You *are* in a state. I don't think I have any rye up my sleeve but I did bring in a loaf of home-made cinnamon bread this morning. Why don't I toast you a slice before you go back upstairs?"

My only response was to hug her. This kind exchange and generous offer was why I love this woman. To us at PWC she is a pretty, mid-forties, somewhat doughy, brown-haired, mother of two kids and wife of a third, who is a nurturing friend to all the tenants here. We sometimes forget she's a seasoned psychiatrist with special training in marriage and personal counselling. It's a gruelling line of work that undoubtedly wears her down from time to time but she rarely lets it show.

"Russell? Russell?" I heard the voice travelling towards the kitchen well before its owner. Didn't anyone in this building work for a living? "Russell, you walked right by me. I know you heard me." Alberta. She looks like a younger version of Beverly except for tons more make up, hairspray and peculiar fashion choices. Today it was bangles and boots.

I looked up from where I'd fallen into a chair, awaiting my toast. "I'm sorry, Al, I wanted to see if I could catch Errall."

"I know. I could have told you she wasn't here."

I have never come to a conclusion whether or not I believe in Alberta's psychic powers. I have no doubt she believes she has a special gift. She's no con artist. I'm just not certain she isn't just plain ol' crazy.

I grabbed the cinnamon toast as it hopped from the toaster and headed back upstairs. "Thanks gals. Gotta go." I had to get out of there before Alberta pulled me into some fascinating but long discourse on astral projections.

Now that I knew Tom could have been killed as early as the day of his wedding, I had to re-evaluate each of my suspects and perhaps add or delete a few. So far I had people who had seen him alive and well up to about 1:30 or 2:00 p.m. which is the time Kent Melicke told me he left Tom's apartment. Also Mrs. Coyle said Tom left his apartment at 2:30 and never came back. Assuming none of these people were the killer or in collusion, I had to figure out what happened to Tom after 2:30 and who had alibis for that time of day and who didn't. It was going to be a long day.

I spent the next few hours reviewing my notes on every potential suspect that I'd investigated. I made countless phone calls confirming and reconfirming information I had already gathered and wheedled out more. By 4:30 my brain was fried. And to top it off I wasn't certain I'd accomplished anything useful. I locked up the files in my desk, grabbed my coat and headed down to my car and back to Innovation Place.

This time when I walked into the Quasar reception area Jacquie's smile was not so welcoming. But it wasn't because of me. The woman looked worried.

"Jacquie?" I said when I sidled up to her desk. "I'm here for my appointment with Mr. Biddle."

Her deep brown eyes held mine but I wasn't certain of the message they were conveying. "Yes, Mr. Quant. I'm afraid we'll have to reschedule that meeting."

"Oh? Is there a problem?" The second time I had asked her that question.

For a moment she seemed speechless, as if this circumstance had never occurred before and she didn't quite know how to deal with it. "No problem at all, but unfortunately Mr. Biddle has had to leave the office on some unexpected business and will have to reschedule his meeting with you."

I didn't know this woman at all but I could tell something wasn't as it should be. I furrowed my brow and said slowly, "Jacquie, is there something wrong?"

Although I'd never seen or heard another person in the two times I'd been at Quasar, the woman looked around nervously as though concerned about being overheard. She then leaned in closer to me and said, "This is very unlike Mr. Biddle."

"To miss an appointment?"

"Not just that. Mr. Biddle did have meetings scheduled all day—which he attended as planned. But right after he came back here for about a minute and then left again. He said he'd be back within the hour, in time for his meeting with you. He's always very meticulous about keeping me informed of his whereabouts. But he hasn't come back, Mr. Quant. And he hasn't called. I'm beginning to get very worried about him. I just called Rhonda—his wife— and she hasn't heard from him either. I suppose he could have had car trouble or something…but you'd think he'd have called."

Was this tied to Dave Biddle's earlier refusal to see me? Did it have anything at all to do with Tom Osborn's death or was it just an unfortunate coincidence? Was he hiding something? Was he...running away? I didn't think his secretary would be any help. I assured her as best as I could and left. I returned to my car with a sense of urgency but as soon as I started the engine I realized I had nowhere to go. I had no idea where Dave Biddle could have gone. I tried reaching Randy Wurz at QW to see if he'd come up with anything but there was no answer there. I checked my watch. It was almost 5:30. I was stymied and frustrated. I was about to point the Mazda in the direction of my couch, big screen TV and fattening food but at the last moment I gave myself a mental spanking and drove the few blocks to the YWCA. It was time to get rid of some of my frustration the old-fashioned way.

Most people think the YWCA is a women's only facility, but actually the gym and swimming pool are coed. I like working out at the YW rather than one of the ubiquitous trendier spots. Sure they have newer machines, juice bars and enough mirrors to check yourself and everyone else out from every conceivable angle, but I find the clientele at the YW more laid back and comfortable to be around. Everyone from eighty-year-old grandmas with arthritis to handicapped teenagers to flabby yuppies work out at the YW. No one is particularly interested in flexing muscles or letting off pheromones. Most everyone is there to exercise and that's all. What I secretly like most about the place is that, on occasion, not often, but sometimes, I am the hunkiest guy there. And there is no way that is ever gonna happen at one of the other places.

Twenty minutes of cardio on a stationery bike, stretching, then four sets of twelve reps of various muscle grinding feats, another fifteen minutes cardio, stretch and hit the showers. That is my routine. Ninety minutes later I was drenched but high on the reju-venated feeling only this kind of self-mutilation provides. As usual the gym was less than half full and the men's locker room was empty. I took a leisurely, hot shower. I had thrown a towel around my waist and was applying various overpriced products to my skin and hair when I heard the door to the pool area open and close. As I continued my ministrations at the mirror, I looked beyond my reflection for the newcomer and was rewarded as an Adonis came into view. Depending on the angle at which I stood at the mirror I could see the first shower stall and part of the drying area outside the shower room where the man was now heading. At first I quickly glanced away, embarrassed to be invading the man's privacy. Being as this was the YWCA and not the YMCA, the men's locker room is not big. There are four showers, two bathrooms, two sinks and about eighty lockers. Aside from bright blue curtains on the individual showers, privacy and personal space is not easy to come by. So while smoothing some cool, gel-like substance under my eyes I peeked again. He was still standing in the dry off area between the showers and lockers. His back was to me. But what a back it was. Broad at the top and narrowing in perfect V-formation to an emerald green Speedo. With even the slightest movement, muscles rippled beneath lightly tanned skin. Long, long legs, slightly hairy, nicely-shaped. This guy had spent some serious time in the squat cage. He was slowly, deliberately drying himself off with a white-and-blue striped towel. I could hear his breath as he recovered from an exhausting swim. He had been working it.

I looked away and chastised myself while I searched my shaving kit for hair gel. "How desperate is this?" I asked myself. "Cruising a gym locker room! How pathetic! Was no one safe from a horny Russell Quant?" I smiled as I thought about Mr. Emmeline. Everyone at the YW knows about the old guy. He has to be one-hundred-and-two if he's a day. He comes to the gym every morning for a swim. However, he spends about five minutes in the water and forty in the locker room. This is partly because he doesn't move fast, but mostly because he's a flasher. And everyone is fair game. He doesn't discriminate based on age, race or sexuality. He has one trick, which he plays over and over always assuming his victim is someone he's never met before. Poor eyesight is a handicap he uses to his advantage. The first time it happened to me, I thought I was helping this kindly, old grandpa-type. I had just arrived and was changing from my street clothes into gym shorts and a T when old Mr. Emmeline shuffled over to me with this look of utter helplessness on his wizened face. He was wearing a baggy pair of swim trunks and his pear-shaped body was damp from a recent swim. He asked if I'd be a good boy and give him a hand. Of course you can't say no to someone like that. He told me he'd torn his swimsuit while getting out of the pool and was now trying to get out of them but his hands were too arthritic and he couldn't untie the knot in the drawstring. And sure enough his gnarled hands were tugging away at the string that kept his shorts up and indeed there was a nasty knot. A little weird, but what are you going to do, let the old guy stand there forever in his torn, wet trunks?

I leaned over and began working on the knot. That's when he showed me where his shorts were torn. Right at the crotch. And in exposing the gaping tear, he also exposed his century-old frank-and-beans. For a moment I was stunned and kept working on the knot, trying not to look at his pride and joy. But then things began to change size. I stepped back, pulled a pair of cuticle scissors out of my shaving bag and suggested he cut the cord. Of course his hands were too arthritic to do that either, so I accommodated him one more time and added twenty minutes to my workout that day. I really didn't believe his guile until he did the same thing to me about two weeks later and has done it to me about once a month ever since. I've now watched him do it to several other guys. The dexterous actually get the knot undone before he can give them a peek, but the wise just tell him to keep trying it on his own.

I feel sorry for Mr. Emmeline. I don't know if he's gay or just wants someone to look at his package for some other reason. But the YWCA is not a meat market kind of place. It certainly isn't known to be where the buff gay boys work out. I sometimes wonder if I should suggest one of the other gyms to Mr. Emmeline.

I decided catching a glimpse of an attractive body through a mirror was a far cry from accosting another guy with torn swim trunks. But looking at this guy's strong, brown back one more time, I giddily wished I had the guts to try it. I was going to die! The swimmer had finished towelling off and was now bending over to peel off his trunks. I had to watch. I had to. I definitely could not move from my spot at the sink. I needed the...support of the counter for a while. I felt like a twelve-year-old discovering the Playboy Channel. A rivulet of sweat ran down my forehead. He was turning around. It all happened in slow motion. I had little time left before being caught. I was going to make the most of it. My eyes travelled up from his muscular thighs to the wonders of his freshly exposed manhood. Couldn't stay there too long without being branded a pervert. A quick trip up the rippled abs towards the mounding chest and...

I couldn't believe what I was seeing. I stared.

My eyes fastened onto the object in question, my fear of discovery forgotten.

A half-heart pendant.

The journey my eyes had begun in lust now ended in astonishment.

Things only got worse. Above the pendant was the face of Father Len Oburkevich.

Chapter 16

"RUSSELL?" THE VOICE WAS FAMILIAR but sounded as if it came from underwater. I saw the smile on the handsome face, the pronounced cheekbones, nose and jaw. I couldn't help but look back down at the mountainous chest, still heaving from the exertion of recent exercise. And the pendant. Half a heart. The other half of the one I found in Tom Osborn's apartment? What did it mean? "Russell?" he repeated. I could see him walking towards me in the mirror, fastening his towel about his narrow waist. "It's me, Father Len."

I turned and smiled as if I'd just caught sight of him. Detectives are sometimes required to be actors. "Father Len," I said as I held out my hand. "I hardly recognize you without your…your regular clothes on."

"I stopped wearing my collar in the pool. The chlorine in the water was turning it pink," he said.

I laughed. "I have to admit, I've never seen a priest in a gym before."

"How do you know?" Good point. "We're everywhere!"

He had a sense of humour. I liked that. I was growing to like everything about this taboo package. I could see by the strain on his face he wasn't up to his best game. The words were clever and the smile was there, but he couldn't hide the fact that he was a man in mourning. His eyes were sombre and the corners of his mouth fought against turning upwards. "How are you doing?" I asked in such a way that he'd know I meant it as more than just a polite question.

"Well, I'm glad I decided to come here today. Exercise was just what I needed to take my mind off things for a while."

"Making your body hurt as much as your heart does?" I couldn't believe the sap coming out of my mouth, but I wanted to keep talking to this guy. Without the black robes and starched white collar I felt as if I was talking to an entirely different person. He was just another human being. A hunky, male one. But despite all that, a burning question loomed in my mind. Why was he wearing the half-heart pendant? Did it make him a suspect in the murder of Tom Osborn? One brother killing another—fratricide? One a Catholic priest, one a gay man. Pretty different lifestyles and points of view. It wasn't too much of a reach to imagine they could be enemies. But mortal enemies? And didn't priests take a vow not to take another life? I was pretty certain it was one of the Ten Commandments. I'd have to watch the movie again.

"I'll be okay. Thanks for asking. Are you still working on my brother's case? Still not convinced Harold killed him?"

"Yes, I'm still chasing around a few leads." I watched his response to this. Was it making him nervous that I was still snooping around, or was he glad?

"I'm glad," he said. Phew! "Listen, if there's anything I can do, please call me. I want to help if I can." With that he raised his hand to my bare shoulder and gave it a quick pat. I tightened the nearby muscle group. "I have to rush. I'm meeting my parents for dinner. But I hope we talk soon."

"Yes," I said. "That would be good."

I returned to my mirror, watched Father Len get into the shower, felt the scalding burn where he'd touched my shoulder and let my mind do a few somersaults. What about the pendant? Why didn't

I ask him? When Kent Melicke left Tom at 2:00 p.m. he said he'd seen no sign of it. But it was there when I searched the apartment. How did it get there? The murderer? Was it Father Len? Yet the salesclerk at the jewellery store said a woman, not a man, purchased the pendant. Who was that woman? Or did the pendant mean nothing at all? Perhaps Tom had it hidden until he was alone, pulling it out after Kent left. A gift from his brother he'd never get a chance to wear? Or was I getting soft about this because I had a woody for Father Len? How ridiculous. The man was a Ukrainian Catholic priest for chrissakes…I mean, for Pete's sakes! And nevertheless, I couldn't allow personal feelings to interfere with a case. That was a basic rule of being a private investigator that should never be broken. So why didn't I just ask him? Tongue-tied—or did I just want a reason to see the sexy priest again?

Barbra greeted me at the door with quiet dignity, but I could tell she was excited to see me. I let her out and by the time I'd filled one of her bowls with kibble and another with fresh water, she wanted back in. It was 8:30 and I'd missed supper. The message light on my answering machine was blinking with the same insistence as the growls in my tummy. I hit the play button and began a search through my fridge and cupboards for something edible.

The first message was from Errall, sounding rushed and out of breath. "Russell, I need to talk to you. I spoke with Solonge Fontaine. Wait until you hear this! She still identifies the man she met as Tom Osborn—even after seeing a picture of him! So either somehow or other he was really there after all or Solonge Fontaine is lying through her teeth! Call me as soon as you can."

I dropped whatever I was holding and stared at the phone. Had I heard Errall correctly? I was trying to decipher the message when a second one interfered. "I see lights and I'm betting you haven't had time for dinner yet." It was Sereena. "Open your door."

I glanced over my shoulder at the back door. Barbra was already staring out the window at my neighbour who was holding aloft a container of something undoubtedly delicious. I grinned and ran over to let her in. Barbra gave our guest a quick nuzzle, sniffed the air near the container and then retreated to a favourite spot to curl up in. She was well-acquainted with Sereena and instinctively knew that whatever was in the bowl was not about to end up in her belly.

"I was at this thing tonight where they served way too much creamy, lobster goop," she said, handing me the offering as she passed by me. "I'll trade you for a glass of something brisk and exotic." Her voice fit the description of the wine she ordered.

"It's a deal. Should it be heated?"

"I generally prefer my wine at room temperature, but suit yourself."

"Har har har, I meant the goop."

"I prefer it cold. Only because it shouldn't be. Try it and see." She disappeared into the next room to select a bottle from my meagre collection while I found a fork and tried out the leftovers. Not bad. Sereena returned with a nice California white and two oversized glasses, and proceeded to empty the contents of one into the others. For a peaceful moment we sat atop the stools beside the kitchen island and enjoyed consumption.

"You look preoccupied," she said.

I nodded as I took a healthy swallow of my wine. "I'm trying to make sense of a phone message that came in right before yours. I'm afraid I'm going to have to be rude and make some phone calls."

She shucked her head to one side. "I asked for your wine, not your company." She said it in a tone that made me wonder whether or not she was being serious.

I reached for the cordless and quickly dialled Errall and Kelly's number while chewing on a forkful of meaty lobster. No answer. I left a message on the machine. Just in case she was working late I tried Errall's office number and was diverted to a computerized switchboard operator.

I was dumbfounded. How could Solonge Fontaine have identified Tom Osborn as her visitor? Had I been fooled again by the passport? Was it a fake planted there for me to find for some reason? I was getting more than a little fed up with the constant flip-flopping of facts. Yes Tom was in France, no he wasn't, yes he was, no he wasn't…which was it? Had Tom Osborn been in France or not? He couldn't have been! His passport proved that, didn't it? Damn! This case was driving me crazy.

I reached into a nearby cupboard drawer and pulled out a City of Saskatoon phone book. I found the "W's" and a listing for R. Wurz on Saskatchewan Crescent. Swanky neighbourhood. I dialled and reached his wife who told me Randy was working late that night. I tried the number for QW Technologies but reached the answering service. I wondered if Randy was still in Tom's office trying to find something on his computer that might give us a hint as to what had been in the TechWorld lab.

"You're doing the right thing, Russell," Sereena murmured as she carefully inspected her flawless manicure.

I looked over at my guest. Although I knew better than to ever admit it to her, I'd almost forgotten she was there. Sereena Smith is not the type of woman you don't notice, even if you're trying not to. "Excuse me?"

"Continuing to search for Tom Osborn's murderer. It's time well spent."

I laid down the phone and gave my full attention to my neighbour. She wore a simple silk lounging outfit of midnight blue and her dark hair was piled high in a mass of intricate curls. This was "just got back from a fancy shindig" chic. "Why do you say that?" Did she know something about this case? I'd never discussed any details with her, only generalities.

"Harold Chavell is okay in my books. He would not have committed this crime."

I was surprised to hear his name come from her lips. "You know Harold Chavell?"

Her chiselled chin bobbed up and down. I could see the shadow of a long ago scar. "Yes, I do."

"Why didn't you say something before this?" I should have

guessed. It was no surprise Sereena and Chavell would sometimes travel in the same social circles, the same circle as Anthony and Jared. Saskatoon was a small city and the group of elite even smaller.

"You never asked and I saw no reason to mention it before now. He's not my best friend, but we've certainly done the same functions for many years. I know what type of man he is. He may have a peccadillo or two in his back pocket, but who doesn't? He is not a murderer. I can assure you of that." She shrugged as she took a languorous sip of wine. "Whether you believe me or not, of course, is up to you."

I wished a jury would accept those words with as much conviction as I did. Over the years I'd come to rely on Sereena's sense of a person's character. In particular, she could smell bad intentions half a world away. I imagined it was a skill garnered in a once perilous lifestyle. I was glad to know she had come to the same conclusion about my client as I had. My mind fell again to thinking about Randy Wurz. Had he found something? How could I reach him? Was he in danger? I had almost decided to take a run over to the QW offices when the eureka hit me. It was a clue I'd come across days ago but at the time it made no sense.

I pulled the phone book close again and flipped pages until I reached the map section.

"What are you looking for?" Sereena asked.

In my head I recited the acronyms I'd seen on Tom's computer in his office at QW Technologies. QWHD, QWS, MSHD, TWHD and NavyHD. I'd concluded at the time the obvious: QWHD stood for QW Technologies' hard drive which was the hard drive in the computer on Tom's desk. QWS stood for the QW Technologies' server. Although most people save computer information to hard drives and floppies, many companies also have a main server for safer and larger storage capacity. It was the QWHD and QWS locations Randy Wurz had gone off to search today, hoping to find something that would tell us what was in the TechWorld lab. TW had to stand for TechWorld and TWHD had to refer to a

TechWorld hard drive on a computer Tom kept in the TechWorld lab—a computer that was now missing. That left MSHD and NavyHD. I had no idea what these monikers referred to when I first saw them, but now that I was sure I'd figured it out I was angry with myself for not seeing it earlier. The acronyms created by Tom always somehow indicated the locations of the computers where he stored information. At work, QW, in the lab where he tested his video games, TW, and…at home…MS had to refer to Main Street, the address of his apartment. But I'd seen no computer when I was in the apartment. Where had it gone? Would Tom have been planning to take it with him to Europe? Was it at the bottom of Pike Lake along with the rest of his luggage? That left NavyHD. It had to refer to another location where he kept a computer. I had to find it. It was possibly the only computer left that would tell us what was going on in that TechWorld lab.

I glanced up but for a quick second at Sereena. "Navy," was all I told her. All of the acronyms Tom Osborn used related to physical locations or addresses. So it made sense that Navy could be an address or name of a business. "Is there such a thing as a Navy Street or Navy Avenue in Saskatoon? Or a business with Navy in its name?"

My finger moved down the listing of Saskatoon street names: Nahanni Drive, Nash Place, Neatby Crescent. No Navy. I turned to the White pages and found only one listing that started with Navy: Navy League Cadets & Sea Cadets. It didn't sound right.

"There used to be an Army & Navy store downtown," Sereena suggested.

"Yes, but that's gone now. I wonder if I'm wrong. Maybe 'Navy' refers to something nautical, rather than an address or a place."

"Maybe you're looking at the wrong map."

I looked up at her sharply. "What?"

"Maybe Navy *is* an address, but not in Saskatoon."

It was bad news. The physical location of NavyHD could be anywhere in the world. It made sense. Tom likely travelled widely during the course of his work. If he had some reason to want a secret, secure location to store computer information, he could have a computer in any one of countless locations. I groaned out loud and gave Sereena a hapless look. "It could be anywhere," I said.

"Nonsense. Use your head."

I'm sure my eyes doubled in size as the answer suddenly came to me. I had seen the sign only yesterday. When I'd followed Clark Shiwaga into the Pike Lake resort we had turned onto the street where Chavell and Tom kept house. Navy Avenue!

I reached over the counter for Sereena's hand and kissed it with a flourish. "You were right! I was looking at the wrong map. There isn't a Navy in Saskatoon, but there is in Pike Lake!"

I grabbed at the phone and called Detective Darren Kirsch at his home number. Treena told me he was still at work and I reached him in his office, noisily chewing on an apple.

"Darren," I said with a hopefully contagious sense of urgency and import, "would you answer one query, no questions asked?"

He halted his masticating long enough to let out an unnecessarily long and heartless-sounding laugh. I relented and told him bits and pieces of what I'd found out about the computer storage locations and the TechWorld lab which Randy and I had found empty that morning.

"I don't see what all of this means, Quant," he said after I'd finished.

"It means there might be more to Tom Osborn's disappearance and murder than anyone, including the police, know. If there wasn't," I added, looking at my wrist-watch, "why would you still be at your desk at ten o'clock at night?"

"I do have other cases, Quant."

"Okay, okay, I'm not asking you to do anything, I'm just asking for an answer to one question."

He sighed. He'd either put his apple down or was done with it. "What is it?"

"When your guys searched Harold Chavell's cottage at Pike Lake, did they find a computer?"

He sighed again and then I heard him make a stretching sound as if he was reaching for something. "I've got the inventory of stuff we confiscated from the cabin," he said. "There ain't no computer on here. And if there'd been one we'd certainly have taken it. Is that it? I got work t'do."

Damn. Where the hell was NavyHD? It had to be at Pike Lake! I was about to hang up when I heard Darren mutter. "What did you say?"

"Hold on a sec." More reaching sounds. Some pages being flipped. "Yeah... I thought so, here it is."

"What?" I urged.

"I thought there was mention of a computer somewhere. We did get one."

"From his apartment?" I wondered.

"Nope, nothing there. But the divers found a computer in his luggage."

"Divers?"

"Tom's body got free of the cinder blocks it was tied to, but his luggage didn't. We sent divers into the lake to see what they could find and they came up with two suitcases. One of them contained a laptop. It was ruined though. We couldn't even boot it up and we tried removing the hard drive but it was wet toast."

Was that the fate of NavyHD or was the computer in the luggage actually MSHD as I had earlier guessed? There was only one way to be sure. I hurriedly thanked Darren and hung up.

I jumped off my stool and announced, "I'm going to Pike Lake!"

"I'm coming with you!" Sereena declared.

I looked at her. Then I laughed. She joined in.

"Sorry," she said with a dry rasp, "it just seemed the appropriate thing to say in the heat of the moment." She emptied her wineglass, blew Barbra a kiss and sashayed her way out the back door.

I ran to a closet and selected a maroon-coloured, down-filled bomber jacket. I dashed about grabbing keys, wallet and shoes. Barbra followed at a discreet distance as I scrambled about. She wasn't particularly pissed off when I left. She was used to my leaving at a second's notice and easily resigned herself to an evening on her own. As I made my way to the garage I wondered if I should get her a puppy.

On my way to Pike Lake I used my cellphone to try reaching Randy Wurz and Errall again, but neither were answering their phone. I was a little miffed at Errall for leaving me an urgent message to call her back and then not staying by her phone. But then again, this wasn't her investigation and no matter how I looked at things, there was no way I could reasonably expect her to sit by her phone all night waiting for me to call.

It was a starless night but the moon was nearly full and cast a bluish glow on the shadowed streets of Pike Lake. From my earlier visit with Shiwaga I easily found my way to Navy Avenue and Chavell's place. I parked on the same berm as before, retrieved my flashlight and gun and made my way through the caragana moving the flashlight from side to side like a pendulum of fireflies. Before long I was standing on the wooden deck at the cabin's back door. I directed the light into the sloping backyard. Nothing new to see since yesterday as far as I could tell.

I chose the back door for my dastardly chore—break and enter—because it was near the lake end and away from the road. As I expected, the lock was unsophisticated and easy to pick. For some reason, all sense of security and safety goes out of people's heads when it comes to their leisure properties. It's as if nothing terrible could happen to them when they're at the lake. Tom Osborn, for one, had tragically found that to be untrue.

The back door swung open and I stepped again into the comfortable porch area. Although the moon was doing its best to illuminate the room it was still insufficient for my needs. If I was going to try to find something the police had missed, I knew I'd need the full benefit of electricity. Even if someone were to drop by and wonder what I was doing, I was pretty sure I'd be able to come up with a reasonable story. I reached for the nearest light switch and began my search for NavyHD.

It was well after midnight when I gave up. Dejected at my failure to turn up the computer I'd hoped would reveal the secret of the TechWorld lab, I helped myself to a bottle a beer from the kitchen refrigerator. As I sipped the frothy elixir I retraced my steps and made sure all the lights in the cottage were extinguished. I let myself out the door I'd come in, careful to re-lock it, and eventually found myself once more, none the wiser, standing on the small wooden landing that looked out into the narrow back lot and lake beyond. I stood there for many seconds, staring blindly into the abyss of darkness, wondering what to do next. Although getting out of the cold night and jumping into a warm bed were quickly making their way to the top of my list, the fate of NavyHD continued to bother me. If NavyHD was the computer the police had found at the bottom of the lake, then where was MSHD? Was it possible that NavyHD and MSHD were the same computer? Was it possible there'd been nothing important going on in the TechWorld lab after all?

I finished my beer and deposited the bottle on the deck where I hoped a recycler would find it. I was about to illuminate my flashlight for the trip back to my car when I heard it.

An unfamiliar noise.

I felt my skin shift.

This was one of the many reasons I don't like camping or living in a cabin in the middle of wilderness. There's a myriad of unfamiliar noises. I used my flashlight to pan over the yard. Fire pit. Check. Sloping lawn. Check. What else was out there? A squirrel? Possibly. Raccoon. I suppose, although I'd never seen one in person. A bear? No, Quant, no bears in the Saskatoon region. How about a cougar? Hadn't I heard something about cougar sightings near the city this past spring? Or was there a person out there? I straightened my back and asked myself what kind of detective I would be without doing some detecting. It was my job, but even so, there was no need to be unprotected. I moved the flashlight from my right hand to the left and pulled the revolver from my pocket. I stepped off the landing into a squishy mix of grass and soil. I slowly made my foray into the backyard keeping the light one step ahead of me. My ears were hurting with the effort of trying to discern a sound of impending danger. As I got further away from the cabin the ground became steeper and steeper and I knew I would soon be at the lake's edge. I kept my steps as small as those of a blind man without a cane, wanting to make sure I stopped before I found myself in water. But instead of water I found myself on another wooden platform. It was the small dock I'd noticed the day before.

Again the noise!

I twirled around wielding the flashlight like a *Star Wars* light saber.

Still nothing. Damn squirrels.

I moved the light over the surface of the floating dock, half-submerged in the water, and followed a rope from its one end tied to a mooring post to the other now hanging limply in the dark water of the lake. A short time ago the rope was probably used to secure a boat of some sort to the dock. I panned the flashlight onto the shore and indeed, overturned and now landlocked for winter storage a couple of yards away, was a small, wooden skiff. With a sudden acrid sensation in the pit of my stomach I realized that this was where it happened. This was where Tom Osborn had met his end. Someone had marched him out of the cottage and forced him, probably at gunpoint, close to the water's edge (less distance to drag the body) but not so close that anyone on the lake might have caught sight of what was happening. And then they'd asked him to turn away. The last thing Tom Osborn would have seen was the glass-still surface of his beloved Pike Lake. Perhaps there'd been a few late season ducks floating by. Maybe he'd tried to focus on the dusk canoe ride with Harold, the scene from the picture I'd seen in their bedroom. I hoped that in his last moments, when he most certainly would have known he was about to die, he'd buried himself in memories and found some small comfort.

And then he was shot in the head. From behind. The body would have toppled to the ground.

I directed the flashlight to the spot where I guessed his body might have lay. There was no blood left, no sign of a life seeping into the soil. I supposed what the police didn't take with them for evidence had long ago been cleaned up by wildlife and weather.

Darren Kirsch had told me Tom had been tied to cinder blocks. Obviously the killer didn't do a good job of it. And then Tom and his luggage were moved into the skiff, taken for one last ride on the lake, probably not too far out to avoid being seen, and tossed overboard, discarded like garbage.

After one last glance at the ice-cold lake, the intended burial ground that instead had given up its dead, I put my gun back in my pocket and turned to walk away. Despite my lined coat, it was well past midnight on an October morning in the prairies and I was shivering. I felt my leg muscles work a little harder to move my body up the slope. The ground, now greyish with frost, was slippery. I took tiny steps to avoid a fall. I didn't relish the thought of rolling down the hill, over the dock and into the freezing water. I grabbed hold of a stray sapling to steady my progress. And that was when I saw it.

The beam of my flashlight had settled on a spot to my right, about halfway of the distance between the rear of the cabin and the lake. At first I wasn't sure what I was seeing. So I stepped closer and then even closer. I looked down and I knew.

I knew who killed Tom Osborn.

Chapter 17

I TRAVELLED FROM PIKE LAKE TO SASKATOON in a night so dark it felt as if I was submerged in a vat of black oil. Where had the moon gone? Had it hidden its face behind a bank of clouds as if afraid? Was it the same cold, dark fear that filled me now? As I covered the kilometres from lake to city, my mind whirled. I checked and rechecked everything I knew, all the clues I'd collected, along with this last, most damning thing. I knew I was right. But how to prove it? In the cocoon of my car the dashboard clock told me it was now after 1:00 a.m. The perfect time for clandestine activity.

Innovation Place was a glass and girder ghost town. I left my car in the now familiar parking lot and approached the building that housed QW Technologies. I peeked through the glass doors. Good news and bad news. The bad news was that a guard raptly reading a newspaper occupied the security desk. I was disappointed. I'd seen a guard here before, but only during the day and I'd hoped there wouldn't be one at night. The good news was that if there was a security guard, the front doors would more than likely be unlocked. That was a good thing because, although I had few qualms about breaking into someone's home, an office building was another thing. I'd much rather sneak in. Pushing myself closer to the side of the building and into the feathery protection of a handy globe cedar, I slumped down to the ground and began my wait. I knew that sooner or later, either exercise, the john or job description would send the guard off on a walk. Within half an hour my wish came true. Luckily for me he went in the opposite direction from where I needed to go. I tried the door. Yes! It was unlocked! With nary a sound I slipped into the building and away from the security station. I hurried down the series of dimmed corridors.

As I worked on the locked door to QW I knew I wouldn't have to worry about the security guard for a while—he was practically a mile away. I also wouldn't have to worry about an office alarm system. Not only had I not seen any evidence of one on either of my two prior visits (something I'd had the smarts to check for— just in case), but it made sense that if building management put out for a night watchman, they'd feel little need for one in each separate business. After all, this wasn't a Royal Bank. As the door clicked open, I was glad to find I was right and management was oh, so wrong. The reception area sans my favourite secretary was in near darkness except for the red glow given off by an exit sign. I winced when I realized that although I still had my gun in my jacket pocket, I'd left the flashlight in the car. Unlike the cabin I didn't dare take the chance of using the lights, just in case the guard came by. Fortunately I'd been in the office before and pretty much knew my way around. I circled behind the reception desk and let myself into the back. I was in the hallway. More exit signs. I walked down its length to Tom's office and tried the knob. Unlocked. I pushed open the door. Something wasn't right. I was getting the creepy feeling that I was not alone. Slowly I turned my head to look behind me.

Nothing. Only red-tinged darkness.

I stood in the doorway to Tom's office and peered in. The windowless room would have been pitch black if not for the diffused glow of a desk lamp. By now I'd been in the dimness long enough for my eyes to adjust. I could make out shapes and the difference between grey and dark grey and darker grey. Behind Tom's desk with its back to me was the chair I'd sat in while searching his computer. Over the edge of the chair's back I could see the top of a head. For a tension-filled eon of indecision I stood frozen to my position in the doorway staring at the silhouette, but the game of who's gonna move first could not go on forever.

"Hello," I said into the darkness. "I can see you." I felt a little silly, as if I was playing a child's game of hide-and-seek.

The person who'd obviously been using Tom's computer remained silent.

"I can see you," I repeated, slowly inching closer to the chair.

Nothing.

I knew the situation was not as it appeared. The head was too still. Another few feet closer. I pulled out my revolver.

"I can see you!" I exclaimed one more time as I put my left hand on the chair's back and spun it around.

Even though I knew I'd find someone sitting there, I jumped back, startled, as he was revealed to me in the halo of the desk lamp's hazy illumination. I stood ready, in front of the man, my gun pointing at his chest. But he did not react to being in the sights of my weapon. I squinted at the man trying to make out features. Was he dead? Had someone caught Randy delving into Tom's computer and killed him because he was getting too close to the truth? Was that someone still here? Had I been so wrong? I moved a step closer and stared at the familiar face. Familiar but not the face I'd expected.

The body in the chair wasn't Randy Wurz.

It was Dave Biddle.

The local entrepreneur, the owner of Quasar, was sitting straight-backed in the chair, his hands tied together with a man's tie and sitting helplessly on his lap. His feet too were bound. A scarf covered his mouth. And then I saw the most frightening thing of all.

The whites of his eyes.

Dave Biddle was staring at me with a look of utter horror. The pupils of his eyes were moving wildly back and forth from my face to some spot behind me. But by the time I realized what the man was trying to tell me, it was too late.

"Get rid of the gun!"

The voice was higher than normal, probably matching an escalating stress level, but I still recognized it.

I looked at Dave Biddle. His eyes had now ceased their desperate dance and fallen into a gaze of despair. I noticed blood, a red trail from somewhere in the back of his head into the depths beneath his once crisp and white shirt collar. I crouched down slowly and placed my gun at my feet. When I rose I used my right foot to push it away from me. I heard the office door close and then I turned around to face my aggressor. My eyes burned as he switched on the overhead lights, but I did not flinch at the sight of Tom Osborn's murderer.

Randy Wurz was wearing the same suit I'd last seen him in yesterday morning. It appeared as distressed as he did. I could only guess what had transpired in Randy's life since I'd last seen him outside TechWorld, supposedly off to search Tom's computer. In his hand he held a gun. It was pointed at me.

"Randy…" I began.

"Shut up!" he cut me off with a sharp bark. As he stared at me his lips were drawn into a tight grimace, his eyes glittered with a frenetic sheen and his normally precise hair was mussed about his face.

After a moment of silent communion, he finally said, "Why did you come here?" He ran his free hand over his neck. His shirt collar and cuffs were unbuttoned and his tie was missing—obviously it was now around Dave Biddle's ankles. A nice casual look for him. "Why the hell are you here?"

His sleeves were rolled up and I pointedly looked at the underbelly of his right forearm. I was right. But what good was it going to do me now?

Randy glanced at his arms. "What?" he demanded, his voice gruff. "What are you looking at?"

It wasn't much of a rash now, but it must have been a doozy when he first got it. "Poison ivy?" I asked.

He looked at me closely, trying to figure out what I was getting at. "Yeah, so what?"

"You're not even sure where you got it, are you?"

He was silent. He wasn't sure. But he probably had a good idea.

"The cinder blocks," I told him. "The cinder blocks you used to weigh down Tom's body and his luggage. They were in a bed of poison ivy."

He let out a derisive laugh and smirked at me. "Is that all you've got, Quant? That doesn't prove anything!"

"No," I readily agreed. "But it brought me here and I'd say having one man tied up and gagged and another at gunpoint is fairly good indication that you're guilty of something, wouldn't you say?"

"Shut up!" he ordered once more. I've always felt it wise to heed the instructions of a person with a gun. "Sit down!" he told me.

I looked around me. Dave Biddle was in the only chair in Tom's sparsely furnished office. I debated plopping myself down on his lap but thought better of it. Instead I looked at Randy and shrugged.

"Goddamn!" he bellowed, for a moment moving the gun off my heart as he used it to scratch the back of his head. He began a nervous pace back and forth in front of the office door. He swore some more. Things were obviously not going his way today. After a minute of that, he somehow managed to control his adrenaline infusions and leaned back against the door, the gun once again threateningly pointed in my direction. "We need to just relax here."

Yeah right.

He studied me in a way an alien might look upon a human for the first time, as if trying to figure me out. More likely figuring out what he was going to do with me. He'd already killed once. And I was betting he had been planning the same fate for Dave Biddle.

But with me suddenly in the picture perhaps the mounting body count was beginning to bother him.

I decided my best bet for a longer life was to try to get him talking. It would distract him from coming up with a plan to get rid of me and also give me a chance to figure out how the hell I was going to get out of this. "It was you in France, wasn't it?"

"Yes," he admitted almost absent-mindedly. "It was."

Hmmm. Not quite the verbal discourse I was hoping for. He looked frustrated. Worried. What was wrong with him? Didn't all criminals have a senseless but uncontrollable desire to reveal the details of their crimes?

"How did you get Tom to meet you at Pike Lake on the day of his wedding?"

He shrugged and changed his position against the door, crossing his legs. It was an attempt at a casual stance that I wasn't buying. "I didn't have to do a thing. He'd told me he'd be spending the afternoon at the cabin packing for the trip. That's where he kept most of his things, not at the apartment in the city. So I took a cab out there, even went for a little walk. Eventually he showed up. I waited outside, watching him pack through a window and then…" He didn't seem willing to finish the sentence.

So I did. "And then you forced him at gunpoint—with Chavell's gun—down to the water's edge and you killed him."

He said nothing.

"After you shot him you found the cinder blocks which were unfortunately surrounded by poison ivy, tied them to the body and luggage and after a brief ride in the boat you dumped the body and bags into the lake."

"After I got the keys out of his jacket pocket. I needed them to get his truck back to the city and myself into the TechWorld lab."

This was more like it. Talk sucker, talk. "It was the middle of the afternoon. Weren't you afraid someone would see you or hear you?"

He snorted, "Didn't matter, did it? Tom was in France. There was no murder at Pike Lake that day. Besides, I shot him through a pillow. It didn't really make all that much noise and anyone who'd heard it could have mistaken it for all kinds of different things. And I didn't have to go that far out in the boat, just far enough so he'd sink below the surface."

"His ticket was gone, his luggage was gone, Tom was gone. The illusion was complete."

He nodded, his face an expressionless mask. It was almost as if he'd frozen himself into an emotional numbness as he recalled the details of the ultimate betrayal.

"So you attended the wedding and acted as surprised as everyone else when Tom didn't show."

Another bob of the head.

"How could you do this to your friend?"

"Oh for chrissakes!" Aha. A crack in the controlled façade. "You have me unimaginatively pegged as the perfect, evil villain. Well you're wrong. I didn't enjoy doing what I had to do. Tom *was* my friend. I shed my tears. I have my guilt. I'll have to live with that forever."

Give me a break! I couldn't believe what was coming out of this guy's mouth. Was I suppose to feel sorry for all the inner turmoil he was experiencing? What an idiot. But was he an out-of-control idiot? How much time did I have before he shot me? I had to keep him talking until I figured something out. If this had been an episode of *Starsky and Hutch* (me being Hutch), I'd have wisely called for backup before I got there. Or someone I'd been working with on the case, would figure out I was in danger and burst in at the last moment to save the day (and my ass). Perhaps a knight in bulletproof armour? Not likely. Sereena thought I was somewhere on Navy Avenue (where I no longer was), but even so, she had no reason to suspect I was in trouble. Errall? Darren? Nope. I was in this alone. I definitely needed to look into a trusty sidekick arrangement.

I had the grim premonition that only one of us was leaving QW alive. I was hoping it would be me. "But why, Randy? Why did you go through all this elaborate planning to commit this murder? What would make you kill your best friend?"

Randy Wurz pushed himself off the door and took a first step towards me. His gun was pointed at my forehead. I now knew the true meaning of menacing. "Haven't I told you to shut up? I need to think."

I hate bullies. They fill me with more bravado than I should have. "Never mind," I said as if I truly didn't need him to fill me in. "I know why."

He looked at me, his well-tended face creased into a frown. Randy Wurz had not had a good day. And I wasn't about to make it better.

"You double-crossed him, didn't you? Because you needed money."

This got his attention. "What money? I don't need money." His voice was scratchy and he was obviously lying.

"It's no secret, Randy. You live an extravagant lifestyle. The clothes, the cars, the house, the trips. And that's just for your wife. You were running out of cash faster than QW could make it." I didn't really know whether that was true, but it was an educated guess. I remembered Tom's tax returns. It was simple deduction that since Tom and Randy were equal partners in QW Technologies, if Tom's income was down, Randy's probably was too. "Your income over the last couple of years hasn't been what you're used to. You were getting desperate, weren't you? The bankers were getting desperate too, right?"

The lines in Randy's brow became so deep I wondered if he'd need Botox to plump up the furrows. "Where the hell do you get your information?"

Aha. I'd struck a chord, stamped my feet on his manly pride. "What happened, Randy?" I asked. My technique was working. Sort of. As he concentrated on frowning and denying what he wanted no one to know, he was paying less attention to his firearm. On occasion he now had it pointing at the ceiling or sometimes at the desk behind me or at Dave Biddle. This was greatly preferable to my chest (except the Dave Biddle part I suppose). "Tom was working on something important in the TechWorld lab, wasn't he? Something you wanted to sell and make lots of money from...and he didn't?"

"That's not how it happened!"

I continued to push buttons. "And then Dave got in the way," I said with a backhand wave at the incapacitated hostage next to me. "Were you afraid Tom was going to team up with Quasar and leave you behind?"

"That's ridiculous!" Randy shouted. "Dave and Tom were only friends, like I told you...oh hell, what am I doing explaining anything to you?"

"Makes you feel better?" I said with a smile.

He actually growled.

"Randy, you can't believe you'll get away with this! If you kill Dave Biddle, don't you think you'll be the first one the police will suspect?"

He looked at me with interest, as if I was a fellow executive who'd come up with a business scenario he hadn't yet considered. "Why? Other than Tom and Dave's inconsequential friendship that not many people even know about, there are no ties between Quasar and QW or me. If I do this right, no one will even look at me sideways."

I calculated the amount of time that had passed since Jacquie felt her boss had gone AWOL. It had been several hours. "So that's why you're still here? It's taken you this long to come up with something?" I chided him.

He wasn't having any of it. "It took me weeks to plan Tom's disappearance. That's how a smart man doesn't get caught," he told me as if he was a professor of murder and mayhem. "I wasn't expecting any of this today. I had to have time to think. Besides, I knew I'd have to wait until late at night before I did anything." He looked away then, somewhere into the middle distance, but then suddenly turned his bloodshot eyes back on me in full attack mode. "Do you think this is easy for me? Do you think it means nothing to me to have killed Tom and now have to deal with both of you?"

I stood still in my spot and gazed at him, trying not to show any reaction to his outburst. For a full thirty seconds he glared at me, some spittle at one corner of his mouth. We were two skaters skating on a thin sheet of emotional ice. Would it crack?

"Tom had it so fucking easy! I had to scrimp and scramble and try to make more and more sales to keep up while he fiddled around in that fucking lab of his without a care in the world! I have responsibilities! I have a wife and kids and mortgage and car payments and loans for more money than you'll ever have! What did Tom have? He had Chavell and their fucking frivolous lifestyle of the rich and famous and I'm sick of it! I'm sick of being the underdog! I'm sick of being second rate! I'm sick of being behind all the time, trying to catch up! Yes Tom was on to something big in that lab and yes we had a huge deal come our way! Tom could afford to turn it down—I couldn't!"

All this time Randy was waving his gun hand around and small beads of sweat were beginning to form at his temples. The time for action, I sensed, was coming soon.

"But you stupid shit, asshole detective won't believe Chavell is the murderer—even though everyone else does—and then this jerk off ruins it all by seeing what was in the lab!" With this, Randy swung the gun wildly towards Dave Biddle's head. "You couldn't leave it all alone! So yeah, I got a problem. I needed some time to think it through!"

"Well then maybe I should just leave and let you get to it." I grinned.

Randy grinned too. The devil had returned. His gun was back on me. "Actually, Quant, your unexpected arrival makes all of this easier."

"Oh?" I said. "Glad I could help."

"You see, I was considering a suicide for Mr. Biddle. Perhaps remorse over having killed his friend, Tom? Alas, no one would ever know—there'd be no note."

"And now?" I asked, knowing I wasn't going to like the answer.

"Well there's no doubt that I have to get rid of both of you. So I'm thinking murder-suicide. Mr. Biddle realizes you've found out he murdered Tom, so he kills you, but then in a fit of guilt and despair, he turns the gun on himself. You like?"

"Not bad," I said smarmily, "but why would either of us be in Tom's office when this happens?"

Randy scowled at me and said darkly, "Things can be moved."

Oh, oh! My eyes flew to where I'd pushed my gun. Too far away for a quick lunge. I glanced at Dave Biddle immediately to my left. I looked back at Randy, a dozen feet away. Something foreboding about the expression on his face told me I didn't have much time left to save our lives.

"Turn around," Randy ordered.

"What?" Oh shit! This was how he killed Tom. In the head, from behind.

"You heard me, Quant. I want you to put your hands on your head and turn around very slowly."

I did what he said, the entire time my mind ablaze with possibilities—the least of which wasn't "goodbye world." The last look I saw on Randy Wurz's face was not one of malevolent joy or satisfaction but rather blank determination. Killing me was no different than making an unpleasant but necessary business decision. I was to be sacrificed for unlimited credit.

As I rotated I saw Dave Biddle's terrified face. Would he have to watch me die or would I have to watch him die? Behind him, on the desk, was Tom's computer. On the blank screen I could see Randy's sketchy reflection step closer. It wasn't much but it was all I had. I wasn't going to let this sonofabitch get a point-blank shot at me.

In one move I jumped and twisted around, lowering my arms like wings, and kicked out my left foot, hoping for contact with the hand that held the gun. I heard a noise escape Randy's lips, but by the time both my feet were back on the ground I knew that I'd only winged him. But it had thrown him off balance. I dove to the ground and slid toward my gun like a baseball player to home base. I felt rug scrape up my arm, drawing blood, as I reached for the only thing that would protect me from being Randy's next victim.

I missed.

For a millisecond the room was completely silent as the three of us held our breaths. I was laid full out on the floor, my arm extended to its maximum distance, my hand about six inches away from my pistol. Randy had been pushed back by my surprise attack and was managing an odd crouching position while still holding his gun—in the general direction of Dave Biddle's head. Our eyes moved like crazy marbles as we each surveyed the situation and the others in the room. Unfortunately, as far as who had the upper hand, nothing much had changed.

Randy Wurz's face was puffed up and red as if he'd just come off a night of heavy drinking. His left eye had developed a twitch that hadn't been there before. And he was angry. "No more talking," he spit out as he cocked his gun.

"Randy," I pleaded. "Give it up. It's gone too far."

"You're right," he said to my surprise, then added, "It's gone too far to give it all up now."

At that instant the door behind Randy swung open and thumped him soundly on the back. It was all the time I needed. As Randy staggered forward my hand closed on my gun and without hesitation I shot.

Chapter 18

IT WAS A SPLENDID LATE OCTOBER DAY. We were on Harold Chavell's expansive deck that overlooked a craggy gorge through which flowed the sparkling blue South Saskatchewan River. Although the temperature was unseasonably mild, we both wore jackets to protect us from the chill that lurked in the light breeze. Sitting in well-upholstered deck chairs, cupping our mugs of coffee to keep our hands warm, we rarely looked at each other as we talked. After all we'd been through, particularly Harold, we were more than detective and client, but not quite friends.

"I'm going to miss this place," he said, staring at the hills on the opposing side of the river valley.

"Are you sure about the move? Is it really necessary?"

"Well, certainly I could wait out the gossip and innuendo, but I'm not really moving because of 'them' Russell, I'm moving because of me. I need a fresh start."

"Saskatoon's loss is Calgary's gain. I'm still sorry that things played themselves out the way they did. It couldn't have been easy on you."

"None of that really matters much when I think about the price

Tom paid."

I nodded in sombre agreement and sipped my drink.

"I still can't believe it was Randy Wurz. He and Tom had been together as friends and partners for so long. How could he have gotten so desperate?"

"Apparently he was close to being forced into bankruptcy and had a number of banks, credit institutions, not to mention some nasty loan shark-type people, breathing down his neck.

"Although it certainly wasn't your fault, I think he saw how you and Tom lived and he wanted it too. He was jealous and QW was his only source of cash. When he realized Tom was getting close to perfecting a new generation of video games that was gonna blow the socks off of every teenage boy from here to Bangladesh, dollar signs began to appear in his eyes. Financial salvation. What I don't understand is why, when Randy found a deal, Tom didn't want to go along with it? Wasn't that the whole purpose behind QW—to make video games and then sell them?"

"Yes," Chavell agreed, "but not at any cost. Randy Wurz found a company, VidStik, that was interested in Tom's new work. Tom even flew down to California to talk with their people about some developmental problems he was having with the games. But he quickly realized they were interested in a profit-motivated partnership only, not a technologically collaborative one. That's just not what Tom was about. You have to understand, Russell, even without my resources, Tom would never have allowed someone else to take control of the video games he created just for money. And he certainly wouldn't have agreed to the sale of QW. He wasn't motivated by profit. Never was. The luxuries I'm so fond of didn't mean much to Tom. He was a simple guy. He loved his work, he loved me, he loved things the way they were."

"Unfortunately Randy didn't." I shook my head as I guessed what happened next, following my thoughts to their sad conclusion. "Tom's decision not to play ball with VidStik sealed his fate. Randy had to get him out of the picture—so he could make the deal without him."

Chavell tensed his jaw and gave me a tight nod. "I hear Mr. Wurz will survive his injuries?"

"Yes," I said. "Although I hate what Randy Wurz did to Tom, to you—I never wanted to kill the man. But he's lucky I just got his shoulder. Painful, yes, but rarely fatal. It was good fortune that the security guard unwittingly opened the door into Randy's back. He'll be sharing bunks in the Prince Albert pen for quite some time."

Harold Chavell nodded grimly. "I guess I'm thankful for that. It still hurts—man it hurts—but at least there's been justice."

"What happens to QW now?" I asked.

"At first I didn't much care, but QW was Tom's baby. He and Randy created that company from nothing. Although it isn't much without either of them left to run it, there is the matter of the programs Tom was working on. My lawyers have been talking with VidStik. Apparently they had no idea what Randy was up to. They're still interested in making money from the games. And…I'm the last one to think there's anything wrong with that, so I think I'll let them. With the profit from the sale, I'm considering setting up a bursary at the University of Saskatchewan to be awarded annually in Tom's honor."

I smiled. A legacy of love arising from the ruins of tragedy.

Chavell smiled too. It looked odd on his face and I soon realized why. Other than the Pike Lake pictures, it was the first smile I'd seen there.

"I hear your final confrontation with Randy Wurz is all thanks to poison ivy?" he asked with a doubting smirk. "I knew there were some plants in the bushes near the cabin, and I know the cinder blocks were found in a nest of the stuff, but how did you ever connect that with Randy?"

"Calamine lotion. When I was searching Tom's office at QW, I found calamine lotion in the bathroom just down the hall. Although it didn't mean anything to me at the time, it's a peculiar thing to have in a bathroom and it stuck in my mind. That's why I went back to QW that night. And to see if I could find anything more to incriminate Randy."

Chavell gave his head a confounded shake. "How the hell did he pull it all off?"

"I think finding Tom's plane ticket when he attended the rehearsal party was a bit of pure luck."

"But he could never use it."

"He didn't need to. He already had his own ticket. He destroyed Tom's. But it certainly hastened your conclusion that Tom had left on your honeymoon without you. Once in France, he dropped enough bread crumbs to convince anyone that Tom was hiding in Europe."

"I must tell you that I've had quite a bit of squawking from my friend Solonge in Paris. She has registered shock, horror and a fair amount of titillation at having been considered by you as an accomplice in the murder," he said, somewhat tongue-in-cheek. "But why was she insisting that Tom had visited her?"

"An honest mistake. Indeed it was Randy Wurz who visited Solonge, pretending to be Tom. Randy and Tom are quite similar— size, height, hair and skin colouring. Randy knew she'd never actually met Tom, and he had a copy of your itinerary. After I found Tom's passport, I asked my associate, Errall, to send a picture to Solonge to verify that indeed the man she'd met was not Tom. She sent her a page from the QW annual report. That page contained a picture of *both* Tom *and* Randy.

"I know Solonge is a friend of yours, but having met her, I wouldn't call her a real…detail…kind of person. She probably didn't even bother to read the print below the photos identifying who was who. I told her we were sending her a picture of the man who was Tom Osborn but at the same time Errall regrettably also sent her a picture of the man who was pretending to be Tom Osborn."

Chavell nodded then said, "He certainly did a thorough job of setting me up."

"His Plan B. If the body did show up, which it did, it would be found near your property, the murder weapon—which he stole during the rehearsal party and returned the night of the wedding— belonged to you and had your prints on it, and the victim was the lover who'd recently jilted you. The only mistakes he made were arranging for the messengers in France who couldn't speak English and not finding and destroying Tom's passport."

"And I suppose not knowing Dave Biddle had been in the lab with Tom and knew about the games was also a big mistake. If it wasn't for that, under their partnership agreement, Randy could have easily found a secretive way to profit from the games without throwing any suspicion on himself."

"That too," I agreed, happy to acquiesce that Randy Wurz was nowhere near infallible.

Chavell shook his head, took a long slug of his coffee and after swallowing asked, "Is this what all of your cases are like, Russell?"

Although I knew the answer, I deliberated. Had this been a watershed case for me? Had I crossed some sort of line as a detective—no longer a Shelley Hack-type "Charlie's Angel" but a full-blown Farrah Fawcett-Majors? Would all my cases from here on involve more than a missing casserole dish or wayward cat? Did I want them to? "Not all, Harold," I said contemplatively, "not all."

It was late. Friday. Everyone else at PWC had already left for the weekend. I like being alone in the building. And there's something about the utter silence, the dark outside the window, and the headlights of commuter vehicles travelling on Spadina Crescent that inspire me to get paperwork done. I was closing my files on Harold Chavell and Tom Osborn. The case was solved and final bill paid in full (plus some) before I'd even had a chance to make one up. That did not happen every day. But then again, cases like this did not happen every day.

As I often do at the end of an investigation, I couldn't help wondering what to call this case. As I thought about it, I pulled a cold Great West brew from my desk-fridge, along with a frosted mug and one of those tiny juice-box containers of clamato. I mixed the clam and beer in the mug and sat back in my chair. It was a pleasurable feeling. The case was over. I'd caught the bad guy. I had money in the bank. Sure, maybe I wasn't the most experienced P.I. around, but I'd done damn fine for my first big case. And— there was absolutely nothing that I *had* to do.

Until the next case.

I pulled myself back up to the desk where I'd piled the folders. I had used purple ones this time. From a drawer I selected a fine-point black marker and on the tab of each of the purple files I wrote, *Amuse Bouche*. An unlikely name, but I knew it would recall for me every detail: the supposedly jilted lover, the overnight flight to Paris, chasing a ghost across the French countryside, my first experience with *Amuse Bouche*, being taken off the case, being put back on the case, the cinder blocks in the bed of poison ivy and shooting a murderer. It hadn't exactly been a "party in my mouth," but it had definitely been exciting.

I hesitated on the last file. The Herrings file. It still contained one item that beckoned me like the smoke of a denied but much desired cigarette.

The sketch of the half-heart pendant.

A half-heart pendant connoted a certain level of…what? Like? Love? Did the damn thing mean anything at all? I wasn't sure.

I was surprised, and a little relieved, when, instead of Olga, Father Len himself answered the front door of the rectory. But I was taken aback by the unwelcoming look that crossed his face. It lasted only an instant, but it had been there. I looked at my watch. Almost seven. "I'm sorry, Father, is this too late? Or am I interrupting something?"

The charcoal-haired priest smiled his disarmingly sexy smile and stepped aside to let me in. "No, no, no, Russell. Please come in."

I gladly left the chilly night outside and followed him up a staircase to a sitting room.

"Coffee or tea?" he asked. "Maybe a shot of something to warm you up?"

I smiled. Did he mean real alcohol or was he offering me sacramental wine on the rocks? "What are you having?"

"Are you a scotch drinker? I have some Oban that's very nice."

Another smile. "That sounds perfect."

While Father Len busied himself at the liquor cabinet, I looked around the room. Pretty fancy for a house full of priests and Olga. I was expecting a plastic-covered sofa, a black-and-white TV perched on a rickety TV tray, and ragged throw rugs on the floor. I settled myself into the black leather couch and awaited my drink.

Father Len returned holding two cut crystal shorts with a generous splash of rusty amber liquid in each. He handed me one and sat next to me on the couch. Suddenly it felt as if my entire relationship with this man had changed, and along with it, the temperature in the room. I felt hot. His closeness magnetized and repelled me at the same time. I could smell his cologne. Had he worn cologne before? It was nice. Maybe too nice. Like a pheromone eliciting a response I knew I could never allow.

But I was no longer a detective investigating his brother's murder. And he wasn't my parish priest. We were two men having a drink on a Friday night.

"Where is everyone? It seems very quiet."

"Don't tell anyone I told you, but the other priests are out playing bingo." He grinned. "They're addicted. Every Wednesday and Friday night."

"And Mrs. Doubtfire?"

He cocked his head to one side, then chuckled when he got the joke. "You mean Olga?"

I nodded.

"She doesn't live here. She's just down the block though if you'd like me to invite her over."

I grinned. "Maybe next time."

"I'm sorry I was a bit hesitant when I answered the door."

"Oh, that's okay. I get that all the time."

He laughed. "No, really, I'm sorry, Russell. If it wasn't for you, we may never have solved Tom's murder. Or worse, they may have put the wrong man in jail for it."

"Just doing my job."

"It's taking me a while to make peace with God about Tom's death. And it's taken me a while to spend a day without thinking about him every second."

"And then I turn up and remind you."

He winced. "Well, sort of, yes. I was surprised to see you."

"I should have called."

"Don't be silly. I'm glad you stopped over. From here on in I'll think of you as the guy I drink scotch with, instead of the private detective who solved my brother's murder."

"Sounds good to me." And it did. But there was one piece of business remaining. I hated to break the mood, but I wanted to get it over with. "There was one more thing, Father Len."

"Yes?"

"When I was searching Tom's apartment for clues, I found a gift that looked as if it may have recently been opened. It was a half-heart pendant. People who were in Tom's apartment immediately before he left for Pike Lake didn't see it and he never mentioned it to them. Harold knew nothing about it. Neither did Kent Melicke. Yet there it was, fairly obvious, in his apartment. There was no indication where he got it from or from whom. And then I saw its mate…I'm assuming it was the mate…I saw it…"

"…around my neck," Father Len finished my sentence and fingered the chain hidden under the fabric of his shirt.

"Yes."

"You're right. It is the mate to the pendant you saw in Tom's apartment."

"Did you give it to him?"

"No. It was a gift to both of us. From our mother. And I think I can guess why no one else knew about it."

I had recently been considering the merits of a trusty sidekick. Perhaps Father Len was a good candidate, I thought to myself.

"I received my pendant by mail on the Friday before the wedding. I imagine Tom received his on the same day and in the same way. With all that was going on, he likely didn't get around to opening it until Saturday, and probably not until he was alone."

It made sense. He had a visit from Clark Shiwaga, lunch with Kent Melicke and then, before he left for the cabin he opened his mail from the day before. And voila, a package from his mother containing the gift. Possibly an "I know about the wedding and I'm not coming, but here's a little something for you anyway" gift.

"But why didn't he put it on?"

The priest laughed and chucked me on the shoulder. "Would you? Have you seen it?"

I was surprised. I'd never considered Tom, and obviously his brother too, simply didn't like the gift. "But you wear yours."

The smile faded. "It means something completely different now that Tom is gone."

"Of course. I'm sorry."

"Don't be."

"It's…it's an unusual gift from a mother."

"What do you mean? Hasn't your mother ever given you something tacky?"

"It's not that," I chuckled as I spoke. "But the pendant itself…the half-heart thing…it seems more like something someone would give a lover."

"Ah. Yes. I see your point. There's a story behind the half-heart thing. You see, Tom and I are twins."

My head dropped and my eyes pulled up to stare at the man. I don't know why it seemed so inconceivable at the time. I had guessed the two brothers were close in age but I had no idea they were fraternal twins.

"Mom always referred to us as two parts of one heart. I think the saying came from when we were bratty kids demanding to know which one of us she loved more. So I'm sure when she saw the pendants she felt they were made for us."

"That is a wonderful story."

"After the funeral she told me that with Tom gone, she only had half a heart left."

Father Len downed his remaining scotch, pulled the glass out of my hand and headed away to pour refills. As I sat there waiting, all I could do was focus on the warm spot where his skin had grazed mine.

It's like a fever that sets my blood afire and clouds my mind. The cause is always different. It might be a smell, a sight or one of many sensory stimulations or deprivations that drive me into the fever. Before it happens I am only dimly aware of its impending arrival. After it's gone I'm sometimes fulfilled, sometimes guilty, sometimes euphorically sated. But always, I am unable to resist.

The hand felt dry and cool as it buried mine within its cave and led me down unfamiliar hallways into a bedroom. Except for the dull illumination of a floor lamp in one corner, the room was dark. We stopped and faced each other as two strangers. At every point of contact my skin tingled as if it had just received a mild electric shock. Our eyes did all the talking. And they came to a speedy agreement.

The silence was drowned out by the blood rushing into my ears…and other places. Thump, thump, thump. I placed my mouth over his and tasted him. Cinnamon. I tasted of scotch. Oban. I teased his tongue with mine until it fought back. The battle continued for eons. In need of air I pulled my lips off of his and sank them into his neck. He smelled like oranges. My hands sought further excitement. They slipped from the small of his back to the mounding fabric below. I cupped one hand under each buttock and pulled him up and closer to me. He began to breathe deeply, as if winded from running a marathon.

I pulled back from him, but only far enough to watch his face as I unbuttoned his shirt. He started to help me but I gently pushed his hands away. I deliberately left his cuff buttons buttoned so that when I pulled the shirt off his chest and shoulders it fell in a tangle around his hands but would go no further. Captive.

He stood there, barechested, his arm muscles quivering with excitement. I gave him a crooked smile filled with lustful communication that could not be put into words. I approached him and bent forward. His chest reflexively surged forward with each min-istration. Next I followed my tongue to the tender area under each arm. He groaned as I painted him with my saliva. He fought to release his hands from behind his back, but not that hard. He was enjoying the feeling of powerlessness in the face of great pleasure. I found his neck again and then his mouth and then his neck again. And I whispered into his ear in between puffy breaths of air, "I want to taste you. Everywhere." He moaned his acquiescence to my proposal.

As I kissed him more, my hands found his belt and made short work of it. I leisurely slid his pants down over his thighs. And similar to his shirt cuffs at his wrists, I left them as manacles around his ankles. I wanted to control, I wanted to direct, I wanted to give and take at my command, without interference. And he was a willing accomplice. He wore white, ribbed Jockey briefs that stretched attractively over their contents. At first I only observed and smiled in anticipation. He whispered something unintelligible and I gazed at him. As our eyes communed my hands and mouth met their marks. I was pleased by the transformation of his face and felt the trembling of his knees.

He looked at me, mesmerized, as I stepped back. I began to peel off my clothes. It was time for this to become a two-man game. I enjoyed undressing in front of him, revealing what would soon become his toy, like a self-unwrapping present.

"Russell," he whispered.

I looked at the man. I couldn't recall his name. I'd just met him—after leaving the rectory in the full heat of my fever. But in my mind I imagined someone with a name I knew well and I fell upon him.

It was time for *Amuse Bouche*.

Acknowledgements

Johanna and the late Frank Bidulka, my parents, for making me feel I was the best at whatever I did.

Kim, Kell and Kris—the first and best fans of my written word.

Shelley Brown—mentor and enduring supporter (thanks for making it okay to leave and, true or not, convincing me you'd take me back any time).

Laurie Welch, the contest winner (I remembered!).

Those who read my stuff and provided valuable input: Mary Clark, Rhonda Sage, Muriel McFaull—special thanks for the kind words when often none was due; and the many who wanted to read my stuff (I appreciate it).

Carolee Milroy and Darrell Bell for the generosity of their artistic craft.

My many friends in research, including: Shelley (hair), MP (French) and the Palazzo Pants Gals (especially Rod).

Those who offered special encouragement when I needed it most: George, Jill, Bob, Eleanor, Eldeen, Fran, Linda, Trina, Dan, Judy, Holly, Dori, Lynne and Jessica.

Catherine Lake, editor extraordinaire, for striking the right balance, giving and taking, for generosity of time, spirit, kindness and friendship, and for making this happen.

The many writers, in this genre and others, whom I've never met but who inspire me with their diversity, brashness and courage in words.

The readers.

And Herb.